Ruth Fever

Beverly J Scott

PublishAmerica

Baltimore

First printing

ISBN: 1-59129-645-5
PUBLISHED BY PUBLISHAMERICA BOOK PUBLISHERS
www.publishamerica.com
Baltimore

Printed in the United States of America

Dedicated to:

Tracey, Amy and Michelle,
who responded to my first draft with encouragement,

to my husband, Dwayne (Scotty) Scott
for providing me with the nicest Edsels,

to the members of the Iowa Chapter of the Edsel Club
for their unwavering support

Edsel lovers and Classic Car enthusiasts everywhere,
who enhance the hobby with their beautiful restorations,
their sharing of advice, and their Friendly attitudes.

May God Bless each and every one of you.

Acknowledgements

Special thanks:
to Jason Boten and Ken Belzer
for their computer wizardry in the creation of my website
(http://www.beverlyjscott.com) and their ready when-in-need assistance.

To Nicholas Bartlett (grandson)
for his able computer help.

To Russell Wolfe (brother-in-law)
for his aid in clarifying the technical wording of Ruth Fever.

To Estella Swartz (retired teacher)
for her critique and review.

Through out our country, but most especially in the Midwest, glorious summer days, bring out classic car hobbyists who gather at some favorite attraction, historical celebration or the local drive-in restaurant to brag, glorify and swap tall tales while celebrating their enjoyment of cars built in an era when Fords, Buick's, Cadillac's and Chevrolets were distinguishable.

With luck we will pass this unique and joyous preservation of our automotive history on to our children and our grandchildren.

Beverly J. Scott

PROLOGUE

Squealing tires and screeching too-late-used brakes preceded the explosive collision that ripped away the twilight-quiet of the area and left a twisted, smoldering mass of sheet metal and shattered glass. Loud snaps, angry popping, mini salvos igniting tiny individual fires in grassy areas, created a disaster that washed the neighborhood with dissension and vibration. The mangled mass of material that had once been two vehicles lay now in an unidentifiable heap.

Within minutes the sound of sirens reverberated through the streets heralding the arrival of police, ambulance, paramedic's and the fire squad. Police quickly determined that there was no need for rescue. There were no survivors. Lifeless bodies were hastily pulled from the burning wreckage before a major explosion sent rescuers scurrying for cover.

Later, news people would disclose the presence of alcohol at the scene; attest to the fact that the young couple was obviously inebriated. That fact was the single item ever released about the young couple.

Only two obituaries appeared in print, notices that detailed the pertinent facts about Mr. and Mrs. Dennison and Ruth Dennison, their one surviving heir. All other details of the accident, including the names of the other couple involved, were mysteriously squelched.

CHAPTER ONE

"Good Morning, Horse," Ruth said to the large black tomcat sniffing suspiciously at the edges of the new rug she'd placed between the kitchen and the family room. Horse paced back and forth as if contemplating a deep problem then he moved away from the rug's edge and gracefully leaped over it to land with ease at Ruth's feet, his disdain for the new floor decoration evident in his actions.

"Meo-o-ow," Horse rumbled, stretching his neck to stare up at her, his nose twitching with feline arrogance. Ruth's mouth curved in a grin, her eyes twinkled briefly with laughter. She watched him hump his back before extending himself into a full body stretch. Horse's pink tongue slid out to lick around his mouth; he squinted and looked up at her, his eyes aglow with mischief.

"I have work to do this morning," she chided. Horse playfully nudged her leg for attention. She ignored him. The cat's purring motor seemed to stall and Ruth knew he was disappointed.

"Go play," she instructed, turning back to her task and momentarily dismissing the distracting tomcat from her mind.

Ruth deliberated over the words for the newspaper advertisement. Clenching the end of the pen with her teeth, she scrutinized her writing. Today was the first day of 'Spring Break,' her day to tackle the list of tasks she penned last night and planned to accomplish this week. Horse continued to rub against her. His soft cat fur tickled the inside of her calves as he dove between her legs to weave circles through her feet. She was reaching for the phone book to look up the number for the daily newspaper when Horse nipped at her big toe.

"Stop that," she cried, moving her foot away from the cat's sandpapery wet tongue.

Refusing to let his antics interrupt her task, she jotted the necessary phone number on the note pad in front of her and returned the book to its proper place.

Laughter erupted from deep in her chest when Horse tried to push his face up the leg of her slacks. Giving in to his demand for a little attention, Ruth reached down to scratch him behind the ears. Horse's body rumbled contentedly and he rolled over pawing the air. Humor flashed momentarily in the depth of Ruth's eyes as she watched the cat. *Life would be unbearably lonely these days without this conceited tomcat,* she thought.

Ruth leaned over to scratch the tom's belly, "You're a very demanding and arrogant roommate, Horse, pleasant but a definite distraction." She was humming by the time Horse tired of her attention and she could return to her task.

Satisfied, at last, with the wording of the advertisement, Ruth called the Des Moines Tribune. After checking rates, she decided to run the "For Sale, Edsel Station Wagon," advertisement for five days. She repeated her address and telephone number to the sunny voice emanating from the phone then settled the receiver back in its cradle.

Sun streaming through the window splashed a wild riot of color across the desk distributing swirling dust motes around the area but Ruth seemed oblivious to the golden ripples, her mind held captive by memories of her parents and the last time they had driven the old station wagon.

It was a winter picnic; a treat for her students when they had eagerly surpassed their semester's reading goal and that of several other classrooms. Her parents had helped to transport the second grade class for the November affair. Everyone had enjoyed her mom's chili and mini sandwiches. Ruth could still picture the students' eager faces as they devoured every morsel.

Later, she tried to organize games and competitions for the class but the boys were more interested in the old Edsel station wagon and her dad's stories.

The day had been surprisingly warm for November and the park teemed with the sound of migrating birds and furry critters preparing for winter. A flock of geese held the second graders mesmerized when they glided in to rest and feed on the park's pond. Everyone gazed in silent wonder until, in a single glorious moment, the large birds lifted their wings and, flapping gracefully, they flew away.

It was one of the best memories Ruth had of her parents. Listening intently she could almost hear the echo of their laughter as they interacted with her students. She sighed audibly. She missed them, them and that wonderful feeling that they radiated that all-was-right-with-the-world.

Today the mantle of grief she'd been wearing since her parent's death seemed overpoweringly heavy. Even the warm sun splashing red highlights in Ruth's dark brown hair failed to suppress the shiver that overtook her small frame when she thought of the tragedy that had snatched away their life. Ruth understood that other people had troubles but still she could not seem to overcome her despair at their death.

They had always been her support system. When others teased or bullied her during her growing-up years, she always knew that she was loved unconditionally by God and by her parents. Now, she felt only abandonment.

Her common sense kept reminding her that she was being ridiculous, she was an adult after all. It might help if she'd had a brother or sister to share her pain but that was not the case. Ruth's emotions fluctuated between depression, sadness and anger. Thinking about it set her heart pacing like the heartbeat of a tiny rabbit that you'd just rescued from the neighbor's dog. She fervently hoped she would soon learn to forgive the drunken couple who had caused her parents' death. Maybe with forgiveness would come a measure of relief from her relentless hostility.

"God, help me to forgive," she prayed out loud.

Knowing that the driver and her mate had paid with their lives did little to stem Ruth's anger and she wondered if she would always be haunted by the needless loss of the two most important people in her life.

She understood that there was no answer to the why-now of their death and until she could find a way to forgive she was certain that her pain would not diminish.

"I'm twenty-nine-years old, God," Ruth murmured, "I still feel like a lost lonely child. Help me to release my anger, help me to heal."

Ruth brushed a tear from her cheek, mentally reviewed the last few years of her life. Her decision to move back to Des Moines two years ago to help care for her arthritic mother suddenly seemed provident, almost insightful. Now, in such a short period of time she'd lost both of her parents to a senseless accident.

A picture flooded Ruth's mind; it was the image of her parents framed in the open front door. Her six-foot father dwarfing her seated-in-a-wheelchair five-foot mother. Her father stood behind the wheelchair, his hands were resting lovingly on her mother's shoulders. They were wishing her a good day and waving good-bye as she left for school. Their smiling faces, bathed in the glow of early morning sun, were permanently etched in her brain bank of memories.

She silently thanked God for the time that they shared and for her joyous memories. She would never regret returning home or having had the opportunity to spend time with them. Her fingers curled around the coffee mug. Her past, her life rose up to block out the present. Boston and the five years that she spent there teaching second grade, now seemed wasted years and she wondered why it had taken her so long to grasp that she missed Iowa, her family, her home.

Ruth enjoyed teaching and usually her interaction with the students served to distract her from loneliness and grief, still, every day she thanked God for the wonderful months she shared with her parents before their deaths.

"Stop, feeling sorry for yourself girl," she chided. "You have work to do." Ruth checked her to-do list, crossed off item number one before looking up the phone number of a local shelter.

"Hello. I have several boxes of good clothing, can you use them?" The positive answer did little to ease the turmoil of disposing of her parent's things.

"You have pick-up service." Ruth said, surprised yet pleased. "I'll have them ready for you by tomorrow."

Ruth lifted her cup for another sip of coffee and grimaced at the coldness of the liquid. She scanned through her to-do list once more and decided only two items posed any real problem. Number seven: solve the mystery of Jason Winters' behavior, and number eight: make new friends. Where would she start? She already knew most of her neighbors. All were older and had been friends of her parents. They were good people but she needed friends of her own. Lifting her eyes she murmured "God, help me with both of these problems."

Sun streaming in through the colored glass of the window finally caught Ruth's attention and she let the warm ray's splash across her face, content to put off her unpleasant tasks for a few more minutes. She loved sunshine. Loved the way it painted all it touched with a hint of gold. With a sigh she pushed to her feet; stepped over a napping cat, and moved into the elevator where she pushed the down button. A faint hum sounded as the small, wheelchair size elevator glided down to the lower level. Her jaw set in determination; she began the distasteful chore.

She found several large boxes in the basement perfect for closet cleaning and piled them by the elevator. Ruth discovered several boxes filled with her mother's paperback books. Three bookcases upstairs were also overloaded with paperbacks. Apparently in the past her mother had boxed up the overflow and sent it down to the storeroom. Ruth wondered if the shelter might also be interested in the books and made a mental note to call them back and inquire.

Car parts, models, and Edsel memorabilia filled every available space along the walls and again, Ruth smiled. Her mother had continuously teased her husband that he had an unassembled Edsel stored in the basement. After touring the area, Ruth believed the statement was true. *What will I ever do with all of these things?*

She gave herself a mental shake, *one thing at a time, slow and easy.* Ruth grabbed a few more empty boxes, dragged them to the elevator and pushed the open button. While she loaded the boxes into the elevator she looked around the room. Except for an accumulation of dust it would be a great place to entertain. Not that she had anyone to entertain she thought as she surveyed her surroundings.

Her parents had used the room many times since they built the house seven years ago. The walls were covered with automobile memorabilia, including her father's miniature car collection, which was displayed in various glass cases set side by side along the walls. She knew many of the models were worth hundreds of dollars but she had no idea how or where to advertise them properly. Maybe one of the men from the Edsel club could help her with that project.

One more item to add to the to-do list, she thought with a sigh. She stacked the boxes in the elevator, rode up and forced herself to begin closet cleaning.

Now that the house belonged to Ruth, she was not sure she could handle staying here surrounded by so much that reminded her of her parents and their times together. Living in this beautiful place without them was almost as difficult as moving some place else would be.

Seven years ago the Dennison's constructed their dream home, nestling it on twenty-two park-like acres of grass, trees and fresh air. Although built far enough from Des Moines to be considered out in the country, the home was convenient for shopping and entertainment.

Constructed of natural wood and a great deal of glass, the house melted into the scenery so well it was almost invisible to passersby. Created with three bedrooms, each sporting its own bath, plus a master suite that had its own sitting room and a bath designed with a double walk-in shower, benched along one wall for convenience, made the house overlarge for one person.

The large eat-in kitchen was designed with a four-foot wide counter separating it from the adjoining family room. Indian-pictures, plates and dolls covered the walls and shelves in a multi-purpose room always filled with sunshine. It was her mother's favorite place to read or visit with friends.

The living room seemed new and was the least used room in the house. There was a main bathroom just down the hall from the small den where Ruth had set up her computer and where she spent hours preparing class work.

Ruth hummed along with the music drifting from her CD player. She carried one full box after another out and stacked them in the breezeway.

I need a break and a cup of herbal tea, she thought, after dragging the three heavy boxes of books out with the other cartons she'd set out for the shelter. Exhaustion left her almost too weary to prepare her favorite berry spice tea, but the aroma of raspberries and cinnamon released by the addition of hot water drifted upward tantalizing her nostrils and giving her a needed lift.

She moved slowly toward the patio door, careful of Horse who was playfully weaving between her legs with each step she took. Trying not to splash the hot tea on her purring companion, she stopped in the doorway then followed him out onto the deck. Fresh-scented air, rich with the sweet smell of spring, wafted across the deck. Ready-to-bloom daffodils danced in the breeze, their yellow tipped green shoots, along with a multitude of tulips and crocus, added color to the view. A rabbit darted around the grape arbor sniffing at its base until he flushed another rabbit, then they played tag through the yard cavorting in the joyous sunshine. Movement, quick and shadowy, afforded her a brief glimpse of her resident chipmunk.

"It's beautiful here, Horse," Ruth said to the cat sitting on the rail at her elbow. Absentmindedly she stroked Horse's soft fur. She understood the pleasure her parents had found in their home. Nature's beauty was evident everywhere she looked. Deer often grazed in the back yard alongside the rabbits and the squirrels. There was a family of chipmunks nested in the bushes behind the attached garage. Ruth delighted in their antics whenever she was lucky enough to catch a glimpse of them as they scurried playfully under the lilac bushes. She stood listening to God's music drift around her on the light breeze, music created by a myriad of different species of birds flirting and flitting among the budding trees.

Ruth sighed. "I like it here, Horse. It is peaceful." The cat cocked his head and looked up at her, seeming to understand. He lifted a paw to swipe at the smiley face on her cup; she grinned at his playfulness and backed away from his quick movements. Savoring the spring-scented air a moment longer, Ruth prayed that she would be able to adjust to living here without her parents, prayed that she might someday feel comfortable living here all alone.

She settled in one of the padded loungers rimming the edge of the deck and let the brilliance of the sun drive her to hide her eyes behind their lids. Soon the empty teacup slipped from her fingers, nestled in her lap. She napped.

Whirling mists invaded Ruth's sleep, haunting her with dreams of a tall handsome man, an elusive stranger with an invisible face. At times she could almost make out his features then the foggy mist would enfold him and she would once again be alone.

Air, cooled by the setting of the sun, pushed Ruth to wakefulness and indoor. Back in the kitchen, a subdued Ruth faced a lone supper in front of the darkened screen of her television set. A best-selling novel, a paperback worn with many readings, had been rescued from one of the boxes awaiting pick-up and she sat curled in the corner of the sofa, book in hand, content to read until she realized how hard she was fighting to stay awake. She slipped a bookmark between the pages and turned out the lamp.

Ruth opened the French doors and walked out onto the deck, her chores and reading completed for the evening. Looking up she spotted a brilliant winking star. A smile skirted her mouth. Childhood memories surfaced and she recalled all the times she, as a child, had wished on just such a star. Thoughts of her parents, and the wondrous love they shared, left her feeling lost and alone. A tear meandered down her cheek, hung at the edge of her jaw briefly then dropped to the deck. She dried her face with the back of her hand and whispered, "God, will there ever be someone special just for me?"

CHAPTER TWO

Wyndom Winters settled wearily into the only chair available as he waited outside the principal's office. He raked splayed fingers through his dark brown hair to tame the wind blown mass. A glance at his watch told him he was early for his appointment. He rechecked his hands hoping he had managed to remove all evidence of his busy morning.

An entire day at the construction site, working alongside the crew, left him with blistered hands and little illusion about his supervisory abilities. He took a deep breath and strove to stretch the weariness from his shoulders. Bruce Overton, his new foreman, had arrived in town just this afternoon. Thankfully, Wyndom's life could now return to normal.

Bruce came with good references and in two short hours this afternoon the man had taken charge of the crew and accomplished more than Wyndom had the whole day. With Bruce at the job site, Wyndom figured he would be free to concentrate on working out the estimate for their next project.

Wyndom wondered why his son's school principal wanted to see him. After questioning, Jason, Wyndom was still in the dark about the note his son had handed him last evening requesting this meeting.

Wyndom Winters, thirty-four-years-old, six feet tall, lean but muscular, was a very handsome man. Muscles rippled beneath his clothing and, after his morning on the job, Wyndom knew that every one of them ached. His dark wavy hair, dark eyes and broad forehead coupled with square jawed good looks gave him an appearance of youth he definitely did not feel at this moment.

He was totally out of his element sitting in a room surrounded by students. When Wyndom entered the room they were already waiting. The two girls and three boys had been huddled together whispering since his arrival. Had he ever been that young, he wondered as he studied them from behind his newspaper.

They're probably plotting their next bit of youthful mischief; he thought and suppressed a grin at the idea. The inner-office door opened and Wyndom watched an attractive woman step out. Was she the principal? All five students came to attention at her approach. The smile she beamed at each youth started in her eyes spread to her mouth and transformed her attractiveness into beauty. Wyndom's body reacted with a swiftness he had not experienced for some time.

"You have each been selected to drill with the marching band as flag bearers," the beauty said, her voice low and melodious. "Congratulations." She handed each student a schedule for practice and watched them file from the room.

Wyndom heard one of the girls say, "Thank You, Miss Dennison," and he knew she was not the person who had summoned him.

Ruth moved toward the outer door. She appeared to be deep in thought. By chance she looked up, noticed Wyndom seated in the corner. "Mr. Winters?"

Wyndom smiled and nodded ascent. "Mrs. Naylor will see you now, just go on into her office." He watched the attractive woman turn and leave. Apparently she was a teacher. He wondered why none of his teachers had ever seemed so young and lovely.

Taking a deep breath to bolster his courage, Wyndom grasped the knob of the office door. He was an adult now so why was it still intimidating to enter the principal's office?

The woman behind the desk did not look intimidating. Smiling in his direction, she looked more like the ideal grandmother, Wyndom thought, and stepped into the room.

The principal's heart shaped face, surrounded by a short cap of brown curls frosted lightly with gray, radiated warmth. She stood and welcomed Wyndom.

***

"You're Jason's father," Mrs. Naylor said, reaching out to shake his hand. "Have a seat." She nodded to indicate the chair in front of her desk. "I'm sure you're eager to know why I requested this meeting."

"Yes, I am," Wyndom said, settling into the wooden chair and giving the woman his attention.

"Jason is an excellent student, Mr. Winters. He is well behaved and does his assignments without complaint."

"I don't understand, I assumed there was a problem," Wyndom said frowning, his brow furrowed with concern.

"According to Jason's teacher, he has been too quiet, too well behaved, and he seems more withdrawn than usual this year. Apparently his behavior has become increasingly more subdued, withdrawn since the second week of school."

"Withdrawn?"

"Jason had the same teacher last year that he has this year," she explained.

Mrs. Naylor leaned back in her chair and met Wyndom's gaze. "Last year he was a happy, smiling, boisterous first grader. Now he rarely smiles. He isn't interacting with the other students. Miss Dennison says he is overly quiet. She senses something is amiss."

"What do you want me to do?" Wyndom's face reflected his puzzlement. "I haven't noticed a change."

"His teacher is concerned." She paused to let him assimilate the implication of her words. "I trust Miss Dennison's judgment."

Wyndom scowled. Frustration creased his forehead.

"What happened in September?" Mrs. Naylor questioned, then watched the man shrug his shoulders.

"Spend time with Jason. Maybe he will confide in you. If you do figure it out, let us know if we can help." She made several helpful suggestions then stood and ushered Wyndom from her office.

* * *

Wyndom sat in his car contemplating their conversation. Jason's problem was not academic. In a way Wyndom wished it were, he could have handled math or reading, but this? Jason's teacher said he had been withdrawing slowly and quietly since the second week of school. Wyndom tried to pinpoint exactly what had been happening the second week of September.

Jason's mother, Cindy, left them more than three years ago. Two months before school started, he and Jason had moved in with Mrs. Carlyle, Cindy's mother. The woman seemed sincere in her wish to spend more time with her grandson, and Wyndom was relieved to have someone around for Jason when his workload kept him away from the house.

Cindy and her ultra-rich, jet-setting husband had returned to town before Thanksgiving and by Christmas they were both dead, killed in a car crash. During Cindy's return to Des Moines, she had not once attempted to see her son. The incident was traumatic for Mrs. Carlyle but Jason had been so quiet about his mother's continued absence and then her untimely death that Wyndom assumed he was handling the affair very well. Apparently he was wrong.

Wyndom realized he had taken advantage of the situation and started working longer hours. He rarely arrived home before Jason's bedtime. Could it be one or all of these changes in Jason's life that were upsetting him so deeply.

I've been so wrapped up in my feelings of failure, Wyndom thought, *I did not even notice what was happening to my son.* Now he had to find a way to draw Jason out of his depression and back to the loving, laughing boy he used to be.

Wyndom thought about his ex-wife. Cindy Carlyle Winters had left nothing behind three years ago but a note explaining her boredom with being a wife and mother. She wanted more out of life. She wanted excitement. Cindy ran off with a rich jet setter, filed for a quickie divorce, and married her rich playboy, all at whirlwind speed.

Until he and Jason moved in with Mrs. Carlyle in July, they'd lived in an apartment with a myriad of different baby-sitters to watch Jason while Wyndom had to be elsewhere.

Again his thoughts returned to his ex-wife. Two weeks before Christmas she and her husband were killed in a car crash. The authorities claimed that Cindy had been driving the car. She was drunk at the time. Four people were dead because of her rash act.

Cindy had been spoiled, immature, drop dead gorgeous and a bad mother. Wyndom wondered if it was guilt that prompted Evelyn Carlyle to open her home to them, offering to help with Jason's care. At first, Evelyn appeared to make an effort where they were concerned but Wyndom wondered if she had grown uncomfortable with the responsibility of an active seven-year-old in her life. Those first few weeks had been very tense. She was a demanding person but things had settled into a routine and Wyndom assumed they were all adjusting to one another.

For the first time Wyndom realized he didn't have a clue what life was like for Jason at home. He had no idea if anyone was there to meet Jason after school or what Jason did with his time in the afternoons.

I've been too involved with work. Wyndom Winters lifted his arm to check the timepiece on his wrist. He'd sat in the car for half an hour wasting time. He should be home spending time with his son. Mrs. Naylor seemed to think it might help Jason to be with his father. She suggested Wyndom find a hobby the two of them could share.

Wyndom closed his eyes and the image of his son materialized. Jason Winters was a curious seven-year-old with spiky blonde hair, snappy blue eyes that seemed to forewarn of some planned deviltry, a smile that dimpled the corner of his mouth and a face that displayed his every emotion. Still, it took a teacher to notice that the fires had dimmed in his young eyes, that he rarely talked or laughed. She said Jason resembled a young flower closed up against a cold wind. Yet most of the people in Jason's life had not even been aware of the change. It had taken a concerned teacher mentioning it to the school Principal for Wyndom to find out about his son. Now it was up to him. He vowed to find a way to help Jason get back his joy.

A smile curved Wyndom's mouth as he started the car; Jason's teacher was the beauty he'd watched while waiting for his appointment. Lucky Jason.

***

Evelyn's voice was raised in anger, Jason sat at the table cowering in silence until she was quiet, then he whispered, "I'll promise to never do it again, Grandma."

"My name is Evelyn," she retorted heatedly, frowning at the boy cowering in his chair.

Wyndom walked into the kitchen in time to see Evelyn wince at Jason's "grandma" and to see the fear in his son's eyes.

"What's going on here, Evelyn? Is there a problem." The glare in her eye softened at the sound of Wyndom's voice. She shrugged nonchalantly.

He looked at Jason, "Son?"

"I spilled my milk, Dad. I'm sorry, I didn't mean to make a mess." Jason mumbled, refused to meet his father's eyes.

Wyndom walked over, put a hand on Jason's shoulder then ruffled his hair, "It was just an accident, Mother Carlyle, accidents do happen."

"I decided to come home early, have supper with you, Jason," he said and pulled out a kitchen chair and sat.

Evelyn frowned, "Children should eat in the kitchen away from the adults and the formal dinning room."

The look on her son-in-law's face would have shriveled most recipients but Evelyn's whiskey fog lessened its impact, however it did serve to silence her protest. Why, he had never before called her "Mother Carlyle" in that tone of voice. It was her house after all. She was doing him a favor, was she not? She huffed around the kitchen filling her plate with the meal Katie had prepared before leaving. She hated the inconvenience of a servant's emergency. She hated waiting on herself, hated eating alone but she refused to share a table with an unruly child.

Evelyn made a point of ignoring Wyndom and Jason as she carried her meal into the dining room, deciding the two men could fend for themselves.

Jason watched his father fill two glasses with milk and carry them to the table. "Grandmother said I didn't deserve any more milk," he quietly said.

"She was wrong," Wyndom said and patted his son's shoulder. Their conversation during the meal was a series of questions concerning Jason's day at school from the father and mostly yes and no answers from Jason.

"Where is Katie tonight?" Wyndom asked, concerned about the Carlyle housekeeper. This time Jason's answer was, "I don't know."

Together they rinsed their dishes, stacked them in the sink then retired to Jason's room. Once he was bathed and ready for bed, they took turns reading a few of Jason's favorite books to each other, then Jason hugged his father and climbed in bed. Wyndom tucked the covers around his son, kissed him on the forehead and promised that they would try to do something special this weekend.

Wyndom could not get the kitchen scene or the look on Jason's face off his mind. He needed to cut down on his hours, needed to spend more time at home, needed to find out if this tension between Jason and his Grandmother happened often.

Returning to the first floor, he walked into the kitchen just as Katie stepped in the back door. Wyndom had never seen the spry housekeeper look so distracted and weary.

"Mr. Winters," Katie gasped, "I didn't expect you home yet. I just popped in to check on Jason."

"Jason is asleep." Wyndom watched as Katie rebuttoned her coat and turned to leave.

"Is there a problem, Katie?" He saw her hesitate briefly then she shook her head and reached for the back door knob.

"You know you can confide in me. I might be able to help," Wyndom offered quietly before the housekeeper retired.

"I'm too angry to talk to anyone right now," Katie said. She shook her head, and quickly left for her apartment above the Carlyle garage.

Grabbing a cup of coffee from the thermos in the kitchen, Wyndom carried it into the den where he sat down to read the day's newspaper. It was obvious to Wyndom that Katie had a problem. Don't we all, he thought and settled more comfortably into the cozy chair. He reached up to turn on the lamp as the thought, *Lord what a day this has been,* flashed through his mind.

Evelyn found him in the library, paper in hand, deep in thought, "I missed you at dinner, Wyndom, I had hoped we could talk."

"Yes, Evelyn, we do need to get something settled," he said. "From now on I will be having my meals with Jason, we can join you in the dining room or you may join us in the kitchen, the choice is yours. Just be aware that from now on I intend to be home."

She looked at him for several minutes, "As you wish, Wyndom, I'll see to it that you and Jason are served in the kitchen." With that the older woman turned and sauntered from the room—a scowl deepening the lines already etched around her mouth.

Wyndom turned the pages of newsprint, not really seeing the words in front of his face. He had drifted back in time to memories of his life as a boy, constantly left at home alone with servants. His parents were always absorbed elsewhere, his father with the family business and his mother with innumerable charities. Their activities always took precedence, eventually becoming more important than their son.

The only time he recalled not being lonely were the few summer weekends he spent with his grandfather, Simon Winters, camping and fishing. Wyndom had almost forgotten how much he had treasured those times. Most of his youth, Wyndom realized, had been very lonely.

Was Jason having that same problem? he wondered? He glanced at the newsprint amazed to find that he was already to the classifieds. Suddenly a small advertisement caught his attention.

FOR SALE Edsel: Rare 1958 Bermuda Station Wagon, 67,000 orig. miles, push-button shifting, power brakes, windows and seats, drive anywhere, call evenings. 555-2550.

The phone number was local. Wyndom was interested, wondered about the price. His Grandpa Winters had owned an Edsel wagon. Wyndom could barely remember what the car looked like, he did remember though that grandpa had taken much ribbing from the family when he bought the old station wagon.

Wyndom recalled thinking the car was great. He and his grandpa had spent most of that last summer together. They even slept in the wagon on a few of their overnight camping trips. Then during the fall that Wyndom had turned eleven, his Grandfather had died.

Wyndom wondered what had happened to the Edsel. Knowing his father, that was probably the first thing he sold. As memories of that summer began to surface, Wyndom remembered how lonely his life became once again after his grandpa's death, realized that the feeling had lingered until the birth of his son.

Now, according to Jason's teacher, he was withdrawing. Wyndom had to find out if it were really true and find a way to breach that reserve, discover its source. Could it possibly be a problem with his teacher or maybe another student? Spending time with Jason, fishing, camping, maybe even a weekend trip with a school friend could provide the answer. Wyndom took a small notebook from his shirt pocket where it was always handy. He copied the details of the advertisement including the phone number. Early tomorrow evening he would call about the car then he and Jason would check it out together.

Happy memories swirled in Wyndom's mind as he shut off lights and checked locks before retiring. Memories of warm summer days, idyllic times spent with his grandfather, days that he felt loved, resurfaced.

CHAPTER THREE

Horse stood braced against the deck rails, his pointed-chin face peeping between his front paws. The cat recognized the hum of the red cougar before he saw the car pull into the drive. He began purring a happy welcome to Ruth before she climbed from behind the wheel of her convertible, her arms full of papers that needed grading.

Although the cat was not chained, Ruth never worried about leaving him outside. He had been trained not to leave the deck. Jean Dennison, Ruth's mother, wanted to make sure Horse would not bother any of the birds or wildlife in her yard so she trained the cat to look but not chase.

Ruth wondered how long that training would last if a dog ever ventured into Horse's space. It surprised Ruth to discover that the arrogant creature enjoyed his status as watchcat.

She stooped to let the tom climb onto her shoulder before unlocking the door. Horse had come to expect this special treatment from Ruth, seemed to relish the attention.

Papers and briefcase were placed on the entryway table before she turned to watch Horse, his tail stretched toward the ceiling, gallop from room to room saying "Hello" to the house. Ruth smiled, wondered why she had not realized, before her parents' death, that Horse was a great companion. Shaking her head at the cat's antics, Ruth went into the kitchen and pulled out a can of cat food. She opened the can and emptied it into Horse's food bowl, added water to his dish and put her own supper in the oven. *If I hurry,* Ruth thought, *there should be time for a shower before I sit down to supper.*

Ruth stepped dripping wet from the shower just in time to hear the phone ring. She grabbed a towel, wrapped quickly and headed for her bedroom phone, arriving in time to hear the answering machine click in and record the message. Ruth dried herself and her hair, dressed and straightened the bathroom before she turned her attention back to the phone. The message light flashed its red reminder as Ruth walked into the family room. She found a pen and pushed the play button.

"Hello, I called about the Edsel Station Wagon. If you still have the car, call me at 555-1500. I would like to make arrangements to see the Edsel." Ruth replayed the message to make sure she had the number right and noted that the man had not left his name. She sat down at the desk to return the phone call.

He wanted to see the car tonight. Said he and his son would come by at 7:15. Ruth repeated her address and gave simple directions. His voice is pleasant, Ruth thought, not that it would do her any good. He had a son. Obviously he was a married man. Oh well, he wanted to see the car and no one else had even inquired. *With luck,* she thought, *I may at least sell the station wagon.*

The oven timer buzzed and Ruth rushed toward the kitchen to rescue her chicken potpie from the oven before it burned. She stood at the sink, eating and loading three days of dirty dishes into the dishwasher. As she ate and cleaned dishes she wondered if she could possibly work a once-a-week maid service into her budget.

***

Wyndom entered the kitchen just as Katie, her uniform covered by a frilly cobbler's apron, was starting supper. "Jason and I need to be somewhere at seven fifteen, Katie, could you fix us an early supper."

"Sandwiches work?" she asked, smiling her appreciation of his yes answer.

Katie began preparations while Wyndom went in search of his son.

Jason was stretched out on his bed. He lay on his back with his head cradled in his hands, staring at the ceiling. Wyndom wondered what was keeping him so still and inside on such a beautiful day, then he saw a tear slide down Jason's cheek and he knew something was wrong.

"Are you missing your mother, Jason?" he quietly inquired. Jason wiped the tear away, ran across the room and jumped into his dad's outstretched arms.

"You came home early," he said, hugging his father.

"I've an idea I wanted to talk over with you," Wyndom said and sat down on Jason's bed. He drew Jason to his side, slipped an arm around him. "What would you think if we bought a tent, some fishing equipment and started going camping on weekends?"

Jason hesitated. Frowned. "I don't know how to fish."

Wyndom laughingly allowed that he didn't remember how to fish anymore either, but, "We can learn together can't we."

"Okay Dad," he nodded. Hand in hand they went to the kitchen where the table was set for two. A smile lit Jason's eyes when he realized they were eating together.

***

Jason liked Katie. She treated him with kindness. She seemed to like little boys even when their grandmother said they were bad. She made sure there was always a snack waiting for Jason when he came home from school and she talked to him like he was a real person.

"Oh boy, hamburgers." Delighted, Jason bounced into his chair, "With lots of dill pickles, please," he said to Katie as he swung his feet to his own inner music. Even Wyndom enjoyed the simple food Kate prepared for them. The burgers and pickles were gone before Wyndom remembered to tell Jason his surprise.

"I think I've found the perfect camping vehicle, Jason. It's an old station wagon and we have an appointment to look at it tonight." Jason hurried off to wash his face and comb his hair. Then, hand in hand, father and son walked to the garage and took off in the Corvette.

Evelyn stood at the window watching the car disappear down the drive; a scowl marred what could have been a nice face if its owner had learned to smile more often. The quiet of the big old house settled around her and she was surprised to discover how much she missed Jason and Wyndom. Sometimes she understood why Cindy had abandoned her responsibilities, at other times Evelyn wondered how her daughter could just leave her own son for her fast crowd of friends. Now, Cindy was dead. She was lost to her mother and she would never see her own son grow to adulthood.

Evelyn sipped at the drink in her hand and wondered why she resented being a grandmother. Maybe she really didn't like little boys. Cindy was an only child and although she had been spoiled she had been easy to raise.

Evelyn wondered what would happen next to upset her routine; and she wondered why she resented her grandson's presence one minute and his absence the next. It occurred to Evelyn, as she finished her drink and poured another that what she hated most was the knowledge that she was alone in this house. Still, she decided to leave the brochures about boarding schools on Wyndom's pillow. Maybe he would take the hint. Evelyn knew she would enjoy having Wyndom's company at mealtime once more. She sipped at her drink swaying a little as she walked up the steps.

***

Ruth was putting the last dish in the dishwasher when Horse bounded to the back door, and Ruth heard the rumble of a car engine in the driveway. She slipped through the kitchen door into the breezeway, where she left the agitated puff of black fur trailing her, and stepped out into the attached garage.

Ruth pushed the button raising the overhead door and walked outside onto the double wide concrete drive. The man getting out of the red corvette was tall, handsome, and had a rugged, down to earth appearance some women appreciated. Ruth took one look and added herself to the list. She realized that he looked familiar and tried to remember where they might have met.

The twinge of knowing continued to nag until she noticed the little boy climbing out of the car and recognized her pupil. "Hello, Mr. Winters. Ruth Dennison, we met the other day at school," she said, held her hand out in friendship. "I'm Jason's teacher."

She shivered unexpectedly when their hands met and his large warm hand enveloped hers. Tingles whispered along Ruth's arm, left a dozen goose bumps breeding more in their wake.

"Call me, Wyndom, please," he said. His deep, resonant voice, washed heat down her spine.

Ruth looked down at the little boy standing so quietly beside his father and she recalled the devilishly bright and happy child she'd encountered when he first came to the school. She looked up at Jason's father, wondered if some how he was responsible for the dramatic change in his son's behavior.

"Could we see the Edsel you advertised?" he said interrupting her thoughts. Ruth led them into the garage and pushed the button that opened the other overhead door. Carefully, she lifted several blankets from over and around the vehicle. Light from the open doors enhanced the well-kept appearance of the old wagon.

"I can see your husband has taken good care of the car," Wyndom said.

"The car belonged to my parents. I'm not married." Ruth surprised herself with that admission.

Jason tugged at his father's sleeve, "I rode in that car, it's nice."

Ruth explained about the class trip while Wyndom perused the vehicle. He was astonished at how much it looked like the one he remembered belonging to his grandfather.

"Meeow... Meoow," Horse cried for attention, scratched at the screened enclosure. Jason looked around until he spotted the cat watching them from the breezeway. Ruth noticed the brief sparkle flare from the seven-year-olds eyes,

"Jason, would you like to go in and visit with Horse while your father and I look at the car? The door is unlocked and Horse is friendly."

Jason giggled. "He's a cat not a horse."

"You're right, Jason, but he has always been a cat named Horse."

Ruth watched her young pupil enter the screened enclosure and move carefully to the center of the breezeway. Jason stood quietly and eyed the black cat. Minute's later Horse decided to investigate Jason. Within minutes Jason was sitting cross-legged in the middle of the screened porch, Horse lay curled in his lap, the two seemed lost in their own world.

Wyndom studied the Edsel. The exterior body and paint were in excellent condition. The interior was full of surprises. There were five push buttons in the center of the steering wheel, power windows, seats and immaculate upholstery. The Edsel was definitely a beauty and Wyndom knew he was interested in a test drive. He asked Ruth to start the car so he could check out the engine.

She pulled keys from her pocket and tossed them to Wyndom. After several failed attempts to start the Edsel, Wyndom suggested it might have a dead battery.

"I know Dad had a battery charger but I don't know what to look for," Ruth admitted as her eyes scrutinized the neatly arranged shelves along the back wall of the garage.

Wyndom noted the neatness of the garage, noted that everything looked clean and that each item seemed to be stored in its own place. Mr. Dennison must have enjoyed spending time out here he thought, and wondered if Jason knew what had happened to the couple.

"Here it is," Wyndom said. The battery charger sat on the floor under the workbench. Wyndom removed the battery from the Edsel and hooked it up to the charger. "I'll stop by in the morning and check on it if you want," he said, walking back to stand by Ruth. Together they stood and watched Jason somberly rubbing his hand over the black cat.

31

She thanked him and apologized for not being aware of the car's condition. "It hasn't been run since the picnic, and after their accident, memories have kept me away from all my parent's cars."

It was then that Wyndom connected the name Dennison with the couple who'd been killed by Cindy in the accident that had taken Cindy's life as well. Because of Evelyn Carlyle's influence, the incident had been played down and the press had squelched most of the coverage in an attempt to protect the Carlyle name. It was a shock to realize his ex-wife had been responsible for this pretty woman's loss. Now he recognized that it was sadness that lingered in her dark brown eyes.

Both of the adults still stared unconsciously at Jason. Wyndom interrupted Ruth's glance, "He really has changed, I didn't even realize it until you called it to my attention. Thank you for that," he said quietly. "I wish I knew how to make him happy again."

Ruth placed her hand on Wyndom's forearm, "Let him know that you love him, Mr. Winters," she said and quickly pulled her hand from his arm to stem the tingling she felt flare up her fingers.

"It's Wyndom, my father is Mr. Winters," he corrected, enjoying the warmth of her touch.

"You're Jason's only parent right now and he needs to spend time with you. I'm sure he's just missing his mother."

Wyndom did not correct her impression. Did not want anyone to know how little time his ex-wife had spent with her son. Cindy was too wrapped up in herself to care about another person. There had to be a different reason for Jason's withdrawal. Wyndom didn't know what the problem was but he understood that it was his problem to solve.

When it was time to depart, Jason seemed reluctant to leave the purring black cat. Finally he slipped from the breezeway and walked quietly to the car.

"We'll see you in the morning," Wyndom said. He watched Jason fasten his seat belt, closed the door and walked around the car to slide in beside his son. He waited to back out of the drive until Ruth had closed herself safely inside the overhead doors.

CHAPTER FOUR

Ruth was busy putting her briefcase and lunch box in her wine-red '69 Cougar convertible, when the Winters' car pulled into the drive. She wore a pair of silver-gray slacks and a deep purple silk blouse. A suede vest of multi hued purple patches covered the vibrant silk blouse and a charcoal gray sweater jacket topped the outfit. Wind tugged at her pony-tailed hair, causing soft mink-brown tendrils to curl around her oval face. Her mahogany hued eyes brightened and she smiled with welcome as the Corvette slowed to a stop.

Wyndom immediately noticed the sun-splashed reddish-gold highlights in Ruth's hair and wondered, once again, why he'd never been fortunate enough to have such a lovely teacher. Sunshine glazed off the Corvette's hood, bounced through the windshield and momentarily blinded him. Wyndom snapped the visor down enabling him to savor her appearance another moment before he exited the car.

Wind fingers rumpled Wyndom's hair when he stepped from the Vette. Umber waves rippled into locks that fell across his forehead, giving him a boyish air.

"I'll check that battery," he said and hurried toward the garage. "I'm running late this morning. I hope we didn't hold you up." *She sure looks nice,* he thought again, lowering his eyes to disconnect the cables of the recharged battery. He would have liked to visit, spend some time just looking at her, enjoying that fresh, open, friendly appeal he sensed was her essence.

"If you're late, Mr. Winters—" at his raised eyebrow she amended it. "Wyndom. I'd be pleased to take Jason on to school with me, that is if you think he wouldn't mind."

"Thanks. That really would help. I'll ask Jason."

Ruth shut and secured the garage door, turning in time to watch Jason staring after his quickly departing father. His intense gaze left Ruth with the weird impression that the young boy thought he might not see his father ever again. She knew his mother had been killed recently and wondered if Jason was afraid for his father. Death could be very traumatic for those left behind, Ruth knew from experience.

She opened the Cougar's door and motioned Jason inside, showed him how to fasten his seat belt then walked around to slide in beside him. Throughout the drive, the seven-year-old quietly sat staring down at his too-clean sneakered feet. Once they reached the school parking lot, Jason politely offered to help Ruth carry her folder of papers, briefcase and lunch inside to her classroom. When Jason seemed reluctant to join the other students out on the playground, Ruth allowed him to assist her with class preparation.

Splashes of color covered the walls and brightened the second grade room. Pictures, vibrant with imagination and displaying the students' favorite animal or pet, hung on the walls amid the best landscape artwork of each. Their miniature garden grew green and lush in the sunshine spilling across the windowsill and Ruth watched as Jason carefully watered each plant.

A special corner of the classroom was set up for reading. The area's chairs were comfortable, varied in style, and past pupils had painted each a bright color. Books were arranged on shelves within easy reach of the students. Anyone who finished early with his required assignment was allowed the privilege of time in the corner.

Jason spent a good part of each day draped across his favorite beanbag chair intent on his reading. He was a good student: a student who rarely participated beyond what was required, a student who never misbehaved.

Upon entering the classroom each pupil found an envelope on his or her desk. They all smiled up at Ruth while she explained the morning exercise. Together they opened their envelopes and studied their individual word. One by one they walked to the front of the room and wrote their word on the blackboard before turning and regaling the rest of the class with a story, truth or fiction, utilizing that word.

Some of the stories were simple, little more than a few sentences; others were beyond wild as giant carrots ravished the cafeteria eating only girls. Everyone enjoyed the casual atmosphere and the teacher's praise. Ruth silently marveled at the creativity of their young minds.

Jason walked to the front of the room and wrote H O R S E on the blackboard. "Miss Dennison has a cat. The cat is black with white in his ears and on the tip of his tail. When you pet the cat he will sit on your lap and you can feel his motor running. The cat's name is Horse. I met Horse yesterday. I liked him and he liked me."

After Jason's story, his being the last, Mary Lynn asked if Ruth would bring Horse to school for a visit. The students all begged for a chance to meet the teacher's cat.

Mrs. Naylor chose that moment to walk into the room. She handed a note to Ruth before turning to smile at the eager faces of the boisterous second graders. Red haired, freckle faced, Jerry Bartlett, grinning from ear to ear raised his hand, waving it to get Mrs. Naylor's attention. She acknowledged him. "Can Miss Dennison bring her cat to school for a visit?"

Several other students chimed in with "Please."

Mrs. Naylor smiled at the class then turned to Ruth. "It's your classroom, I don't mind. Could be a good learning project."

Friday was settled on as the day Horse could come for a visit. Good-natured cheering and applause followed the decision. Ruth efficiently calmed the exuberant group and passed out the math assignment before she sat down to read the note.

"Call Wyndom during your lunch break. 555-1500"

After ushering the students to the cafeteria, Ruth decided to use the pay phone in the hall since the phone in the teacher's lounge offered her no privacy.

"Mr. Winters?"

"Wyndom, please," he reminded. "I hope your day is working out better then mine."

"Problems?" Ruth inquired, hearing tension in his tone.

"I wanted to test drive the Edsel tonight but find I need to drive to Ames," he said. Ruth heard him sigh. "I won't get out of this meeting until after four. Since I want to test drive the station wagon, I wondered if we could drive the Edsel to Ames? It would solve both my problems. I'll buy supper, fill up the gas tank...If you're not busy."

He waited. "Ruth?"

"You may take the car without me," Ruth offered quietly.

"No! It's still your car. You have to come." Silence stretched between them. "I am serious about purchasing the Edsel," Wyndom said as encouragement.

"Fine," Ruth said. "Would it help if I took Jason home with me?"

Ruth liked the sound of his soft chuckle. His tone was more relaxed when he replied, "Thank you. That would be a big help. I'll see you this afternoon about five."

"Good-bye," Ruth said. She hung up the phone and walked into the teacher's lounge, no longer interested in eating her lunch.

At the final bell Ruth motioned Jason aside, asked him to stay and help clean the room. All her students considered it a privilege to stay behind and feed the turtle, put the books on the shelves in the reading area and straighten the chairs.

Ruth watched Jason quietly complete each chore. Once finished he looked up at Ruth to see if there was more to be done. "Jason, I talked with your father during the lunch break. He's coming over after work to test drive the Edsel; we are going with him. If you want to help me lock up, he said you could wait for him at my house."

Jason's reserve slipped for just a moment, his eyes glowed, and he whispered, "I get to see Horse again."

"Yes," Ruth said, rumpling Jason's hair before handing him her lunch box. She picked up her briefcase and they walked side by side out of the building to Ruth's car.

Once both were buckled in and headed toward home, Ruth complimented Jason on his story. "Would you like to feed Horse for me once we get home?" Although the seven-year-old did not answer her verbally, Ruth sensed perkiness in his attitude when he nodded his head.

Horse watched them from the screened breezeway where he had spent the day. Ruth had left him in this morning because rain was predicted. Horse was not fond of getting wet. The lawn and the early spring flowers looked and smelled squeaky clean after the day's shower. Ruth took a deep breath pausing for just a brief moment to enjoy her surroundings.

Jason had not spoken or even looked at Ruth since he indicated his pleasure at feeding the cat. The three of them, Ruth, Jason and Horse entered the house by way of the garage and breezeway. Once they were in the kitchen, Horse took off at a gallop, the sound of his paws echoing through out the house. After a hurried tour of each room to check that all was well, the black cat skidded to a halt at Jason's feet.

Ruth opened a can of food for Horse and showed Jason which dish held food and which held water. While Jason emptied the can of food and filled the water dish, Ruth set peanut butter, crackers and milk on the table for the seven-year-old.

"Jason, the bathroom is behind that door. Wash up before you fix yourself a snack. You may keep Horse company while I change."

The pained look on Jason's face halted her departure. "Is there a problem, Jason?"

"I might make a mess," he said, his speech halting and difficult to hear because he refused to look up at her. Ruth put a hand on his shoulder, turned him toward the counter and the paper towels.

"If you make a mess, clean it up as best you can, okay," she said.

"You won't be mad at me?" he mumbled.

"Horse makes messes all the time. Don't worry about it, Jason. I need to change. You are in charge out here."

What an unusual young man, it just didn't seem normal for him to worry about spilling milk before it happens, she thought as she left the kitchen. Ruth knew she would have to keep her eyes open where Jason was concerned. Maybe this trip tonight would give her some insight into the relationship between father and son.

Ruth's bedroom appeared large by new home standards but it was not the largest bedroom in the house, that privilege was reserved for the room her parents had used. Ruth could not bring herself to move her things into that room. She continued to use the bedroom decorated for her when the house was first built. Its soft pastel colors calmed her, helped her to feel safe and secure. Feelings she craved even more since her parent's death.

Unsure of how soon Wyndom would arrive, she pulled a pair of rust slacks and a matching sweater from her closet. Changing quickly, Ruth stood in front of her mirrored dresser to comb her hair and refresh her lipstick.

While she hung up her outfit her thoughts drifted back to her student and his father, she hoped Wyndom was not the cause of Jason's withdrawal. She wanted to believe the man's easy grace, rugged features, and natural smile were the window dressings of a man who truly loved his son. Watching their interaction tonight might give her a better understanding of Jason's situation.

Stepping into her penny loafers and taking one last look in the mirror, Ruth went in search of her cat and her guest. Jason stood, steel-post still, in front of the French doors, his eyes luminous, his attitude attentive.

Jason put a finger to his lips with a "shush" and pointed to the back yard. Two rabbits, crouched in a spot of sun, were laying and munching on rain beaded grass. Jason was totally awed by the sight.

Ruth perused the scene. The young rabbits were surround by rainbow hued water beads suspended from grass shoots and dandelion fluff, beads that glistened throughout the sun washed yard creating an almost unreal magic, a marvelous sense of wonder that convinced Ruth that she could not possibly leave this home her parents built. A home she had come to cherish.

Except for the three large garages, the back yard seemed like a park. There were benches arranged strategically through out the area. Places where her mother sat to read or watch the myriad number of creatures flitting about.

Ruth and Jason stood enraptured by the view. They watched two robins play tug-of-war over a worm, watched a chipmunk scurry along the path, stopping every three or four feet to look around, its manner and movements bright and alert. Both watched the furry creature move nose to nose with a slender stalk of dandelion fluff. Tail quivering, the chipmunk seemed to be analyzing a new unexpected treasure or maybe just surveying his bit of the world through the curtain of fluff. Jason had never seen a chipmunk before and the small creature fascinated him.

"I wonder what the world looks like to him?" Jason said. He remained still until the critter grew restless and scampered off into the shadows. Jason continued to scrutinize the back yard while Ruth explained that the tiny mini-squirrel was part of a whole family that resided under her attached garage.

Ruth whispered, "Listen."

The back yard resonated with clamor: singing birds, raucous crickets, wind whistling through trees and grass, insects humming and squirrels vocalizing their backyard gossip. Nature's roar had melted together into a vast symphony.

Jason put his hand in Ruth's; "My Grandmother has a swimming pool in her back yard." Ruth could not detect from Jason's tone if having a pool was a plus.

She smiled down at him; "Do you like to swim?"

"No," he quietly admitted. "I think I like your rabbits and chipmunks better." His quiet tone was suddenly laced with sadness.

Ruth knelt beside Jason, slipped her arm around his shoulders. "I agree," she murmured.

Horse, feeling neglected and in need of attention, pounced on Jason's feet. Swiftly the cat swivelled, galloped to the front door, around the couch twice and then he made a flying leap for his favorite perch, the living room windowsill. Jason's sadness vanished and he giggled at the cat's antics his features as relaxed and happy as a young boy's should be.

When the doorbell sounded Ruth, Jason and Horse were surprised, not having heard the car or Wyndom's footsteps. Jason immediately bombarded his father with a breathless narration of all he had seen in Ruth's marvelous back yard. Wyndom was pulled toward the expanse of glass and he swiftly agreed with his son that Ruth's back yard was marvelous.

"Are those buildings out back part of your property?" Wyndom asked Ruth.

"My father's car collection." Ruth said and smiled when Wyndom's eyebrows raised questioningly.

"There are twenty-some cars out there," Ruth said, unsure of the exact number. "Most are Edsels, plus one '50 Ford convertible and a Ford Retractable in the mix."

Wyndom looked at his watch; "I really want to see those cars. Today, however, I have to meet my foreman, Bruce, at the job site before it gets too dark."

Ruth grabbed a jacket from the closet by the front door while Wyndom helped Jason gather his things. Ruth handed the keys to Wyndom and closing Horse in the kitchen she followed the Winters men through the breezeway and out into the garage. Ruth opened the overhead door enabling Wyndom to back the Edsel out. After closing and locking the door, she joined Wyndom and Jason in the wagon.

CHAPTER FIVE

While the station wagon idled at the edge of the drive, Wyndom climbed out to familiarize himself with all aspects of the old car. Imitation wood panels gracing each side of the exterior, a feature of the Bermuda wagon, were in mint condition, as were the painted portions of the vehicle. The horse-collar shaped front grille gave the Edsel its distinctive design. Wyndom carefully perused the Edsel's body before rejoining Jason and Ruth. Everything about the car seemed to delight him.

"I don't believe I've ever seen any car but the Edsel this particular color red," he said to Ruth as he eased out of the driveway. "My grandfather called it watermelon red."

"My father was partial to red," Ruth said, her voice thick with sadness and grief at the thought of her parents.

Wyndom guided the wagon onto interstate 35. "Car handles like a dream, Ruth. I think you have a real treasure here." He reached up to adjust the mirror.

"What about it Jason, do you think we should buy this car?" He watched his son through the rearview mirror; the affirmative nod of Jason's head was barely discernable.

Jason's emotionless response puzzled and perturbed Wyndom. For a few minutes back in Ruth's living room Jason had been more like his old self. Now, it seemed to Wyndom, that his son was holding himself tightly closed off, acting as if he were terrified to just be Jason. Wyndom was puzzled.

The beep-beep of a horn drew Wyndom's attention. The car in the oncoming lane was alive with waving, smiling people, none of whom were familiar to Wyndom. Movement in the back seat caught his attention and he watched Jason's reflection, watched his son come alert, waving at the passing car.

"Do you know those people, Jason?"

"No, but they like our car. When I rode to the picnic with Mr. Dennison it happened to us a lot and once when we were stopped at a street light some one asked him if he wanted to trade."

Wyndom glanced quizzically at Ruth.

"My father always said the Edsel turned everyone friendly, people always honked and waved at us and wherever we stopped there was someone interested in the car and full of questions."

Wyndom was touched by the way Ruth's face lit up in a half smile as she told of the pleasure she and her parents had encountered traveling in an Edsel. He remembered that it hadn't been like that when his Grandfather drove the Edsel wagon, in fact he recalled several incidents when his granddad had been ridiculed.

Each time the car was noticed by some passersby, Jason came alive. Ruth and Wyndom were pleased by the sparkle that emanated from him at each encounter and Wyndom wondered what he could do to keep his son this way.

Once they reached the job site, Wyndom politely excused himself, leaving Ruth and Jason in the car while he rushed to his meeting with Bruce. Ruth tried to draw Jason out with questions about his hobbies and his activities at home but his answers were short and uninformative. She turned her attention to the beginning structure before her and wondered at its eventual purpose. The structure already stood two stories high with evidence of a third in the process of being built. Layers of brick joined to create a shape like a square cornered "U" with the open end to the front.

Ruth watched the two men. She guessed Bruce to be about the same age as Wyndom. Noted that the men were total opposites in coloring, and although they were about the same height, Bruce was stockier.

Their conversation became animated and Ruth watched Wyndom use his hands to articulate his ideas. When an older man joined the conversation, Ruth would have guessed his age at sixty-eight or so but in truth he was eighty-years-young. The oldster's eyes were bright with intelligence and his movements attested to good health. Ruth wondered if he were a concerned neighbor, and determined to ask Wyndom about him during supper.

She turned to ask Jason about his food preference and was surprised by the intensity with which the boy watched his father. His look seemed filled with such fear, Ruth had to fight an impulse to draw the boy into the front seat, where she could hold and comfort him.

When Wyndom returned he suggested they eat at a local Mexican restaurant and Jason groaned quietly. Jason's plea for burgers and fries drew smiles from both adults and Wyndom turned the Edsel toward the local burger joint.

"This place is really crowded," Wyndom said, searching for a place to park. "Look at all the old cars." Wyndom slowed to accommodate onlookers as once again the Edsel attracted attention.

A young man sporting a fire-decorated car emblazoned T-shirt directed them to a parking space. "Hi folks, here's your three free drink tickets, be sure to register for the drawing. Tickets are available up at the DJ's table." He quickly pointed out the DJ and said, "Have a good time. Thanks for bringing your car to our first-of-the-year Cruise night."

Wyndom turned to Ruth; "Did you know about this?"

"Several restaurants in Des Moines have car nights throughout the summer on Friday or Saturday. I had no idea Ames scheduled theirs on Wednesday. Cruise nights are a popular pastime," she said.

Before they could even climb out of the car two men walked up obviously intent on checking over the '58 wagon. Wyndom's tiredness evaporated. He heard one of the men remark, "It's an old Edsel. I haven't seen one of these in years. Sure is a beauty."

Wyndom willingly showed them the engine; proud at the attention the car was getting. Unhappily he could not answer most of their questions but vowed to learn all there was to know about the car he already thought of as his. Next time he would be prepared.

Ruth took Jason's hand, "Let's go get our tickets for the drawing, we'll leave your father to show off the car."

They easily found the DJ since huge speakers wailing tunes from the rock and roll era bracketed his table. Jason put one ticket in the pocket of his jeans, handed another to Ruth and saved the last to give his dad, once they returned to the car.

Wyndom reached for Ruth's hand put his arm around Jason's shoulder and with a lopsided grin announced, "Let's eat."

The restaurant was crowded but they found a table for three. Wyndom took their food orders and went to stand in the shortest food line. Jason sat quietly, watching through the window as people drifted over to study the Edsel station wagon.

Ruth had not seen Jason this at ease for months. "I hope Dad buys the wagon," he said, almost as if he were talking to himself.

After eating, the three returned to the parking lot. Wyndom squeezed Ruth's hand, "Well, Teach, do we have time to check out these other cars or are you in a hurry?"

When he smiled down at her, Ruth's breath caught, stalled. The air expanded, felt trapped around her heart adding a husky quality to her voice. "Let's stay and look," Ruth softly said. They strolled along the line of parked cars. Wyndom pointed out years and makes to Jason, impressing Ruth when he cautioned Jason to use his eyes not his hands as they circled and studied the cars.

Jason perked up when he heard the DJ announce the drawing. Standing in front of the Bermuda wagon, Wyndom and Ruth were more intent on their conversation with the owner of a 1957 Chevy. Jason listened to the numbers being drawn, bouncing from one foot to the other in anticipation.

"Number seven eight three," the DJ announced.

"Dad, that's my number, I won."

"We'll be back in a minute," Ruth said and reached for Jason's hand. "Let's go collect your prize."

Wyndom watched Jason strut beside Ruth, his eyes shadowed by an adult size baseball cap, his grin, ear to ear. He proudly displayed his hat and a booklet of coupons worth $5.00 toward their next visit to this fast food chain.

"I'd say you're a very lucky person, son," Wyndom said, putting the coupons in his shirt pocket for safekeeping.

"I know, Dad, but maybe you'll get the girl." Astonishment crossed the faces of both adults; it was quickly followed by bursts of barely concealed laughter.

"Television. Too much television," Wyndom said under his breath as he watched the pink of a blush creep up Ruth's cheeks.

"On that note, I think it's time we head for home," Wyndom said, steering Jason toward the Bermuda wagon. Once Wyndom had promised to take Jason to a Cruise night again soon the small boy seemed to relax.

As the car merged with traffic, Wyndom noticed Jason yawn for the second time, "Pull off your shoes son and lay down back there, we've an hour's drive." Ruth could hear the tenderness in his voice each time he spoke to Jason.

Wyndom pulled onto the interstate and, keeping his eye on the speed control, he lowered his voice. "We never did talk price for the Edsel, Ruth. I am serious about buying the car."

"Dad talked about selling the car before his death. He planned to advertise it for $6500.00 in the International Edsel Club national newsletter," Ruth said, a mist of sorrow lacing her tone as she spoke of her parent.

"If you think that price is fair, we have a deal." Wyndom said.

Ruth sighed. Rubbing her fingers lightly over the dash, she looked at the dust glazing her fingertips and Wyndom wondered if she was thinking about her father. Wyndom decided not to dicker about the price and after a brief discussion, they agreed on a time to get together and transfer the title.

Ruth looked into the back of the wagon. Jason was curled in a corner of the seat; his new cap was clutched to his chest. Wyndom saw the same picture when he looked in the rear view mirror.

In a voice so quiet she barely heard, Wyndom said, "What can I do to help Jason?"

"Do things together, Wyndom. Let him know you love him. He seems to be afraid of something. If you spend more time with him maybe you will uncover the problem." Ruth reached out and touched his hand. "Tonight was a good start." Wyndom tipped his hand and caught her fingers, his clasp firm but restrictive. He rubbed his thumb over the back of her hand, enjoying the contact. He felt young and invincible one minute and old the next. Still he refused to release her hand. In fact he hoped that she needed a little human contact as much as he did.

Slowly stars popped one by one from their night windows and all around the Edsel the country road resounded with the buzz of multiple insects singing their thanksgiving to God for the perfection of the night.

Wyndom and Ruth, fingers entwined, were steeped in the revelry as they journeyed home, both aware of a blissful magic long absent from their lives. Once the car was parked in the garage, Wyndom reluctantly released her fingers and exiting the front seat he opened the passenger door and lifted his son from the car.

"I'm serious about trying to help him, Ruth. You work with young people all the time so if I'm doing something wrong or if you think of a solution, please, I need help."

They walked side by side toward his car and Ruth held the door while he belted Jason into the seat. She set Jason's new cap in his lap then carefully closed the door, eager to walk with Wyndom to the driver's side to share an idea.

"I've considered inviting parents to spend a day in the classroom to help and to observe," she said. "If you could take the time to visit for a day I think it might mean a lot to Jason."

He studied her face, and then leaning close he kissed her cheek and said, "How about Friday?" *She looks so beautiful in the moonlight her eyes widened by surprise,* Wyndom thought, unable to stop staring down at her.

"Friday is great," she murmured, caught up in emotions she'd never experienced before. Emotions stirred to life by her pupil's father. She stood motionless. Wyndom climbed in beside his son and she watched him drive away, unaware that her hand was still touching the place he'd kissed.

Ruth absentmindedly entered the house through the garage making sure to lock all the doors in her wake. She floated through the house steeped in the joy of her evening until it suddenly dawned on her: Friday! Friday both Horse and Wyndom would be in her classroom.

CHAPTER SIX

Jason sat in the kitchen, his chin resting in his hands his elbows on the table and his feet swinging back and forth, occasionally bumping the chair rung. Milk and cookies sat untouched in front of him. Today was Thursday. He was remembering how much fun he'd had at the burger place last night with Dad and his teacher. She was nice. She smelled good and she never ever yelled at him...course she never yelled at anyone in her class.

"Jason! Jason, stop kicking!" His feet froze and he visibly stiffened at the sound of her voice, his hand jerked and his glass of milk splattered across the table.

"First you scuff my chair then you spill milk everywhere. You're disruptive and clumsy," Evelyn snapped, her voice louder than necessary. "No wonder your mother left you, you're always such a naughty boy."

Jason scrambled for the paper towels, tears sparkled unshed in his eyes at his grandmother's comments. He swiped at the milk, his efforts only making the mess worse.

"Stop it, Jason. You're impossible. Just go to your room. Now!"

When Wyndom arrived home it was already starting to get dark. He had stayed at work later than usual making it possible to spend Friday at school with his son. He had decided not to mention his plan to Jason until he knew it would be possible, now Wyndom was eager to give him the news. Wyndom entered the too-quiet house, went in search of people. He walked from room to room until he found Evelyn in the library.

She was stretched out on the divan listening to classical music, her face covered with a heat mask. Wyndom recognized it as her standard treatment for a headache and quietly closed the door. He hurried upstairs hoping to find Jason playing in his room.

The door hung ajar, the room lay in darkness and echoed the quiet of the lower floor. Wyndom pushed against the door, spied Jason, sound asleep in the middle of his bed. Scruffy, his stuffed bear, was clutched to his chest, there were tear tracks staining his cheeks.

Looking at him, so small and vulnerable, Wyndom was jolted by the force of the love he felt. He wondered what had happened tonight to cause Jason tears, wondered what he could do to keep his son happy.

Wyndom thought about the brochures that he'd found strewn across his bed. He knew that Evelyn had left them for him. It angered Wyndom to think that Jason's grandmother wanted to send him away and knew he needed to speak to her about the situation. If Evelyn couldn't handle having Jason around, they would move.

Wyndom unfolded the blanket at the foot of Jason's bed and covered boy and bear. He sat watching Jason sleep for a long time before he left the room. Slipping down the stairs, he walked into the kitchen, made himself a sandwich, ate it quickly then went up to his room to make a telephone call.

***

Ruth sat at the kitchen table sipping her morning coffee, captivated by the beauty visible from her patio doors. Sun splashed a golden glaze across the emerald hued grass, enriching the brilliant yellow of the dandelions and turning the dew into a kaleidoscope of color. Joyously, Ruth asked God to bless the coming day. She thanked him; for the beauty spread before her, for her life, and most especially for a certain tall handsome man and his son. "Thank you for relieving the intensity of my grief." After her silent 'amen' she finished her coffee and walked to the sink to rinse her cup.

Horse did not appreciate his traveling enclosure. His cries of distress sounded almost human as they reverberated through the entryway. Finally the knock at the front door distracted the cat in his plea for freedom and he peeked through his cage in expectation. When Ruth opened the door to Wyndom and Jason, Horse was so delighted to see his new friend that he ran circles in his cage.

Last evening Ruth had explained to Wyndom about the cat coming to class and they determined that the station wagon was the appropriate means of transportation for the day.

Ruth handed the owner's manual for the Bermuda wagon to Wyndom, "I found this among some of Dad's books I thought you might enjoy the information."

Wyndom flipped through the pages. "Thank you," he said. Ruth smiled as he pocketed the manual.

"My reading assignment for the day?" Wyndom said, lifting his eyebrows in an exaggerated question to comply with his tone of voice.

"Of course," Ruth said in her best school teacher tone.

Wyndom picked up the caged cat and waited for Ruth to open the garage door. Horse's distress diminished when Jason joined him in the back of the wagon.

***

As each child entered the classroom, he or she was greeted by Horse, sniffed at, circled cautiously, and with the highest disdain, nose in the air, the cat would sauntered over to curl up at Jason's feet. All the students handled the episode with laughter and Jason glowed at the cat's attention.

Obviously Horse received more notice than the tall, good-looking, man lounging in the reading area, his nose buried in the Edsel owner's manual. When Mrs. Naylor entered the room minutes before the starting bell; Horse scrutinized her, as he had everyone else, but this time he rubbed against Mrs. Naylor's ankles and purred contentedly.

It was obvious to the entire class that the snooty cat approved of their principal.

"I can tell already that you are going to have an interesting day," she murmured to Ruth. "An arrogant cat, and the attractive Mr. Winters." Mrs. Naylor picked up Horse, eyed him nose to nose and said, "You mind your manners today young man." She set the cat back down at her feet, turned and waved at the giggling students before she excused herself and continued her morning inspection.

After the pledge of allegiance, the day started in earnest. Ruth worked with some of her slow readers on their phonics while Wyndom made himself available to the rest of the class if they needed help with math workbooks. The morning went smoothly and Ruth was as surprised as Wyndom at how easily the students accepted and utilized his presence.

During lunch, Ruth and Wyndom sat together in the cafeteria. She noticed the stir he was creating and the envious stares of her fellow teachers. When Wyndom took her hand in his after a quick wink, she knew he too was aware of the attention directed their way.

"We might as well make it look good," he whispered, a mischievous gleam in his eyes. Wyndom watched a blush wash across Ruth's cheeks at his open flirtation. It became more and more difficult for Ruth to suppress her laughter at Wyndom's exaggerated antics and boyish grin. Thank heaven most of his exaggerated actions were out of sight of the students. He directed his mischief solely for her colleagues. Refreshed by the food, the relaxing camaraderie and the brief break from the classroom, Ruth and Wyndom strolled back to the classroom, hand in hand.

Ruth kept occupied at her desk and Wyndom settled in a corner of the reading room to wait for the students to come in from the playground. It took several minutes for the class to settle in and get ready for their lesson. They had each been previously instructed to find out where they were born: the state, county, city and name of the hospital. Now each stood and recited what they had learned. Most said the same thing, Iowa, Polk county, Des Moines and the name of one of the four hospitals in the area. However, one of the girls had been born on an army base in Germany, another in Central America and Jerry Bartlett, whose parents were missionaries, had been born in South Africa. The large map above the blackboard was pulled down and these areas were pointed out and discussed in a combination geography-social studies lesson.

Ruth passed back several graded papers before announcing, "Wyndom Winters, Jason's father, is helping out today in our classroom, maybe we can persuade him to come up and tell us about his career. Wyndom?"

He walked casually to the front of the room, ran his fingers through his hair nervously and said, "No one told me I'd have to give a speech, do you really want to hear this?"

The students yelled "Yes" simultaneously.

Raising his hands in surrender, Wyndom began. "I design and construct buildings. At the present time we're working on a project for Iowa State University," he said, looking from one eager face to another.

"The building will have living quarters for senior citizens, a nursery, a cafeteria and a combination adult and child day care center. We'll have a playground and designated plots for both vegetable and flower gardens to encourage everyone to spend time outside."

"I don't understand about the nursery," Ruth said when Wyndom offered to answer any questions.

He told them of the group of senior citizens who were concerned with the alarming number of drug addicted and AIDS babies left unwanted in hospitals.

The senior citizens were intending to foster parent and care for a few of these children.

"The older people believe their lives will be enriched along with the lives of the babies," he said. "The University offered to help fund the project if they could study the effect of the interaction on both the seniors and the babies."

"My grandfather tells the best stories," one the girls offered. "The babies will like the stories."

"The seniors have appointed a liaison to work with my crew. He's had some very valuable ideas to insure our project meets the needs of the older people." Ruth immediately pictured the older gentleman she remembered from their visit in Ames.

"Do you have more questions?" Ruth asked the students.

Wyndom treated each question seriously and Ruth could see he was surprised by the students' interest. Because they seemed so curious, he promised to bring a working model of the building to the class in the near future.

Ruth passed out boxes of colored markers and paper and asked each student to draw a scene from the story read to them before lunch. She moved through the room offering advice and praise as the pupils bent their heads to the art project.

School was about over when Horse grew restless and took to prowling.

Quick as lightening, Horse galloped from one corner of the room to the other, around desks and feet, intently investigating the whole. He stretched up on his hind legs to peek inside the glass home of Theodore R., the class turtle. Suddenly the case tipped surprising Horse and spilling the turtle onto the table.

Theodore R. landed on his back. He began rocking to right himself and came too close to the edge of the low table. Thankfully, the turtle landed on his hard-shell back, bounced once then flipped upright. Stunned but pleased to be free from his glass home, the turtle poked his head out and began to survey his surroundings. Horse watched all of this, mesmerized by this unfamiliar creature. The cat studied the turtle for several minutes then he poked his nose at the slow moving animal. He sniffed once, backed off momentarily and circled twice. Straining forward, Horse nudged the turtle with his nose.

The startled turtle snapped its jaws.

Horse jumped backward.

With unusual bravado, the turtle snapped again.

Horse hissed.

The turtle stretched his neck, and shuffling toward the cat, he snapped once again.

In one swift movement, the black cat turned and leaped, hitting a startled Wyndom in the chest broadside.

Wyndom lost his balance and toppled backwards onto the reading room's one and only bean bag chair.

With a pop, the chair exploded, spewing popcorn-like debris everywhere.

Laughter burst from the students, while embarrassment momentarily tainted Wyndom's cheeks red. However he was soon hugging the shaken cat and chortling loudly with everyone else.

Ruth, unable to resist, joined in the laughter, amazed at how appealing Wyndom looked sprawled ridiculously across the floor.

Jason was still gloating about the incident in the classroom when they drove the Edsel to the courthouse to transfer the title. Wyndom's face positively glowed when he discovered his grandfather's name listed on the document as a past owner. His memories of the summer they spent together were his happiest and the Edsel wagon had been an important part of their activities.

Both Winters men were almost jovial as they drove Ruth home and Wyndom was delighted at Jason's open, teasing manner.

"This has been a good day," he said when they pulled into Ruth's drive.

Wyndom looked down at his watch; "I'd love to see your father's car collection, Ruth." He studied her face waiting her acquiescence.

I do not want to go home, Wyndom thought as he and Jason followed Ruth in to get keys. Horse was released from his cage and fed before they walked out the back door.

They moved slowly through each of the large buildings. Most of the cars were convertibles and Wyndom especially admired the Edsels. He and Jason also admired a 1950 Ford convertible, several Cougar rag tops and a 1967 Mustang convertible.

"It's obvious your father liked red," Wyndom said, noting the number of cars in various shades of that color.

Ruth moved from building to building locking each. "Dad had a hard time turning down a red car, Mom often teased him about it."

"That is quite a collection, Ruth," Wyndom said as he watched her lock the last door. "Is the '73 Cougar the newest car here?"

"Yes, nothing newer and except for the two Cougar convertibles, they're all Fords," Ruth commented comfortably as they strolled through the yard back to the house.

Wyndom easily talked Ruth and Jason into another trip to Hardee's. Jason seemed relaxed, bouncing from one side of the back seat to the other chattering about his day. Watching him reminded both adults of the happy child he was a year ago.

***

The drive-in overflowed with cars, most 1970 or older. Hand in hand the three walked from one car to another pleased with the variety of make, model, style, and color. Everyone driving in a classic car received a Star Trek glass and Jason insisted on using the coupons he'd won in Ames.

People, music and, most of all, the man walking at her side, transformed the evening into magic for Ruth. She knew by the easy manor, with which Wyndom fielded questions about the wagon, that he had digested the owner's manual she'd given him before school. Pride of ownership gleamed from his eyes every time he talked about the car to anyone interested.

They feasted on burgers, hummed to the music and enjoyed the evening. Soon the absence of the sun created a chill in the air and robbed the day of light. Everyone seemed to know that it was time they left the drive-in.

Wyndom slowed the Edsel, stopped in front of Ruth's garage. He opened his car door then hers and walked Ruth up to her front porch. He unlocked her front door and gave her a bear hug, whispering, "Thank you, for the best day I've had all year. May I call You? We could go out on a date."

Ruth chuckled at his effervescent mood and said, "Yes."

Wyndom grinned. He leaned down to give Ruth a swift kiss on the mouth before returning to the car and a sleeping Jason nestled snugly in the back seat.

Driving home, Wyndom tried to figure out what had made the evening...no the whole day, so very special. It took a while to understand that it was being with Jason and Ruth. She was talented at making him and everyone else around her feel important. She radiated natural warmth that made others feel important and comfortable. Wyndom silently admitted that he enjoyed their time together. Cindy, his ex-wife, had been beautiful and exciting to be with at first, but she always had to be the center of attention.

Wyndom had not dated anyone since Cindy left him. There had not been anyone he was interested in until now. And he was interested in Ruth, he admitted to himself. He chuckled, recalled her blush in the lunchroom today. By the time he and Jason arrived home and he carried Jason to bed, Wyndom had mentally planned his first date with Ruth.

Jason did not once wake up while his father removed his shoes and tucked him beneath the covers. A smile settled on Wyndom's mouth at the picture of Jason trying to master a Hula-Hoop for the kids' contest at Hardee's. Wyndom had a feeling Jason would master the hoop with just a few more tries.

When the thirty-four year old left his son's room, his thoughts returned to the image of Ruth. She knew how to make a Hula-Hoop sing with the gyrations of her hips. Ruth had promised to dig out for her old hoop for Jason to use. "You'll master it easily once you have one to practice with," she'd assured Jason. Wyndom was touched by the easy way she interacted with his son.

Monday, after school, Wyndom and Ruth planned a trip to the bank, intending to transfer the funds for the Bermuda wagon into Ruth's account. Wyndom wondered if Ruth realized how unusual it was to transfer title before transferring funds. She had explained that school would be out early Monday and indicated she did not want that amount of cash laying around over the weekend.

Wyndom undressed, prepared for bed, his mind busy with the puzzle of his son's behavior. He wanted Jason jubilant and boisterous. This evening he glimpsed a smidgen of the Jason of the past. Wyndom drifted off to sleep his thoughts on Jason and his son's interesting and beautiful teacher.

* * *

Ruth stood on the deck, dressed for bed but not tired. Her mind kept flashing pictures of Wyndom: his smile in the cafeteria, the nervous way he pushed his fingers through his hair while addressing her class and his reaction to the exploding chair. He was a very sexy man, a man with a sense of humor and the ability to laugh at his own foibles. Ruth visualized Wyndom lying sprawled across the broken chair, laughter pealing from his gorgeous shaking body.

Would he really call? she wondered. "Thank you, God, for this wonderful day," Ruth whispered to the heavens before entering the house. She locked the patio doors and slipped off to bed.

Flashes of lightning and the rumbles of thunder drove the black cat to slip quietly into Ruth's bedroom. Leaping gracefully onto the bed, Horse circled the space at Ruth's back several times then settled next to her warm body. The arrogant tomcat remained alert until the storm cell passed overhead. Once nature's fireworks finally diminished, the cat slept.

CHAPTER SEVEN

Gray, low-drifting, moisture-puffed, clouds obliterated all evidence of the sun. Now and then the whimsical drizzle grew serious and huge drops of rain pelted the earth. It was cold and it was definitely dreary.

Ruth spent the early part of the morning going through file cabinets in the basement, sipping hot tea to ward off the chill as she sorted. She uncovered several more Edsel related manuals, which she set aside for Wyndom; her parents income tax records, which she re-filed; and more car parts. Everywhere she looked down in this room she found car parts.

Ruth opened the door to a storage area and unearthed her dusty old ten-speed. Against the wall behind the bicycle leaned her striped Hula-Hoop.

"You're going to have a new home," she murmured as she dusted the peppermint stripped plastic circle and tried it out to make sure it still worked. Ruth carried the Edsel material and the hoop up to the family room.

It seemed cool and damp in the house so Ruth brewed another pot of her favorite blend, pulled an afghan up over knees and settled on the couch to savor the brew.

The scent of Cinnamon Twist wafted through the air adding the ambiance of comfort to the room. Ruth nestled into a corner of the sofa, relishing the sense of warmth that enveloped her with each sip. Horse was curled up next to her and she absent-mindedly stroked the cat behind the ears while she carried on a silent conversation with God, her own personal form of meditation.

The sound of the phone startled both Ruth and the cat from their reverie. Ruth had conversed with Martha Tate, one of the Iowa Edsel Club members, for several minutes before Martha reminded her of the next scheduled meeting.

"I sold the '58 wagon to a very nice gentleman," Ruth said, her voice wobbly with her effort to thwart a yawn.

"Bring him to the meeting," Martha suggested.

"I'll try, Martha. He might enjoy the club."

"Are you taking care of yourself, Ruth?"

Martha heard the catch in Ruth's voice when she said, "Yes."

"We haven't seen you since the funeral and Ed and I we're worried. He told me to offer his assistance if you need help with anything."

"I just spent the morning in the basement. There's Edsel stuff everywhere. I have no idea what to do with any of it." Ed Tate was well informed about Edsels and Edsel memorabilia and Ruth figured he would be a big help if she decided to start disposing of it.

"Tell him 'Thanks' for me Martha," Ruth said. "Maybe I will see you Saturday."

She sat contemplating a phone call to Wyndom when the phone rang once again.

"Are you enjoying these May showers?" the male voice questioned at Ruth's Hello.

Wyndom's deep baritone sent delightful shivers along Ruth's spine and she smilingly responded, "Showers that bring flowers are always appreciated. However," she quipped then admitted with a sigh, "I prefer my showers interspersed with sunshine."

"Jason and I spent the morning going through catalogs of camping equipment," Wyndom said, "Now we're bored." Cradling the phone to his ear, he pictured Ruth curled on the couch her rich brown hair falling in waves around her shoulders. "I'd invite you over for a picnic lunch but I left my umbrella at the office," Wyndom said into the mouthpiece.

Ruth could picture the exaggerated sad-dog look on his face as his words penetrated her ears. "My breezeway is dry, we could picnic out there by the grill," she offered, surprising herself with the suggestion.

"We'll be there with the food in fifteen minutes," Wyndom hurriedly replied.

"That quickly," Ruth said in amazement.

"We hoped you'd invite us," he playfully admitted.

Ruth barely had time to comb her hair and add a touch of makeup to her face before Wyndom and Jason were knocking at her door. A sack with hot dogs, buns, marshmallows, chips and packets of pink lemonade Kool-Aid rested in the crook of Wyndom's elbow.

Ruth led the way through the kitchen to the breezeway. The grill was uncovered and Ruth prayed that its tank had enough fluid to barbecue their meal.

Jason went looking for Horse while Wyndom and Ruth cleaned carrots, chopped onions and sliced enough tomatoes to complement their picnic menu.

"Don't forget dill pickles," Jason quietly said from where he sat against the wall of the screened porch petting Horse.

"Wash your hands, son, everything is ready to eat," Wyndom said, carrying a plate of sizzling wieners to the picnic table. He stepped over the wooden bench seat and sat, twisting this way and that until he was comfortable.

The soft steady drumbeat of drizzle continued throughout the afternoon but Ruth dug out her old Monopoly board and she and the Winters men forgot about the weather in the heat of the game. Jason's mouth lifted crookedly in a proud smirk and he seemed almost content as he counted up his winnings.

Ruth watched through the fringe of her lashes, as Wyndom stretched the stiffness from his too-long-quiet muscles. The softly faded denim of his blue jeans fit his lengthy lean legs like kidskin gloves and the long sleeved turtleneck T-shirt molded itself to the ridges and ripples of his corded chest. Unconscious of Ruth's gaze, he lifted his arms and continued the tension relieving stretch.

A tiny warm smile settled around Ruth's heart at the familiarity of Wyndom's agile movements. He shifted and arched with the arrogant assurance of a big sleek cat. His mannerisms easily mimicked those of Horse.

When the drizzle threatened to become a heavy blanket of fog, Wyndom knew it was time to return home. Jason thanked Ruth for the Hula-Hoop barely listening as his father cautioned him several times to use it only out of doors. When Ruth handed Wyndom the stack of Edsel manuals she'd found in the basement, she was reminded of her conversation with Martha Tate.

"There's an Iowa Edsel club meeting next Saturday. Would you be interested?"

Wyndom thumbed through his appointment book. "Sounds intriguing," he said, pleased to find his schedule unfettered. "Could we join you?"

Silence stretched between them. "Yes," Ruth said, leaving Wyndom puzzled by her hesitation. Silently, Ruth wondered if she could handle being with her parent's friends for a whole afternoon without resorting to tears. Being with Wyndom might make the day easier. "If you don't object to riding in the wagon again," Wyndom said, "we'll pick you up at eleven." Her parent's death flashed into his mind and he wondered if she was reluctant to attend the meeting for that reason.

Wyndom's fingers curled under Ruth's chin and he turned her face up so he could look into her dark chocolate eyes. He brushed the soft pad of his thumb along her bottom lip setting her body on fire. "I'd be more comfortable with you beside me at the meeting, Ruth. You know all those people." Wyndom smiled, appreciated the pink blush that curled up her cheeks.

"You're blushing, how lovely," he murmured, his eyes taking in every inch of her face.

"I don't blush," Ruth quietly replied.

A chuckle rumbled up from the depths of Wyndom's chest and he quietly insisted, "Yes, Ruth, you do."

Wyndom dipped his head and used his mouth to follow the trail his thumb had already blazed. Ruth's body tingled, tiny flames licked along her skin and she felt aglow with life. A soft sigh of pleasure slipped from her lips.

Wyndom whispered "Monday, 2:30, don't forget," in her ear, then the Winters men were racing through the milky drizzle toward their Corvette.

Ruth's fingers rested against her lips and she relished the feel of Wyndom's mouth over hers. When she remembered that Jason was watching, the slight blush deepened and rose clear to her hairline. She prayed Wyndom's actions had not upset Jason. She set about straightening the family room while mulling over the afternoon. She acknowledged her attraction to Wyndom Winters, acknowledged that that attraction both terrified and titillated her. She was twenty-nine years old and for the first time in her life a man was making her feel the way heroines felt in romance novels. Her emotions seemed new, wonderful and a bit scary. Ruth had dated some in collage, however, most of the time she was too busy with her part-time job and her studies for socializing.

She dated a few men in Boston once she started teaching but most of them made it clear they were not interested in permanency and Ruth had not been interested in one-night stands or short affairs. Unhappy memories resurfaced, memories of the pain those dates had inflicted.

Chided for her morality, berated for her archaic attitude and accused of being frigid, Ruth stopped dating all together. N*one of those men ever made me feel the way Wyndom does. Wherever we touch, with hands, lips or eyes, Wyndom makes me tingle.*

Ruth stood before her patio door not really aware of the view, her mind a turmoil. Pleasure at Wyndom's attention; worry about Jason's reaction to that attraction and concern for her student's well being swirled vicious circles in her thoughts.

***

Drizzle slowed, seemed to be abating yet the foggy fingers surrounding the car thickened. Wyndom rubbed his hand over his face and struggled to concentrate on the road instead of enjoying the mental pictures of Ruth he'd managed to store up through out the day.

A brief glimpse of red taillights glimmering off and on through the mist alerted Wyndom to another vehicle ahead on the road. He moved his head around fighting the tension in his neck, took several deep breaths in a struggle to stay alert. His fingers tensed on the wheel with the strain of keeping the red taillights within sight until finally the Corvette moved safely up the Carlyle drive.

Jason sat hunched next to his father in the Corvette's contoured seat. The seat belt held him motionless but his mind swirled a myriad of sharp candid snapshots, all of them identical. *My Father kissed my teacher. Ruth is my teacher; the best teacher I've ever had. Please God, don't let Dad mess that up.*

Jason agonized over what this might mean to his life. *If the kids at school find out that Dad is kissing Ruth, would they'd tease me and make my life miserable? What if Dad really liked Ruth and they got married? She would be my Mother. I might like that. What if Ruth doesn't want a little boy? What if she is just pretending? Grandmother doesn't like little boys. I know.* Jason figured that sometimes his grandmother even hated him.

Grandma Carlyle scares me. Especially when she says my father will leave me, just like my mother did, if I'm not good. What if my father marries Ruth and neither one of them want me any more? What if they both leave me?

Thoughts, murky swirling thoughts, ran rampant through Jason's mind and drew him into a troubled sleep. His body twitched and harsh jerky grunts slipped from his mouth. Wyndom pulled the Corvette into the garage, punched the button to activate the door opener, pulled the key from the ignition and wondered what demons troubled his son's sleep. He unbelted Jason and, holding his slender seven-year-old son close to protect him from the elements, Wyndom dashed for the house.

Fog pushed the shadows of night in around the Carlyle estate, the air was damp, bone chilling. Wyndom carried Jason into the bathroom and toweled the moisture from his hair before undressing him and tucking him beneath the covers with his favorite stuffed animals; a raccoon that Jason had named BooHoo, and his bear Scruffy.

Wyndom wandered restlessly through the downstairs rooms of the Carlyle mansion. He went to the kitchen in search of food; hoped eating might dispel the empty ache gnawing at him. Leftover roast beef had provided him with the means for a sandwich; next he nursed a can of lemon flavored sparkling water. The ache remained.

Drizzle escalated once again turning into a full-blown storm. Moisture pelted the house with the cadence of stampeding cattle. Wyndom stopped before the patio doors and watched the patterns of rain rivers crisscrossing the panes of glass.

Soon the rain frosted glass disappeared, replaced by mind pictures of Ruth Dennison. Wyndom remembered the way her eyes lit up with laughter moments before her mouth curved into a smile. Remembered how her soft, chocolate-chip-colored eyes, glazed with unshed tears while she peeled and chopped onions. Wyndom knew he was enchanted by the agile way she moved tending hot dogs at the grill; the way she stooped to sweep an attention seeking cat up into her arms; and the loving way she brushed the hair from Jason's face.

Wyndom could not remember the last time he'd felt so comfortable and relaxed with anyone. It had been such a long time since he had enjoyed just being with a woman. When Cindy left, Wyndom withdrew from society. All his contacts with people became work related. Even then he rarely accepted the social invitations from the men with whom he worked.

Wyndom had not realized, until this moment, how much he'd cut himself off from others. Now he understood that he'd not really been in love with Cindy. She swept into his life with the force of a twister and before his physical being had calmed and returned to normal, Cindy was pregnant and they were married.

Once Cindy figured out Jason was a little person who required a great amount of care instead of the toy doll she'd anticipated, she lost interest. Instead, she went looking for a good time. She quickly become disillusioned with her attractive husband, a husband who seemed more interested in work than partying.

Wyndom carried his empty can to the kitchen and rinsed it before tossing it into the recycle bin. He climbed the stairs to his bedroom, his thoughts elsewhere. He stopped at Jason's door to check on his still-sleeping son.

Love swept in like thunderheads and overwhelmed Wyndom with its force as he gazed at Jason's angelic expression. *I want so much to make you happy son*, he thought. *I want to give you more than I ever got from my parents.* He closed Jason's door, admitting that the only way he knew to achieve his goal was to spend more time with his son.

Wyndom sat on the edge of his bed and removed first one shoe then the other. The splatter of rain against the house had lessened and Wyndom let the soft gentle rhythm of the water beads lull him to sleep and into elusive dreams haunted by the face of a lovely second grade teacher.

***

Sunday dawned bright and sunny. Miniature rainbows blossomed across the lawn caused when the rain beaded grass burst into color from the sun's rays. While Wyndom watched, a light breeze wiffled through the shoots of new grass bouncing the crystal water beads hanging from their tips into a miniature waterfall of diamonds.

Jason stopped dressing just long enough to appreciate the spectacle that lay beyond his window. He searched the yard for signs of playful creatures but not even a bird dared to land on Grandmother Carlyle's pristine pampered lawn. Jason sighed and turned from the window to finish buttoning his white shirt.

Wyndom entered the room in time to help Jason with his bow tie. They descended the stairs side by side. As usual on Sunday they joined Evelyn for the ride to church. Wyndom drove. He and Jason discussed possible activities for the upcoming afternoon. Evelyn ignored them and their conversation.

Hours later, after taking Evelyn home and changing vehicles, Jason meticulously dipped each French-fry in ketchup before stuffing it in his mouth. He finished his burger and watched the two men out in the parking lot walk around ogling the Edsel wagon. Jason drained the last of his soda pop then plopped the last fry into his mouth, squirming restlessly and waiting for Wyndom to finish his meal.

"Why don't you gather our empties and carry them to the trash barrel," Wyndom suggested, rubbing his hands with a napkin and licking the chicken crumbs from his fingers. He studied Jason, watched his son meticulously busy himself with cleaning up the table. Wyndom prayed the afternoon would be entertaining for his son, prayed that their time together provide some insight into what ever was troubling Jason.

63

Before driving to the park, they stopped at Wal-Mart and purchased a colorful kite that assembled quite easily under Wyndom's deft fingers. Jason bounced eagerly around his father as he watched the kite take shape.

Several times Jason tried to launch the brightly colored boxed-frame skyward but the kite refused to cooperate. Breathless and frustrated, he handed the papered frame to Wyndom and begged him to try. Wyndom, definitely winded and feeling old, sat down on the ground to rest after dragging the kite into the right updraft to carry it aloft. Handing the looped string to Jason he stretched out on the grass and used his raised arms to pillow his head. Wyndom was content to lay quietly and behold the wondrous change in his son's attitude.

Jason's face glowed with happiness. Laughter bubbled from his mouth as he danced through the grass, the kite string clenched in his fist. He darted effortlessly through the open area of the park his attention riveted on the wind-driven man-bird in the sky.

Wyndom marveled at the play of emotions sweeping across his son's face. Jason was completely relaxed, happy and oblivious to the world around him. Eyes bright, he cavorted across the lawn beckoned by the bright flash of color fluttering aloft, The kite, held prisoner by the boisterous wind currents in the sky and by the string Jason controlled, looped and tugged in a dance for independence.

Wyndom winced inwardly when Jason tripped and the force of the fall snapped the kite string. Jason rolled over, staring wide-eyed as the kite got smaller and smaller. When the bit of red was no more than a dot in the sky, Jason turned to his father and grinning from ear to ear he sighed, "That was fun, Dad."

With the flashing speed of small boys, Jason landed on Wyndom's chest and they wrestled in the sun-warmed grass. "I'm hungry again, " Jason managed to say between giggles as Wyndom found all his ticklish spots.

A stop at the local ice cream parlor solved the hunger problem for both of them. Wyndom licked drips from his ice cream cone and speculated on how Ruth had spent her day. Jason lingered over the chocolate cone he held, reluctant to end the outing, reluctant to return to the Carlyle mansion and reality.

***

Ruth popped pizza into the oven, set the timer and grabbed the paperback she had been enjoying since her return from church this morning. She would finish the book while she ate her solitary supper than do her class preparation for Monday.

Now and then her mind strayed from the words in front of her and Ruth thought of Wyndom, wondered how he'd spent the day.

Horse leaped onto Ruth's lap, nudged her book aside, circling twice before squirming into position. Ruth returned to her book. She tried to turn a page but the cat covered the words with his paw then used his head to push the book out of reach. Not really minding the interruption, Ruth set the paperback aside and scratched behind Horse's pointy ears and under his chin. When Ruth stopped her ministrations, Horse nudged her palm with his nose demanding more.

"I didn't mean to ignore you, Horse," Ruth said and rubbed the soft, shiny black hairs along the cat's back.

"Are you lonely tonight?" Ruth's rubbing movements turned to scratches and she recalled how much her mother doted on the cat. Soon contented purrs resonated through out the room. Horse playfully wormed his head under the afghan laid across the arm of the sofa causing Ruth to chuckle when he continuously peeked out at her from under the cover as if to say, "peek-a-boo."

Horse shook his head, sneezed, and launched his sleek shinny body from Ruth's lap. Arching his back into a perfect "U", Horse yawned twice then he extended his front paws into a full body stretch. Swishing his tail he glanced once at Ruth and arrogantly sashayed from the room. It was his mealtime. Just as Ruth reached once more for her book the oven bell sounded. Her pizza was ready.

Later, when her lesson plan was done and the students' papers corrected, Ruth prepared to shower. She stood under the steamy flow letting the water rain down on her soapy body. She poured shampoo into her palm and massaged the scented creme into her hair. She would see Wyndom again tomorrow. They were going to the bank to transfer the money for the Edsel into her account. Ruth wondered if she would see Wyndom once the transaction was completed then she remembered the Edsel meeting the coming Saturday and accepted that Wyndom was not yet out of her life.

The thick thirsty towel drew the moisture from Ruth's long brown hair. Slipping on her nightgown she settled in front of the mirror. She brushed her curtain of hair into burnt umber silk and fantasized about Wyndom's kiss.

Just the briefest touch of his mouth to hers had ignited a fire in her body.

No man had ever made her feel quite so soft and feminine. Ruth remembered the way Wyndom's touch made her senses reel. In his presence, she felt beautiful. Color rose to Ruth's cheeks when she silently admitted how much she enjoyed just looking at Wyndom Winters. He seemed special; still there was much she did not know about the men, this man in particular.

Wyndom appeared to love his son but Ruth knew Jason had problems and she could not yet rule out Wyndom as the cause. Her mind busily pictured each incident of her time with the Winters men as she checked the locks and turned off the lights in all but her bedroom. Cool sheets enticed Ruth to slide into bed. She was reaching up to turn off the light when the phone rang.

"Hello, Ruth. Hope I haven't called to late."

"Your timing is perfect, Wyndom," Ruth said, leaning back against the headboard, the receiver cradled to her ear.

"Have supper with me tomorrow night, Ruth? I know this perfect place on the edge of lake Panorama where the food is even better than the view," Wyndom said.

"I promise to have you home early. I realize it's a school night," he cajoled.

Ruth smiled at the wistfullness she heard in Wyndom's voice. She chuckled softly and told him, "Yes."

They talked for a few more minutes. Wyndom described the kite-flying afternoon he shared with Jason and the awe he'd experienced at seeing him happy. With Wyndom's "good-bye" and "I'll see you tomorrow," the phone call ended.

Ruth slid down under the covers, her mind busily examining her wardrobe for the perfect attire for an evening's outing as well as a day in the classroom. She drifted off to sleep wondering if Jason would spend the evening with them. She realized it should not matter but she graciously admitted that it would seem more like a date if she were alone with the handsome Wyndom Winters.

CHAPTER EIGHT

Wyndom stood alongside the Corvette storing up the picture of Ruth hurrying across the school parking lot in his direction. Her dark brown hair flowed around her shoulders like a mink cape; its gloss reflecting shimmery fingers back toward the warm May sun. Her emerald green dress complemented her complexion and highlighted the green flecks in her brown eyes. The dress, nipped at the waist with a wide matching-fabric belt, accentuated Ruth's slender frame. She wore a matching pair of green suede shoes. With each step the full skirt swished sensuously around her legs.

The picture she created while walking toward Wyndom left him breathless and seeking air. He had forgotten just how beautiful she was and, as Wyndom watched, the notion struck that maybe she had dressed especially to attract attention, hopefully his.

***

Ruth felt pretty. The flirty little skirt of this dress always made her feel sexy and just a tad reckless. Boldly studying Wyndom's face as she walked toward him, she saw a smile curl his mouth and light his eyes and she relaxed. He wore dress slacks and a jacket that draped his body perfectly. This was her first glimpse of him in semi-formal attire and she savored the knowledge that he was as attractive in a suit as he was in his hip hugging Levi's.

Wyndom met her halfway across the parking lot. Offering her his arm, he bowed as if to royalty and said, "Hello, beautiful."

Ruth noted that Wyndom had arranged for Katie to pick Jason up from school and she was pleased when Wyndom introduced them. Ruth liked the housekeeper immediately. From Jason's attitude, she figured he did too.

It took very little time to accomplish their mission at the bank then they were back in the car flowing through afternoon traffic toward the man-made lake. Once they left the congestion of the city behind them conversation flowed more easily. They talked about music, literature, and little boys. In less than an hour they reached their destination.

Hand in hand they walked around the lake, waiting for the time of their reservation to approach. The late afternoon sun had glazed the lake with a golden sheen that changed slowly into an effervescent shimmering rainbow hued reflection of the vibrant unmatchable mixed coral and hot-pink sunset.

Poised on the edge of the lake, the restaurant featured open decks and large windows that served to enhance the panorama of the lakeshore and its remarkable view. Their meal lived up to Wyndom's promise of surpassing the vista, an astonishing feat after the spectacular sunset that they had thoroughly enjoyed. Their conversation before, during and after dinner remained constant and interesting.

Ruth and Wyndom shared dessert then returned to the car and began the trip back to Des Moines.

"I'll drop you off at school so you can pick-up your car," Wyndom offered through the soft sounds of the radio.

"Thank you," Ruth said. Her eyes were closed and she drifted on the edge of the music more content then she remembered being for months.

"I'll follow you home," he remarked, once they reached their destination.

"That's not necessary," Ruth softly said, reluctant to break the cloak of pleasure surrounding her. Still, Wyndom's gentlemanly insistence pleased her.

***

Jason found an end of spaghetti and sucked it into his mouth. Katie, busily cleaning the kitchen, paid little attention to the seven-year-old. Jason missed his father. He played with his plate of food, eating one piece of the sauce covered pasta at a time, feeling left out and alone. He watched Katie cleaning up and wished that just this once she would sit down and talk with him.

"Jason, stop slumping and eat properly," Evelyn demanded when she swept into the room to hand the housekeeper a list of chores. Jason swirled up a forkful of pasta and shoved it into his mouth.

"Now that your father has a girl friend you'll be eating alone again and I expect you to remember your manners. Do you understand?" Evelyn said.

She scowled at him, stared until he had swallowed his food.

"Yes, grandmother," Jason whispered.

"Just pray he doesn't decide to marry her," Evelyn slurred, finishing the drink in her hand. "Nobody wants to raise someone else's brat. They'll send you off to boarding school and promptly forget about you." his grandmother warned before stumbling back to the dinning room for a refill.

Jason pushed his plate away. His father was out with his teacher. Miss Dennison seemed to like all of her students but if she married his father maybe that would change.

A tear slipped down Jason's cheek and he rushed from the kitchen. His father had just started to pay attention to him. Jason recalled the special times, their nights at Hardee's, the Edsel and his beautiful kite. The seven-year-old scrubbed at his tears with sauce stained fingers and worried that his grandmother might be right. Worried that he might be going away soon.

Jason slipped into his father's bedroom and climbed onto the huge bed. Colorful pamphlets lay strewn across the nightstand and he reached out to grab them. Jason Winters sobbed himself to sleep once he figured out what the papers were that he clutched in his grubby fist.

***

Wyndom's fingers wove through Ruth's; he matched his steps to hers and walked her from her car. She wondered if he felt the current of electricity that flowed from his fingers along the length of her arm. Hand in hand, the two moved toward her front door where he turned and took her into his arms. They stood face to face, each enjoying their view.

Wyndom's hands were splayed across Ruth's back; their warmth seeped through her wrap. Tenderness and caring flowed from his gaze and suddenly a great gapping hole of loneliness welled up inside Ruth and she prayed that Wyndom might be the one to bridge the emptiness she felt mired in. She longed for him to drive out the ache of loss and grief that constantly plagued.

Wyndom lowered his head and slid his tongue along Ruth's lower lip. He felt her body tremble. He licked the curvature of her upper lip then drew her lower lip between his and sucked on its fullness. Skyrockets exploded inside Ruth and the vivid colors drove all thought from her mind. She sighed. Wyndom pulled her closer uniting them in a heart-shocking kiss. Ruth's arms slid up around his neck and she clung to him, needing support for her boneless body. Wyndom finally broke off the kiss, granting both the opportunity to breathe. He nibbled along Ruth's ear and down the side of her neck, affording each of them time to regain their equilibrium. Wyndom stepped back drew apart from Ruth.

"I need to…Ruth, are you involved with anyone?" Wyndom stumbled over the question, afraid of her answer.

Ruth was speechless, shocked by the intensity of his tone.

"I'm not meaning to pry, its just that I want to spend more time with you if…if you aren't committed to someone else."

"There is no one, Wyndom."

"Then the men in this town must be idiots," he whispered and reached for her hand.

"I have tickets for the symphony Friday night, Ruth. Will you go with me?" he questioned, watching for her response, holding his impatience in check.

"Yes, Wyndom, I'd like that," Ruth whispered. The huskiness of her tone betrayed the depth of her emotional turmoil. She took a deep breath in an attempt to steady her inner confusion.

"Thank you, Ruth," he said and leaning close kissed the tip of her nose.

"Friday. Seven o'clock." Wyndom smilingly said, before reminding her to lock the door. He turned and was soon gone.

Ruth floated through her preparations for the next day's class. Her mind overflowing with images of a tall ruggedly handsome man as she dressed for bed and drifted off to sleep. The dreams that rode through her slumber kept her restless and feeling overly heated.

***

Wyndom felt younger than he had in years. He was jubilant, felt as if he could jump high enough to land his own double axle, as if he could literally dance on air. Euphoria remained with Wyndom throughout the drive home, carried him all the way through the house to his bedroom where it burst into a storm of doubt at the sight of the small, dirty-faced child curled up in the middle of his king-sized bed.

Wyndom pulled the crumpled papers from his son's hand, wishing he'd thought to toss all this boarding school junk in the trash. It was obvious Jason had been crying and Wyndom silently berated himself. It was also obvious that Jason had had spaghetti for supper. He scooped the sleeping child into his arms, carried Jason to his own room and lay him on the bed.

Wyndom dampened a cloth with warm water, washed and dried Jason's face and hands.

Jason stirred at his father's ministrations. He rubbed his eyes and mumbled, "Hi Daddy."

Wyndom pulled him into a hug then he pushed the hair from Jason's eyes.

"It looks like you had a rough night. Jason, were you upset by those brochures you found? Someone else gave them to me. I meant to toss them in the trash, I just forgot. I promise you, son, I have no intention of sending you away," Wyndom said with all the force he could put in his tone. He hugged Jason, held him close for several minutes.

"Okay, Dad," Jason sleepily mumbled, the words almost lost in a big yawn.

Wyndom settled his son in the bed, handed him scruffy and tucked the covers around him. He prayed that he had assuaged Jason's fears, remained by his bed until assured the boy slept. Wyndom returned to his room wondering what had happened that Jason had sought comfort in his father's bed. He gathered the boarding school advertisements that lay strewn across the spread, staring quietly at them for a moment. Wyndom carried them quickly down the stairs and into the den where he proceeded to burn them in the fireplace.

The last red ember slowly faded into black ash and Wyndom stirred the crispy black curls to assure himself the fire was dead before returning to his bedroom. Fatherhood weighed heavily on Wyndom's shoulders as he undressed for bed. He loved Jason, wanted to do the very best for him but somehow Wyndom knew he was failing miserably. He and Jason seemed to be getting closer. Suddenly it dawned on Wyndom that whatever had troubled Jason, he had at least turned to his father for comfort.

***

Steam from the cinnamon scented tea in front of Ruth wafted upward titillating her nostrils. She ate the last bite of her toasted, cream-cheesed, bagel. Early morning tea enervated Ruth; she sat at the table savoring each sip. The huge patio doors beside the table afforded her a breathtaking view of her lawn, brilliantly aglow and golden with streaks of sunshine. Bright color caught her eye and she watched a Cardinal flit from tree to tree hunting the perfect breakfast for his mate.

A tap-tap rhythm drew Ruth's eyes to the oak shading the back deck and she smiled softly to herself as she watched the redheaded woodpecker beat a discordant rhythm in his search for hidden insects. Spring had come to the backyard, flown in on the wings of a returning woodpecker. It was a beautiful morning, a feel-the-presence-of-God morning, and Ruth wished she had time to just sit and savor it.

Draining the last dredges of tea, Ruth cleaned the table and gathered her lesson material for the day. It was time to leave for the classroom. She hummed to herself as she locked the house and loaded the car, totally unaware that she was beginning to slough off the sorrow that had such a deep hold on her since her parent's death. Ruth opened all her car windows to the freshness and wondered if the day's perfection was related in any way to the perfection of last night's date.

***

Jason rinsed his toothbrush and returned it to its holder. He tried to comb his hair but it was hard to do a proper job when the mirror was too high for him to see into. Words kept reverberating through his head, first his grandmother's warning next his father's reassurance. Jason remembered his father saying that someone else had given him the brochures and Jason wondered who that someone was. Could it have been his teacher?

Katie set a bowl of cereal in front of Jason and admonished him to eat. The seven-year-old was still playing with his food when it was time for him to leave for school. Wyndom watched Jason; he sat in the car fidgeting with his backpack. "Jason, is there a problem?" The question was met with silence, so Wyndom tried again.

"You must have wanted me for something last night son, I found you asleep on my bed."

Jason was reluctant to talk to his father about what grandmother had said, instead he mumbled, "I don't remember."

Jason remained unusually quiet for the next several days and Ruth tried, with out success, to discover the problem. Wyndom made a point of being home for supper with his son each evening and Katie made him special treats. By Thursday Jason was convinced his grandmother must be wrong and he began to relax.

Friday night, Wyndom arranged to have an early supper with Jason. The seven-year-old was watching a new video about dinosaurs when Wyndom left to pick up Ruth for their date.

Jason had just set the VCR to rewind when Evelyn Carlyle entered the family room. "Where's your father, Jason, I need to speak to him for a moment?"

Jason walked over to remove the tape from the machine. "I don't know," he said.

"Left you alone again," Evelyn said, turning her back on him.

She did not see Jason shrug or hear his sigh. "I suppose he's out with that woman again," she mumbled to herself as she hurried from the room.

Suddenly all of Jason fears resurfaced.

***

"You look beautiful," Wyndom said when Ruth opened the door to let him inside. He helped Ruth on with her wrap, relishing the fresh floral scent she wore.

"Thank you," she said and handed him the key to her front door. "You clean up very nicely too," she said. Laughter edging her tone as she grinned up at him.

"Anything to please my lady." He quipped, slipping his arm around her waist. Guiding her outside, he turned, locked the door and walked her to the passenger door of the Corvette.

Both enjoyed the musical selections the symphony chose to play and the featured soloist. They lingered in their seats; making meaningless chatter until the crowd thinned and they could easily leave.

Both refrained from talk about Jason, preferring to bask in the glory of the night and their being together. Earlier they had parked the car on the far end of the river bridge, now they enjoyed their leisurely walk back. The rich scent of spring filled the air intermingled with the scents of green grass, new flowers and Ruth's perfume. Twinkling lights of downtown Des Moines surrounded them, creating beautiful reflections on the water flowing gently below the bridge. They stopped halfway across, leaned on the parapet and watched the river rushing bank-full beneath them.

Excessive rains in the northern part of Iowa had strained the limits of the river and broadcasters had begun to hint at possible flooding, but tonight, to Ruth and Wyndom, the river appeared lovely, smelled of spring. The city's restless bustle faded away leaving them momentarily isolated in the shared pleasure of togetherness. A group of teenagers crowded past on the sidewalk and the magic of the moment passed. Ruth and Wyndom continued their unhurried trek to the car. Wyndom opened the car door for Ruth, silently sought for a way to prolong the magic of the evening.

"I'm ready for dessert," Wyndom suggested once he'd maneuvered the Vette into traffic.

"Sounds good," Ruth agreed. City lights flashed by her window and she relaxed into the car seat quietly humming along with the radio. Wyndom found a parking spot and soon they were seated across from one another at a windowed booth. In minutes, their pie and coffee arrived.

"Do you like opera?" Wyndom said before slipping a bite of cherry pie into his mouth.

"Opera, classical, country and pop," Ruth said. "I love all kinds of music."

Ruth was delighted to discover Wyndom's taste in music was as eclectic as hers.

"Simpson Collage begins their opera festival in a few weeks," Wyndom said. "I'll get tickets for us."

I'm a part of his future, Ruth thought with wonder. Delightful tremors traversed Ruth's arm; beat a path to her heart the minute Wyndom covered her hand with his.

"What time should we pick you up tomorrow?" Wyndom said, draining the last of his coffee. "Do I take anything to an Edsel meeting?"

"Eric and Brenda Jacob live in Newton, the meeting is at their house. Everyone brings something for the food table," Ruth said.

"Any suggestions?" Wyndom asked. Ruth helped him select a pie for the local Edsel Club meeting. They agreed to leave her place the next day at eleven AM.

On the drive home, Ruth mentioned her concerns for Jason. "He seems quieter than usual this week," she said to Wyndom.

"I found him asleep on my bed Monday night," he said. "It was obvious he'd been crying."

"Did he tell you why?" Ruth noted Wyndom's furrowed brow as he shook his head negatively.

"He'll be with me all day tomorrow, hopefully there will be other young people there and he'll have a good time," Wyndom said.

Wyndom's goodnight kiss left Ruth breathless and tingly clear to her toes. She relived the kiss over and over in her mind as she gathered the ingredients for a pasta salad that she would make in the morning, before she dressed for the meeting.

***

Wyndom set the boxed pie in the refrigerator before going up to check on Jason. He switched on the stairway light, set his foot on the bottom step.

"Wyndom."

He heard Evelyn call to him from the living room. He pulled the knot from his tie, unbuttoned the top button of his white shirt and walked in to find out what she wanted. Wyndom watched her struggle to rise from her chair. She grabbed the edge of the table to steady herself; the odor of stale whiskey assailed his nostrils as she swayed toward him.

"Where have you been?" Her slurred speech caught Wyndom's full attention. "I'll not have you use me as a baby sitter," she said angrily.

"Did Jason give you problems this evening, Mother Carlyle?" Wyndom said, stressing the word mother and watching Evelyn wince and stagger unsteadily.

"I walked in while he was watching a movie," she admitted, "I haven't seen him since."

"You didn't have to tell him to go to bed?" Wyndom said in a low quiet voice. "You didn't tuck him in or tell him goodnight?" His question hung as an accusation in the silence of the room as he wondered if Evelyn was always this inebriated in the evening.

"You know I didn't," she snapped, unwilling to let anyone think she was the grandmotherly type.

"Jason is very responsible," Wyndom said. "What's the problem?"

"Did you look at those brochures I gave you," she said, grabbing the arm of the davenport for support. "They're the very best schools."

"Jason will not be leaving this house unless we both leave, Evelyn. Is that understood? Do you want us to leave?" Wyndom asked his voice and manner rigid.

Evelyn looked at the strong handsome man staring at her and realized her dream of them being close was foolish. Still, she did not want him to leave. Then she truly would be alone.

Wyndom watched her head dip and heard her whisper, "No." He noticed that she had taken particular care with her make up and attire. In her attempt to look younger she had donned a Dolly Parton style wig, a too-tight black dress and bright red lipstick. He briefly wondered what was going on in Evelyn's head, but he didn't have the inclination to pursue the issue and, shrugging his shoulders in puzzlement, he hurried from the room, anxious to check on his son.

***

Saturday morning dawned cool and drizzly. Huge black clouds scurried across the horizon as Jason and Wyndom worked inside the garage polishing the wagon. Jason crouched beside a tire intent on cleaning the wide white-wall while Wyndom waxed the exterior of the Edsel. By the time the Winters men had finished the work, the car's mirror-like surface reflected their image.

Wyndom looked at his watch. "We have to pick Ruth up in an hour, Jason. I'll bet you a root beer float that I can shower and dress before you."

Jason jovially raced from the garage determined to win his favorite treat.

***

Ruth slipped the Iowa Edsel newsletter into her purse. Wyndom would need it for the map to the Jacob's residence. She set her pasta salad in the refrigerator to cool, cleaned the kitchen hurriedly and shoved a couple of magazines under the sofa where they would not be seen. I've got to dust one of these days she thought as she walked to her closet to collect her water-repellent jacket. She stopped in front of the mirror to check her appearance.

She studied her features, saw nothing but plainness. Her eyebrows were a bit thick but Ruth could not endure the pain of plucking. She thought her eyes were too big, they seemed to overpower the rest of her face. Her hair was brown, her eyes were brown, her nose was average and her mouth was nothing special. Ruth pursed her lips, pleased that they were full and well shaped, still it would be nice to be just a little pretty.

She made a face at the reflection staring back at her, then smiling broadly she walked out of the room, forgetting her flash of vanity.

Ruth had just finished feeding and filling Horse's water dish when she heard the Edsel pull into the drive. Wyndom was lifting his hand to knock when Ruth opened the door. He took the keys from her, locked the front door, dropped the keys into her shoulder bag and escorted her to the Bermuda wagon. Wyndom set her dish in back with the pie and Ruth climbed into the front seat.

"You did a great job with the Edsel," Ruth said. "The car is glowing."

"Me and Dad polished it this morning," Jason said from the back seat.

Ruth shifted sideways in the seat so she could see the seven-year-old. "You must have worked very hard," Ruth said and smiled at Jason. His blue eyes sparkled briefly while he described his part in the process.

Ruth eyes glistened with mirth at Jason's appearance. It was obvious he had tried to tame the spiky shoots of hair sprouting straight up from the cowlick at the base of his part. His unruly blonde mane added to the false imp image of Jason's features. He slid across the back seat. "I beat Dad dressed too, we had a race and I won," Jason said quietly.

"What did you win?"

"A root beer float," Jason said the sparkle already absent from his young face.

Halfway to Newton the clouds parted and sunshine bathed the scenery along the roadway. The wet leaves of the young corn stalks glistened like emerald sateen in the brilliant rays. May, in Iowa, vibrated with rich-hued spring colors.

"Will there be other kids there?" Jason asked, squirming against the back seat, his face void of all emotion.

"Eric and Brenda Jacobs have an eight-year-old son and a six-year-old daughter," Ruth answered. "There could be others."

With the aid of the map, they found the right house and Wyndom found a place to park across the street. Although there were several cars parked in the driveway only two of them were Edsels.

Everyone had contributed to the table full of food and after eating their fill the members circled in the family room to began the meeting. Ruth introduced Wyndom and Jason and each person in turn gave their name and the city where they lived.

"Wyndom bought dad's Bermuda Wagon," Ruth continued when it was once again her turn.

"Are you selling all of your dad's cars?" Eric Jacobs asked what the other men in the room were thinking.

"Not yet," Ruth quietly stated. "I wouldn't even know where to start."

"If you need any help, Ruth, let us know," one of the other men said, not surprised at the indecision he read on her face.

She watched most of the men in the room murmur their assent to the offer and understood they were offering her their friendship just as they had to her parents.

"Martha Tate called this morning," Brenda Jacobs said. "Ed's in the hospital."

Everyone expressed concern and Ruth made a mental note to send him a get-well-card. Brenda continued to reiterate what she knew of the situation.

The meeting was lively and both the Winters men enjoyed themselves. They were welcomed by all present. Soon Jason and Bobby Jacobs excused themselves to go play video games. Wyndom eagerly talked Edsels with the men gathered. Before leaving he paid dues to join both the national and local club.

Hours later, as the three of them left for the trip back to Des Moines, he kept Ruth busy satisfying his curiosity about various members. Wyndom admitted to enjoying his conversation with the short, eccentric, matronly, woman who served as club president.

"Does Mrs. Jean always wear such sparkling attire," he said, picturing the short, plump woman dressed in deep sparkling purple.

"The louder the better," Ruth admitted. "She's always in pain from her arthritis, I expect the bright colors help to keep her cheerful."

A warm breeze from the open window tugged at Ruth's hair and she brushed it from her face. She leaned closer to Wyndom. "I know the perfect place to get a root-beer float," she quietly said and directed him to an ice cream shop in Altoona.

Loud fifties music reverberated throughout the Sugar Shack parking lot. An area in front of the restaurant was cordoned off and a variety of well preserved antique and classic cars sat gathered on display. Wyndom was directed to a parking spot among the other vehicles. They had apparently stumbled upon another Saturday night summer ritual. Wyndom looked around as he climbed from the wagon. Theirs was the only Edsel present and Ruth saw Wyndom's chest swell with pride.

Jason delighted in his earned treat, Wyndom delighted in the rich variety of cars on display and Ruth delighted in being with Wyndom and Jason.

Ruth quietly sang along with the music while they walked around the lot admiring the cars. She promised to help Jason learn all the words to the "Witch Doctor" song, and he worked on the words as he walked among the cars, careful not to touch any of them. Again Ruth noticed the gentle way Wyndom cautioned Jason about his manners around the old cars. Their loving interaction was a welcome sight for her.

Wyndom reached for Ruth's hand. Fingers intertwined they circled the lot inspecting each vehicle, silently Wyndom rejoiced that the Bermuda wagon belonged to him. Several people stopped them to ask about their Edsel and to swap tales of the joys and horrors of owning an older car.

Night settled softly around the parking lot, the music ceased and slowly the cars and their owners left the Sugar Shack. Ruth, Wyndom and Jason drove in contented silence through the out skirts of Des Moines. A multitude of stars twinkled above the car as Wyndom slowed the Edsel and pulled into Ruth's driveway.

Jason was still very wide-awake and energetic when Wyndom walked Ruth to her door. He gave her a quick kiss and promised to call, then he turned and walked back to the car.

Jason watched his father kiss Ruth. He didn't know a lot about kisses, except he never intended to ever kiss any girl, still he did wonder if his father was serious about Ruth. He sat quietly in the back seat remembering his grandmother's words. Would his father really send him away if he decided to marry Ruth?

CHAPTER NINE

Ruth looked forward to tonight. She and Wyndom were spending the evening together. She stood before the floor length mirror, circling slowly to check her appearance. The sleeves of the black dress hugged the outside of her shoulders leaving her arms bare while the neckline dipped to a seductive point at her cleavage. The bodice of the gown fitted perfectly down to where it nipped Ruth's slender waist. From the figure-hugging top, the skirt flared into flirty folds that swished fashionably just above Ruth's knees.

The top edge of the bodice and the bottom edge of the frilly skirt were decorated with brilliant black bugle beads that flashed fire when she moved under the light. Ruth grabbed a piece of ribbon and, using a small sparkling butterfly pin, she secured the black ribbon as a decoration at her throat. Her black pumps were simple, elegant and surprisingly comfortable. Wyndom said they would be dining out but he'd refused to elaborate further on his plans for the evening. Ruth brushed her brown wavy hair back from her face and secured it with a black glitter glazed butterfly comb. She had just finished daubing her favorite scent to her pulse points when she heard Wyndom's knock.

The gleam in Wyndom's eyes when she opened the door gave Ruth the confidence to swirl slowly in front of him. His low, slow whistle elicited a bright laugh from Ruth and she flowed easily into his embrace. "I'm glad we'll be alone tonight," Wyndom said, his lips glazing her temple. "I don't want to share you with anyone."

A tingling sensation skittered along Ruth's flesh at the husky timbre of Wyndom's voice and the wind-soft brush of his lips. "It's good to see you too," she said. She handed him her wrap in an attempt to quell the trembling timbre of her voice and the jitters of her fingers.

He placed the colorful shawl around Ruth's bare shoulders, used her keys to secure the front door, and escorted her to the waiting Corvette.

Ruth and Wyndom sat at a small table skirting the dance floor. Soft, seductive music from a live band wafted easily over the room. Once they gave the waitress their food order, they joined several other couples on the dance floor.

"Do you like to dance, Ruth?" Wyndom asked.

She turned into his arms, put her hand in his and began to follow his lead. "I paid my way through college working with Arthur Murray Studios in Boston."

Their steps synchronized into a harmonious journey around the floor. "They're having a dance contest tonight," Wyndom said against Ruth's ear. "I thought we might watch, now I believe we should enter. We are good together," he mouthed over the music, as their steps carried them close to the raised platform where the musicians gathered.

Ruth pulled back to study his face. The idea of competing intrigued Wyndom; she recognized excitement in his expression. *Why not*, she thought and nodded her ascent.

"Tell me about this contest," she said matching Wyndom's intricate maneuvers perfectly. "It's been years, I'm a bit rusty."

Wyndom twirled her out and back, drew her close then bent her over his arm in a deep dip. Neither of them hesitated or missed a beat, a fact that secretly surprised both of them and attested to their abilities.

The music ended. They walked back to their table, sat down and the waitress arrived with their food. Over their meal of grilled chicken breast and vegetables in a Dijon mustard sauce, Wyndom clarified what he remembered of the rules posted out on the marquee. They would compete in a series of dances until only one couple, one very accomplished couple, remained on the floor. "There's no entry fee or entry deadline."

"Do they have dance contests here often?" Ruth forked a piece of chicken, turned it into three bites while waiting for his response.

"This is the first," Wyndom said. "Still, it's amateurs only and I think we have a chance." He shoved his empty plate aside.

"You up for the challenge?" he asked, watching Ruth savor her last bite of chicken before she spoke.

"I'll be your shadow every step of the way," she promised. "How did you hear about this?"

"The owner mentioned the contest when I stopped by to make reservations, he indicated it could become a monthly event if the turn out was good and there was enough interest, so I stopped on my way out and read the rules."

While the waitress cleared their table, Wyndom sought out the maitre d´ and added their names to his list of contestants. They sipped lemon laced ice water, scrutinized the competition, and Ruth, who understood the importance of attitude, tried hard to picture them winning.

The contest began with the two-step and none of the couples were signaled off the floor as they danced to the music. Fox trot tempo swept across the floor invigorating the dancers. Ruth and Wyndom moved through the steps with confidence, felt like they had danced this way a million times. Laughter ebbed and swelled around them from the competing couples, swirling in pleasure, and from the intent observers.

The sparkle in Ruth's eyes matched the sparkling beads decorating her dress and she laughed with delight when Wyndom lead them into a lively waltz. They circled the floor effortlessly, their steps perfectly matched. Ruth's ability to anticipate Wyndom's every move gave the aura surrounding them a sense of the surreal.

The floor became less crowded, exhausted and disillusioned competitors dropped out, the less coordinated were eliminated. Ruth felt feather light in Wyndom's arms. He controlled their movements with the mastery of an expert, leading them effortlessly through the steps of each new dance. The gracefulness and symmetry of their actions gained admiration from their observers.

Ruth had forgotten how wonderful it was to move around the floor in perfect sync with your partner. Wyndom, who seemed to know each dance, continuously amazed Ruth with his flawless innovations. He kept their steps in perfect unison to the beat as they whirled across the floor. Ruth's brown eyes twinkled with pleasure when Wyndom again swept her into an elegant dip. Their laughter echoed around the room and it was easy to see they were enjoying themselves.

Wyndom smiled down at Ruth. She sensed he was having as much fun as she was. His smile, his touch, the way they moved together all served to make Ruth feel beautiful, also breathless and ready for an intermission.

Wispy tendrils of wavy brown hair slipped from Ruth's butterfly comb, framing her face. *She is very beautiful tonight,* Wyndom thought, pulling out a chair for her.

"You're a great dancer," Ruth said after a long drink of ice cold sparkling water.

"Every Saturday morning while growing up, I was banished to dance class," Wyndom said, using a clean napkin to wipe the perspiration from his forehead.

"You hated every minute, right," Ruth lightly teased.

"I wanted to be out playing baseball," Wyndom admitted. He covered her hand with his. "From now on I promise to be grateful for Mother's insistence and to all the girls I partnered."

"You must have been the most popular boy in the class."

"Make that the only boy in the class," Wyndom said his voice rich with laughter.

Ruth pictured him surrounded by party dressed young girls all wanting to be next and felt a pang of envy. She wondered if that was how he'd met Jason's mother.

"Are you having a good time, Ruth?" Wyndom watched the smile start in her mahogany eyes before spreading like sunrise over her entire face. His body stirred to life and he silently acknowledged his attraction to this beauty opposite him, the teacher of his son.

They took advantage of the intermission to catch their breath and quench their thirst. The magic they created on the dance floor united them and there seemed no further need for conversation. Wyndom looked around the room at the array of competitors taking a respite. One couple must be close to eighty, and there were two jean-clad couples, obviously still in their teens. All seemed to be enjoying the activity. Wyndom watched and admired the older couple living it up on the dance floor, considered them their greatest competition.

Ruth studied Wyndom through the fringe of her lashes. She guessed his age at thirty-three, noted that the pleasure of their evening gave his face a boyish glow. The effect was enticing. Wyndom covered her other hand with his, their eyes met and he drew her hand toward his mouth to nibble kisses across her knuckles. Gooseflesh roughened Ruth's arm. Wyndom turned her palm to his lips and planted a kiss in the circle of her hand. Heat curled through her body, made her a prisoner of his touch. He held her gaze. Tension built, flowed from one to the other, binding them like a silken web.

Music burst through the quiet breaking the spell caging them. They stood simultaneously and Ruth slipped into Wyndom's arms. The dances that followed were Latin and lively. Ruth and Wyndom's movements grew sharp, exact and meticulous. Their bodies, twisting and whirling in faultless rhythm, created a heady sensation.

Communication flowed between them, unspoken but nonetheless articulate. The hypnotic cadence of the music united them in a dance of love, a dance of thrusts and perries, a dance of challenges issued and met. They stomped, swirled, separated, then flowed back together.

Shoulder to shoulder they drifted in fluid motion, never missing a beat. Then the tempo changed and they were engrossed in a fast stepping lively Jive. Wyndom murmured his intent to Ruth before tossing her over his shoulder. She slipped down his back then reached her hands between his legs and he pulled her through and up into his arms once again. He twirled her above his head, their every movement in perfect time with the music.

Everyone in the room watched in awed silence, mesmerized by the magic Ruth and Wyndom created. The music stopped and the silence took over.

Ruth and Wyndom, entrenched in the mood of the moment, stood, lost in each others gaze, unaware the music had stopped until applause erupted all around them. They hurriedly stepped apart, Ruth's face reddened in a lovely blush. They looked around to discover only the elderly couple still on the dance floor with them and both were pleased to watch them receive the first place trophy then turn and bow to a room of admirers. Ruth and Wyndom were given a trophy and also a round of applause.

The quiet purr of the engine was barely audible to Ruth and Wyndom as they rode hand in hand through the brilliant star-glazed night. Wyndom had lowered the Corvette's top before they left the restaurant, exposing the night to view. The breeze flowing around them felt warm and heavy with the wonderful aroma of full-blown spring. Glow from the full moon softened the scenery, iced it with silver. Cruising through the balmy night wrapped Ruth and Wyndom in a mystical world of fairies and invisible little people, a world enriched by the voices of nature flowing past, a world that silently spoke of an enticing ready-to-emerge summer.

The Corvette slowed and pulled to a stop in Ruth's drive. Wyndom turned to look at her. He gently squeezed the hand he'd held during the trip home feeling suddenly shy and tongue-tied. He lifted his other hand, used the back of his fingers to caress Ruth's petal soft cheek. "Thank you for a magical evening," he whispered, leaning close enough to brush his lips over the rim of her ear.

"I believe I should be thanking you, Wyndom Winters. I've never enjoyed myself more," Ruth said softly. She angled her head, offering up her mouth for Wyndom's kiss.

The kiss was unhurried, languorous and exploring. Tonight there was no audience, no seven-year-old eyes to hinder Wyndom's approach. He lightly grazed Ruth's bottom lip with his tongue then his teeth, learning its contours. The world receded; delightful shivers robbed Ruth of the ability to think. Wyndom kissed one corner of her mouth then the other before joining them in a powerful kiss that effected both of them alike, leaving each breathless and seeking air.

Ruth sought to regain control of her senses. Wyndom's kiss had ignited a myriad of flash fires through out her body. She fought her confusion, wanted the kiss to continue and at the same time wanted it to end. She was in uncharted waters, had no familiar path to guide her actions. She leaned closer, seeking support and the trophy, resting between them on the seat, jabbed her in the ribs. She jerked back, emitted a sharp cry of pain.

Wyndom, grabbing for the prize to toss it in the back seat, cracked his elbow on the gearshift. Despite their pain they both broke into laughter. "Next time I'll bring the station wagon, it's front seat would be perfect for necking," Wyndom said, causing Ruth to avert her eyes and blush at the appropriateness of his words.

"It's time I went inside," Ruth murmured, "I'm teaching Sunday School in the morning and I need to review the lesson."

Wyndom helped her from the car and they strolled toward the house hand in hand. Neither of them eager to dispel the magic of their evening. He unlocked the door and held it open before lowering his mouth for a quick goodnight kiss.

Ruth smiled and in a voice barely above a whisper said, "Thank you, Wyndom."

She watched him turn and wave before getting into his car. Watched while he started the Corvette and began to back out of her driveway. She closed and locked the door, listening until she heard his car accelerate and drive off into the night before extinguishing the exterior light and walking into the den to give the morning's lesson a once over.

Deciding her efforts were useless, Ruth abandoned the study guide and went to her bedroom. Her thoughts, as she unpinned her hair and undressed for bed, centered on Wyndom and the marvelous way they bonded on the dance floor. He had offered her the Trophy but Ruth assured him Jason would want to see their prize.

The more time Ruth spent with Wyndom the more convinced she became that he was not the cause of Jason's depression. By accident she discovered that Jason dreaded summer vacation, he indicated as much when she worked one-on-one with him yesterday. She groaned aloud her frustration over Jason, wished she understood his problem and knew how to help. Wyndom Winters was carving a special place in Ruth's heart and she knew it would hurt tremendously if it turned out he was abusing his son. She opened her window a few inches. A gentle breeze carried the night symphony from her backyard to her ears and she stood listening in appreciation a moment before sliding in bed and saying her prayers. She fell asleep mentally listing all the events of the day for which she was thankful.

***

Wyndom drove through street-lit byways and rehashed the evening, projecting random pictures of Ruth onto the screen of his mind. He cherished the way the silken sheen of her hair brushed his cheek as they danced around the floor, the way her eyes flashed glints of umber and topaz fire as he bent her over his arm, but most of all he cherished the way their bodies meshed in exquisite harmony as they flowed across the dance floor. Wyndom understood that this evening would be hard to forget.

CHAPTER TEN

Katie was just coming up from the basement, her arms full of clean laundry when the kitchen phone started ringing. She dropped her bundle on the table and grabbed for the receiver. She knew Mrs. Carlyle hated being bothered before dinner.

"Mom, I need you. Can you come and get me right now, please?"

"Karen, what's wrong?" The housekeeper heard uncontrolled sobbing on the other end of the phone line and was engulfed with fear.

"Karen, hush baby. Talk to me. What happened?"

"Jeffrey c...c...came home d...drunk. He lost his job and he blamed me," Karen said between sobs.

"Did he hit you, Karen?" Katie questioned, trying to keep her emotional upset from coloring her speech and hindering her ability to think clearly.

Karen took a couple of deep breaths, in an effort to control her tears and contain her fear. "Mom, I'm spotting. I need to get to the hospital right away." Karen moaned.

"Where is Jeff?"

"He's passed out at the kitchen table. I'm afraid to wake him. I'm too upset and shaky to try and drive," she said, biting her lip to stifle a moan. "Please, Mom, hurry!"

Katie heard her daughter's struggle to control her pain and her fear. "Pack an overnight bag and wait for me on the porch," Katie said, "I'm on my way."

The housekeeper returned the phone to its cradle and went in search of her employer. She prayed that this time Karen would leave her husband, for the sake of her baby if for no other reason. Katie prayed it wasn't already too late.

Evelyn sat, feet propped up on a hassock, sipping a glass of sherry. She glowered at the interruption when Katie rushed into the library. "I've an emergency Ma'am, I have to leave for awhile," Katie said.

"Did you feed Jason?" the woman inquired harshly.

"I don't have time..."

"Do it before you leave if you want a job to come back to," Evelyn ordered.

Katie went in search of Jason. Anger marred her features. Anger at Jeffrey and at her employer. Katie's speech was brisk as she pushed Jason toward the kitchen. "I have an emergency, Jason. Come to the kitchen with me, I'll make you a quick sandwich before I leave."

Katie pulled the peanut butter from the cupboard, jelly, butter, bread, and milk from the refrigerator. She muttered under her breath as she rushed back and forth gathering necessities. She returned to the cupboard for a glass and a knife, perturbed by her inefficacy.

"I can fix my own sandwich," Jason quietly offered, tuning in to her distress.

Katie wished Wyndom were here, she hated leaving Jason alone like this. Still, she had no choice.

"Thank you, Jason, that would be a big help." She gave him a quick hug before running out the back door.

Jason bit at his bottom lip in concentration, working to spread the stiff, cold, peanut butter evenly without tearing his bread. He dipped the knife into the jelly and tried to scoop out enough to cover his bread. Finally he succeeded in pulling a glob of grape jelly out of the jar only to discover, when it landed on the bread, that it was a tad more then he needed. Jason eyed it for a minute then just covered the mass with the other slice of bread and squashed the whole together with the heel of his hand.

Sticky fingers uncapped the milk and Jason poured his glass full to the rim. He leaned over to sip from the glass before screwing the lid back on the milk. Picking up the sandwich, Jason took a quick bite. He scooped the bottle of milk against his chest and carried it to the refrigerator.

Jelly dribbled from his sandwich, plopped to the floor. Unaware, Jason stepped onto the blob. He tracked spots of purple across the floor to the chair and settled on his knees so he could lean over and sip milk from his too-full glass.

Jason bounced and hummed contentedly. Eating with zest, he consumed his meal. He licked jelly from around his mouth and drained the last drop of milk from his glass. Jason scooted from the chair, put lids back on the jelly and peanut butter jars and shoved both into the door of the refrigerator.

I'm still hungry. He stood at the open door of the fridge, licking jelly off his fingers, and perused each shelf looking for something else to eat. Cake. It was perfect. It had been shoved to the back of the shelf, almost out of reach.

It looked yummy. Jason grew hungry just looking at the cake. It sat tall and smooth on the plate, like a regal treat waiting just for him. Pink icing glazed the top and sides of the confection. Chocolate sprinkles were scattered evenly edge to edge across the top. *Cake, the perfect ending for my supper.* He studied, looked for the easiest way to get at the mouth-watering beauty.

Jason meticulously shoved several items out of the way so he could reach the cake. He slid both hands carefully under the cake dish and carried the dessert over to the kitchen table. He gently tugged the plastic wrap loose and lifted it away from the enticing confection, eager for a first bite.

Jason stepped back from the table and studied the pink and chocolate beauty. He had never cut a piece of cake but he'd watched Katie and it had not looked too difficult.

He picked up the knife he'd used to make his sandwich and tried to push it through the pink glaze. The frosting crackled into spider-web fissures from the knife's movement but all it did to the angel food underneath was scrunch it. Jason worried at the tip of his tongue, tried to remember how Katie had used the knife. He moved the knife back and forth in a sawing motion to no avail. Jason shook his head and deliberated once more. He looked around the room, spied a knife holder and pictured the knife Katie used. It was the third knife he pulled from the holder and he carried it to the table. This knife easily pierced the frosting and the crust of the cake.

Jason finished his first piece and was busy cutting himself a second generous slice when Evelyn entered the room. She immediately noticed the mess on the floor, the table and Jason's face. She scowled her anger. Last of all, Evelyn spied the cake Katie had baked for her Sunday afternoon tea and she flew into a rage.

"You brat," she screeched, rounding on Jason.

"That cake was for my party tomorrow. You've ruined it." She repeatedly stomped her foot demanding attention. Grabbing Jason by the shoulders, she held him immobile.

"Who gave you permission to eat my cake," she growled, shaking Jason erratically to emphasize her words.

Jason yanked away from Evelyn, cowered against the wall, pulled the chair in front of him. He was rigid with terror, wished Katie had not left. He had never seen his grandmother so angry.

"I'm sorry," he whispered and wished he could think of some way to appease her.

"You're always sorry. Just look at this mess." Suddenly Evelyn's hand shot out and she slapped Jason hard across the face. The sound seemed to explode in Jason's ears and his face burned. "Go to your room. Go to your room, now. Stay there," Evelyn said through clenched teeth.

Tears streamed down Jason's face. He fled the kitchen, still clutching the offensive piece of cake. He slammed his bedroom door shut and huddled in a corner, his face on fire where his grandmother had hit him. *Surely she won't come up here after me. She never comes to my room. I didn't mean to make her angry.* Tears washed unheeded down his cheeks as Jason replayed the shouted words his grandmother's had flung at his retreating back.

"*Your father will leave you just like your mother did. You're an evil child, an unruly brat, you don't even know how to behave properly.*"

Jason munched the piece of cake clutched in his fist and worried that this time his father would change his mind and send him away.

He absentmindedly licked frosting from his fingers no longer enjoying the sweetness and fought against the tears that continued to flow. Jason scrunched down to remove his shoes then, clutching Scruffy tight to his chest, he crawled under the covers to hide from his world.

***

Rage consumed Evelyn, she felt herself shaking. The kitchen was a disaster, her beautiful cake ruined. Katie had no right leaving her and Jason alone. She stalked over to the table, grabbed up the cake and spitefully dumped the remainder into the sink. *Katie will just have to bake another one in* the *morning if she wants to continue working here.*

Evelyn trembled, on the verge of tears. She was so tired of always being alone, tired of feeling like a failure. Stumbling back to the library and her glass of sherry, Evelyn thought of her husband, well ex-husband to be exact. He'd left her three years ago. He'd relocated and remarried. Even her millions were not enough to hold the man. She had not been able to hold Cindy either. Evelyn grasped that she had failed at marriage and motherhood. She accepted failure as just punishment for her excessive wealth.

Now Cindy was dead and Evelyn shared her house with Wyndom and Jason. Wyndom was never around and Jason, Jason reminded her of her failure. Evelyn longed for attention. She wanted a man around to assuage her ego, make her feel young and beautiful again. Wyndom was supposed to be that man, supposed to be here, keeping her company, commiserating with her.

Evelyn set the sherry decanter beside her on the table, and one drink after another, she wallowed in her misery. Not once had she ever laid a hand on Cindy, what possessed her to strike a child? The image of her handprint on his cheek would not go away, eyes open or closed it floated in front of her face. She had to use both hands to steady the glass so she could finish her drink.

***

Wyndom shook the memories of Ruth and the way they had meshed on the dance floor from his mind. He maneuvered the Corvette into the garage. He considered putting up the top but decided to leave the task for another time. If he hurried he might get to tuck Jason under the covers, put him to sleep with the story of their second-place trophy.

The lower floor of the huge house blazed with light and Wyndom wondered if Evelyn was hosting a party. Silence met his ears as he entered the back door and he knew he was wrong. Wyndom pulled the tie from his neck and moved from room to room extinguishing lights.

The kitchen was a mess. Crumbled remains of a nearly whole cake lay abandoned in the sink. Irregular shaped sticky spots scattered around on the floor looked like jelly. *What happened here tonight? I can't believe Katie would leave the kitchen in such disorder.* Vowing to corner the housekeeper in the morning, Wyndom continued his trek through the house. Soft snores drifted from the open door of the library and Wyndom found his mother-in-law sprawled on the sofa, an empty sherry bottle lay on the table beside her. Evelyn had passed out. It was becoming more obvious every day that the woman had a drinking problem and he sighed with relief that Katie had been here to watch over Jason. Wyndom laid an afghan over Evelyn, extinguished the light and wondered if he should confront her about her drinking. Shaking his head in disgust, he went up to check on his son.

***

Karen sat huddled on the emergency room table while the nurse cleaned the cut under her eye. She looked frightful, her lip was swollen and her eye would be black by morning. She bowed her head and prayed silently for the umpteenth time that God would protect her baby. "I'm scared," she admitted to herself, caressing her belly.

Finally the curtain parted admitting the doctor. He carried a folder containing her history in his hand. Karen trembled with tension as he perused her face and the bruises dotting her arms, face, and neck. He shook his head sadly, clipped the x-rays of Karen's arm and shoulder to the lighted wall screen, and studied them slowly. Just then a technologist shoved a piece of equipment into the tiny room. "You'll be uncomfortable for a few days," the doctor said quietly. "You were lucky this time, there are no broken bones."

"What about the baby?" Karen asked wishing her mother were in here instead of in the waiting room.

"We'll do an ultra-sound and check on the little one now," the doctor said, gently patting her on the back for assurance. A tear slipped from the corner of Karen's eye. She trembled with terror for her unborn child.

"Are you here alone?" the doctor questioned.

Karen explained about her mother and the doctor immediately sent the aide to fetch her. Karen's round belly was being covered with conductive jelly when Katie stepped through the curtain. The older woman quickly moved to stand by her daughter and they clung hand to hand while the doctor slid the scanner over Karen's slick flesh.

They both sighed with relief when the doctor pinpointed a steady heartbeat. Katie tissued off the conductive jelly, alert to the doctor's command that Karen must spend the next two days in bed.

The doctor turned to leave, changed his mind instead and walked to Karen's side. "Did your husband do this to you?" he inquired gently.

Karen swiped at tears, sighed, mumbled "Yes."

"Are you going back to him?" he said, concern written across his face. Karen's "No" was strong and determined.

"Good girl," the doctor said. He was mumbling to himself and shaking his head when he walked from the room.

Katie slipped her arm around her daughter and they hugged tearfully, "Are you having any more pain?"

Karen shook her head negatively and leaned against her mom.

"Do you want to tell me what happened?" Katie said as she supported her daughter.

"He was so angry." Karen pulled a tissue from the box next to the bed and blew her nose. "Jeff went to an advertising meeting this morning, apparently he was drunk and got fired." Tears pooled in Karen's eyes, she swiped at them repeatedly. "He said it was my fault, said that I loved the baby more than him and…and he hit me."

"What are you going to do?" Katie said. She brushed the hair away from Karen's face and silently prayed her daughter would make the right decision.

"I have to leave him, Mom. I knew it the minute he knocked me to the floor and kicked me in the stomach." Karen crossed her arms over her rounded belly. "I love my baby. I will have to find a place to stay, get a job. It won't be easy," Karen said, managing a weak smile.

"You're coming home with me tonight," Katie said firmly.

"Mrs. Carlyle would probably fire you if she found out, I don't want to make trouble for you."

"She is a harridan for sure but, even if she pays well and Mr. Winters and Jason are nice and seem to need me, you are more important to me than any job."

Mother and daughter were hugging when the intern slid the curtain back and entered the cubical. "The doctor left you a prescription for a salve and orders to call immediately if you have any more bleeding." A wheelchair was secured for Karen and they were dismissed.

"Do you need anything else from your apartment?" Katie said as she started the car.

"I can't go back, Mom. Jeff will start crying, say he's sorry. He always does. I have to stay strong for the baby," Karen said, she leaned back and closed her eyes.

"You make a list of what you need and I'll pick it up for you tomorrow." Katie reached over and patted Karen's hand. "I'll help all I can."

"I won't go back to Jeff unless he admits that he needs help managing his anger and his drinking."

***

Light shone from beneath Jason's door and Wyndom hoped his son was still awake. He opened the door quietly and scanned the room. Walked in to investigate and lifted the blankets from the lump in the bed. Jason, his face food stained and tear streaked, lay fully clothed and curled up around scruffy bear. Jason shuddered in his sleep and Wyndom wondered if he should wake the boy, find out why he had cried himself to sleep. While contemplating his options, he heard a car in the drive. Wyndom removed Jason's shoes, recovered him, switched off the light and went downstairs to check out the noise in the driveway. He turned on the back porch light and stepped outside.

"Katie?"

Karen was leaning against her mother and they turned as one person when they heard Wyndom's voice.

His shocked expletive at the sight of Karen's face echoed through the stillness of the illuminated driveway. Anger jolted Wyndom and he spit out the one word question. "Jeffrey?"

Karen's affirmative nod was followed by a groan of pain as she shifted her bruised body.

"I'm just trying to get her upstairs, Mr. Winters," Katie murmured. "She can't go home."

Wyndom walked over and scooped the pregnant woman into his arms. "I'll carry her Katie, you get the door open and the lights on." He gently settled Karen in an overstuffed chair in Katie's combination kitchen living room.

"We need a cup of tea, Mr. Winters, would you care to join us?" Katie asked, scurrying around the kitchen brewing tea and fixing a plate of oatmeal cookies for them to munch on.

"What are you going to do now?" Wyndom asked the disheveled young girl.

Katie explained that Karen had to stay in bed for a few days, "I hope Mrs. Carlyle won't be upset."

"If she says anything to you Katie, tell her I gave my permission. In the morning I'll straighten it out with her," Wyndom offered.

Karen started to sniffle again; she reached for a tissue, acknowledged, out loud, that she needed her own place to stay. "I need a job," she murmured to the room at large.

Wyndom thought about Bruce and the way he'd groused this afternoon that he needed an assistant. "We have at least three months of work yet at the job site in Ames. Bruce, my foreman, claims he needs help someone to stay in the office, answer phones, call suppliers and handle accounts. If you're interested, Karen," Wyndom reiterated, "there's a vacant trailer, on site, where you could live."

As the three sipped their tea, Wyndom pieced together the events of the evening from snippets of the conversation.

Before Wyndom left the apartment he arranged to drive Karen to her new job, as soon as she felt comfortable out of bed. Both women quietly thanked Wyndom and he returned to the house. He wondered once again what had happened in this house to upset Jason and he knew that Katie had not been here so he could not ask her. He wondered what the woman would think when she saw her kitchen. Wyndom unsuccessfully searched for a mop to clean up the sticky purple spots but eventually had to settle for paper towels. It took several but finally the floor looked halfway presentable and Wyndom went up to bed.

The next morning, Wyndom dribbled water across Jason's back as he knelt by the bathtub and helped Jason to bathe. "What happened last night while I was gone, son?" he inquired.

Jason hung his head, explained that he had made grandma mad and she had sent him to his room. He did not explain about the cake or tell his dad about being hit. Did not want anyone to know how bad he had been.

Later, when Wyndom had the opportunity to confront Evelyn, she played down the incident, barely remembering the evening.

CHAPTER ELEVEN

Over the next week, Ruth prepared her students for graduation, Wyndom started a new project in Cedar Rapids and Jason grew more quiet than ever. Summer arrived in a wave of heat and humidity that sapped the energy of humans and speeded the growth of field after field of corn.

Jason sat on the front porch wondering what to do with his days now that school was over for the summer. Suddenly he remembered the hula-hoop leaning against the wall in the garage. He was hot and sweaty before he even managed to keep the ring spinning at his waist for just a few minutes. Jason figured his dad might take him to Hardee's for Cruise night if he could master the hoop. Temperatures soared, scorching moisture from trees and grass and heating the expanse of double drive where Jason wrestled with the plastic circle.

"Are you ready for a snack?" Katie said, pushing through the back door with a tray in her hands.

"Oh boy," Jason said as he ran to the back steps, "strawberry Kool-Aid and cookies."

Katie handed the boy a frosty glass of red liquid. Jason drained the glass in one try. She filled his glass again, then sat down beside him on the top step. Pushing the damp strands of hair from Jason's eyes, Katie smiled at him. "What have you been doing to get so hot?"

He sipped the cool drink and munched on his second cookie while he told her about the Hula-Hoop and Hardee's contest. When his thirst was quenched and he had devoured all the cookies, he said, "Thank you, Katie. Do you want to see what I can do?"

Katie studied his method carefully. "Jason, once you get the hoop circling your waist try and slow your movements just a little, maybe that will work," Katie coached.

Jason concentrated and, while Katie watched, he found his rhythm and managed to keep the plastic tube circling for at least two minutes. The housekeeper clapped her hands in approval then picked up the dishes and went back into the kitchen. Throughout the afternoon, Jason continued to practice.

Wyndom turned into the drive and slowed to a stop. He watched Jason gyrate his lithe young body, the Hula-Hoop steadily circling his waist. The seven-year-old was totally involved with concentrating on his movements. When Wyndom honked the horn startled Jason, he jumped and dropped the plastic ring. Recovering quickly, he picked up the hoop and hurried to the edge of the drive so Wyndom could garage the Corvette.

Minutes later father and son sat at the kitchen table feasting on chicken salad sandwiches, deviled eggs, and slices of cantaloupe, honeydew, and watermelon. They discussed another trip to Hardee's. "Would you mind if I ask Ruth to join us?" Wyndom quietly said.

"I want her to see how good I am with the Hula-Hoop," Jason said in the way of a yes before he stuffed the last deviled egg into his mouth.

"You have a birthday coming up in a few weeks, Jason. Is there something special that you would like to do?"

Jason went very still, considered his father's question. Wyndom could see the wheels turning in Jason's mind as he worked through his options.

Jason's spiky blonde hair seemed even more unruly this afternoon and his blue eyes sparkled with intelligence. Wyndom realized how empty his life would be with out his son. He stood and gathered the empty plates, glasses and silver from the table. While he stashed all of them in the dishwasher, he silently prayed for help that he might give Jason a happier life than the lonely existence Wyndom himself remembered.

"Could we go camping?" Jason asked hesitantly.

A smile washed the worry lines from Wyndom Winter's face as the idea, once planted, grew and blossomed with possibilities.

Jason and Wyndom left the artificially cooled kitchen for the breezy comfort of the back yard. Together they made plans for the trip. They would have to purchase a tent, sleeping bags, a camp stove, and fishing gear. Already both of them were excited by the idea.

Jason eagerly jumped up and down at his father's side as Wyndom pulled a small calendar from his wallet. They huddled, head to head, and mulled over Wyndom's schedule looking for a free weekend. Jason asked to take a friend along, his father said yes. They walked into the house and Wyndom helped Jason find Jerry Bartlett's phone number. Jerry was thrilled at the idea of camping out and Wyndom took the phone from Jason to explain their plans to Jerry's mother and get her consent.

It took quite a while that evening to calm Jason down enough for him to fall asleep. Wyndom shook his head, marveled at the exuberance of a seven-year-old.

Bedtimes could be very exhausting.

Before climbing between his cool sheets and giving in to his weariness, Wyndom called Ruth and made arrangements to pick her up Friday night for another Hardee's date. He set the phone back in its cradle, stifling a yawn, and extinguished the lamp.

Wyndom slid between the covers. He'd been up since 5:30 this morning, knew tomorrow would be another long day. He fell asleep with the remembrance of Ruth's melodious voice pleasuring his thoughts.

***

Ruth replaced the phone and picked up the novel she was reading. She held the book open on her lap and fantasized about another evening in the company of Wyndom and Jason. Her smile was unconscious, full blown, as she worked through the flashback of their last date and the wonder of being in Wyndom's arms. She thought of Jason and realized she was also eager to spend time with him, she missed seeing him now that school was out.

By the age of twenty-nine, Ruth assumed her dreams of romance, the kind of emotions you read about in novels, were just hogwash. Then Wyndom Winters kissed her and her dreams took flight. She thought about her relationship with Wyndom, wondered what the future held or if it were only her pipe dream that they even had a future.

I enjoy looking at him, get all tingly when we touch. He dances like Fred Astaire and best of all he kisses...How do you describe the power of a kiss when you just discovered they had power. Ruth shook her head at her wayward thoughts and set her novel on the coffee table, reading fantasy no longer as satisfying as reality. Still smiling, filled with a warm glow and thoughts of Wyndom Winters, she prepared for bed.

***

Ruth noticed the Hula-hoop clutched in Jason's arms the minute she slid into the red Bermuda wagon. She gathered from the size of Jason's grin that he had mastered the plastic ring.

Crowds of car enthusiasts and their vehicles ringed the Hardees' parking lot. More then a hundred old cars and trucks were parked on the concrete and in the grass that surrounded the fast food restaurant.

The Edsel was directed to an empty space and the host handed them three free drink tickets. Wyndom also received a ticket for a drawing especially for drivers. Ruth, Wyndom and Jason decided to eat first then check out the rest of the cars. When they walked passed the DJ's table, they were stopped and each one of them received a door prize ticket. Jason seemed jubilant as he walked between them, anxious to participate in the scheduled contests.

After sharing double cheeseburgers, fries, and chocolate shakes, the three exited the restaurant, surprised to see another Edsel enter the parking lot. Ruth smiled, waved at the young couple and led the Winters' men over to meet the owners of the dusty pink '59 two- door hardtop. The two Edsels were parked side by side and Wyndom spent a great part of the evening visiting with Walter Holly, the '59's owner and other car enthusiasts interested in the Edsels.

Ruth put her hand on Jason's shoulder and steered him toward the DJ's table. "Your father is busy with Edsel talk but I want to see you make that Hula-Hoop sing."

"I've been practicing," Jason said. He watched impatiently as several young people gathered for the contest, eagerly waiting for the signal for them to start.

"I'm sure you can do this," Ruth said. "I'll be cheering for you." She stepped back out of the way just in time. Music signaled them to start and Ruth watched the young people begin to move in sync with the melody. She watched as one after the other contestants were eliminated. Some by dropping the Hula-Hoop others by running out of energy. Standing still became difficult as the music throbbed all around her.

"I won. I won," Jason said. He held up the T-shirt for Ruth to admire. She hugged Jason and they decided to wait by the D J's table while winning numbers were announced. When they walked back to where Wyndom stood, there were fewer people standing around the car. "You did great up there, Jason," he said, hugging his son and mouthing thank you to Ruth. Evening shadowed the area as the crowd thinned and it came time to leave.

Jason sat in the back seat singing snippets of old tunes. It was easy for Ruth and Wyndom, their fingers laced together on the front seat, to tell that he had had a good time.

"We could do this again tomorrow night," Wyndom suggested to the car's occupants when he had pulled to a stop in Ruth's drive. Ruth and Jason looked at him questioningly.

"The Sugar Shack," he said as a reminder to both of them.

Ruth looked at Wyndom. "You don't—"

Wyndom squeezed Ruth's hand then quickly leaned across the seat and kissed her on the mouth. "Tomorrow night," he said firmly and reached to open her door.

Jason watched until Ruth was safely inside the front door before vaulting over the seat and snuggling next to his father on short drive back to the Carlyle house.

***

It was Saturday night, barely 5:00 P.M. when the Bermuda Wagon turned into the parking lot in front of the Sugar Shack. Obviously something special was happening here tonight. The parking expanse bustled with activity.

For a five-dollar fee they entered the Edsel in the car show. The Sugar Shack's owner was providing roast pork sandwiches and chips to all entrants. As usual they received free drink tickets and the three sat in their lawn chairs, eating barbecue and drinking root beer.

Jason looked down at the ticket he held to check the number. Groaned when the number called did not match.

"Give it time, son," Wyndom said. "Look at all the prizes stacked on that table."

"I want another sandwich," Ruth said. She stood. "Can I get anything for either of you?"

"I'm ready for more," Jason said. All three of them walked to the side of the building and stepped into the fast moving line. Ruth carried Wyndom's sandwich and he went to get root beer refills. While they continued their feast they listened to the up-beat music and studied the new arrivals.

"Look at that car, dad, it's purple," Jason said, his eyes following the shiny purple lead sled, circling, looking for a space to park.

"Finish your drink and let me have the cup. I'll put all this in the trash and we'll go look at the cars," Wyndom suggested.

Jason listened to the DJ announce another number. "We won, we won," he said and showed the ticket to Wyndom before he ran up to gather their prize. Each car had been assigned a number and the DJ was kept busy playing music and handing out the donated prizes.

"Thanks," Wyndom said when Jason gave him the envelope with a ticket for two free dinners at the large store across from the parking lot. He slipped them into his front pocket, smiling at how delighted Jason was with the idea of winning food.

The purple lead sled's exterior was smooth. It had no door handles and the back doors of the sixty-year-old four-door vehicle had been leaded shut. The top was cropped and Jason expressed curiosity about the visibility from the narrow windows. All three agreed that the owner had done a great job with design and restoration. They continued their trek through the cars, stopping often to admire and visit with other owners.

"We're ready for the wet T-shirt contest," Wayne, the DJ announced.

Ruth and Wyndom watched Jason soak the T-shirt with water and carry it six feet to a milk bottle. His goal, to squeeze as much water as possible into the bottle. The participants were all young and they all enjoyed their wet game.

"See what I won." Jason's eyes sparkled, he waved a 'dollar off' coupon good anytime at the Sugar Shack. Before leaving Jason used the coupon towards a three-dip cone. Wyndom had a banana split and Ruth enjoyed a dip of double-chocolate-almond ice cream drenched in butterscotch syrup.

"Oo-ee-oo-aa-aa," Jason sang off key from the back seat of the Bermuda Wagon as they drove through town toward Ruth's. "We're going camping for my birthday," he told Ruth, his grin relaxed and carefree.

"You sound excited," she said, twisting in the front seat to get a better view of Jason's face.

"Jerry Bartlett gets to go with us," Jason said.

Wyndom pulled the Edsel into the Carlyle driveway. "I hope you don't mind," Wyndom said, "It's bedtime for Jason."

"Aww, Dad," Jason said in protest.

"Go tuck him in, I'll wait right here, " Ruth said, She leaned her head against the back of the seat and closed her eyes.

Ruth was fantasizing, reliving those moments she and Wyndom shared, whipping around the floor in a brisk waltz, when the car door opened and he slid in beside her. The fire in Wyndom's mahogany eyes blazed a path to Ruth's heart and she moved easily into his arms for a kiss that curled her toes. "Will you go dancing with me again tonight, Ruth?" he murmured against her mouth.

"Anytime, anywhere," she answered between his kisses. He nestled her body against his side and started the Edsel.

"How did you know?"

Wyndom looked at Ruth, his puzzlement indicated by a lifted eyebrow.

"I was remembering the thrill of our first waltz, while I waited for you to return."

They sipped 7-Up between dances, each totally relaxed and comfortable with their surroundings. A spiritual bonding drew them together and they moved as one to the steady beat of the band. Tonight, music was all the communication necessary for either of them.

The space between them diminished. Ruth relaxed, mesmerized by the magic of the music and her companion. Wyndom wrapped her securely in his arms and she felt content. The hint of after-shave lingering on his flesh tantalized, she savored the moment, wanted time to stop for just a little while.

Wyndom buried his nose in Ruth's coffee colored curls breathing in the "Lily of the Valley" fragrance of her shampoo and dreamed of carrying her to a satin-sheeted king size bed and showering her with love.

To Ruth and Wyndom it seemed mere minutes before the band stood to case their instruments. The enchantment of the evening followed Ruth and Wyndom from the dance floor all the way to Ruth's front door.

His kisses grew insistent.

Ruth struggled to catch her breath and calm her equilibrium. "Let me stay with you tonight," he groaned against her mouth.

Suddenly her body stilled.

Wyndom pulled back to search Ruth's face. A deep blush stained her cheeks at his scrutiny. "Am I reading the signals wrong here, Ruth?"

Wyndom stroked her petal soft cheek with his finger, "Am I the only one here burning up with desire?"

Ruth's eyes were luminous and she met Wyndom's gaze with reluctance. Slowly she moved her head from side to side then she groaned and dropped her head to bury her face in his shoulder.

"I've never been with a man before," she murmured against his shirt, "I'm not sure I'm ready." *Why am I admitting this now? He's going to decide there's something wrong with me and I'll never see him again.* Her thoughts set off an emotional turmoil that left her unsettled, started tears slipping silently down her cheeks.

Her muffled response momentarily startled Wyndom until he understood that she was not rejecting him and with a freeing sense of relief and renewed hope he lifted her chin to study her face, he caught a tear with his finger. Mesmerized she watched his tongue dart out and sip it up. Her breath stalled and she saw laughter lurking in his chocolate eyes. "You're a virgin." His whisper held a hint of astonishment and a great deal of respect.

"I've never been with anyone, until now, that even tempted me to break my pledge of waiting until after marriage," Ruth quietly said, praying he would understand.

"I find the idea as intriguing as I find you," Wyndom said, cradling her gently in his arms. "I don't know many people with such strong principles," he stated. "I do like hearing that I at least tempt you," he admitted.

He brushed the pad of his thumb along her bottom lip then he covered her mouth with his.

"Goodnight, Sweet Ruth," he said against her lips. Then he turned and fled to the car, much in need of a cold shower.

Ruth watched him back out of the drive. Wondered if she would ever see Wyndom Winters again.

She sighed deeply; thinking about the way his kisses left her limp with longing. His touch ignited her with unfamiliar feelings she both hesitated and longed to explore. Maybe she should have set aside her principles and invited him into her bed. She believed that he was a man she could love for a lifetime.

Tears sparkled unshed in her eyes. She prayed that Wyndom would still be interested. Prayed that this time there would be understanding instead of ridicule. Ruth gnawed nervously at her lip trying unsuccessfully to suppress the worries that coursed through her as she absentmindedly undressed and prepared for bed.

***

Tepid water pelted his naked body. He adjusted it, hoping the cold would cool the heat in his loins. Never before had a woman declined his attempt at seduction because she was a virgin.

Ruth was far too beautiful not to have had other offers, Wyndom thought to himself. He always considered women a fair challenge, some easier than others. To him, Ruth was an enigma, and he shook his head in wonder when he realized how much he wanted to cherish her.

He rubbed water from his torso with brisk strokes, deep in thought about his next move. She was truly a special woman and he resolved to let her know that was how he felt.

***

Ruth was reaching to extinguish the lamp when the phone sounded. Her hand shook in anticipation. She lifted the receiver to her ear. "Dennison residence," she announced into the phone.

"I'm calling to talk to a very special lady, I believe her name is Ruth," Wyndom stated huskily. "Do you know her," he teased.

Ruth giggled lightly warmth encasing her heart. "I might," she admitted.

"Would you tell her 'thank you' for the beautiful evening?" he said.

"I will," she said in her best coquettish voice.

"Please ask if she'll join me for a late dinner tomorrow," he murmured into the phone.

"She is agreeable," Ruth responded, "she would appreciate a time."

"I'll be there at four," he said.

"Now kind sir if you would just give me your name," Ruth said a light teasing quality to her voice.

Wyndom's chuckle echoed through the line, "Sweet dreams, Ruth," he softly said then disconnected.

He wondered if he might be falling in love, he shifted his pillow to attain maximum comfort, and stretched out to sleep.

Serene with relief, Ruth snuggled beneath the sheet and drifted into a peaceful sleep, a sleep invaded often by an illusive image of the handsome man she wanted in her life. She awoke to the sun shining into her room, prying the fog of sleep from her eyes. She moved joyously through her Sunday morning routine, feeling young, light, and very happy, humming "Amazing Grace" all the way to church. Her thoughts straying continuously to the handsome and understanding Wyndom Winters.

***

Jason watched the pile of supplies necessary for the camping trip grow. They'd spent the last two hours choosing a tent, sleeping bags, stove, lantern, and etceteras. Now Wyndom and the very young and inexperienced store clerk were checking the list to make sure they had everything they would need.

Wyndom had not realized how complicated a chore choosing the proper fishing equipment would be.

"Is it really almost four o'clock?" Wyndom said, surprised at how quickly the camping trip had eroded the afternoon. Cheerfully the young clerk rang up the total, already mentally busy spending his commission from this sale.

Wyndom decided to pick up Ruth before dropping Jason at home. He sensed it would cause her undo tension if he were to pick her up late today. He shoved the credit card back into his wallet, then he, Jason and the young clerk loaded all the paraphernalia into the back of the Bermuda wagon.

Ruth's joy at seeing Wyndom diminished when she spied Jason ensconced on the back seat of the Edsel. She wondered if the seven-year-old was Wyndom Winter's way of distancing himself from her.

With his hand at her elbow, warm and inviting, he guided her toward the wagon, and Ruth silently agonized about the real reason for today's outing.

"Hi, Jason," Ruth said in greeting to him as she scooted into the front seat.

Jason bounced across the back seat, "Have you ever been camping, Miss Dennison?"

She turned to easier look at the young boy and noted the load of equipment behind the back seat. "No, Jason, I've never been camping."

Wyndom slid into the front seat of the wagon just in time to hear Ruth's admission. It started him thinking. Jason's boyish chatter filled the vehicle. He regaled Ruth with the plans for his birthday trip. His manner, his entire attitude seemed light, more like the youth Ruth knew when he'd first became her student.

Tension slipped away from Ruth's body when the wagon pulled to a stop in the Carlyle drive. Wyndom helped Jason from the Edsel, walking him to the back door and leaving him with a smiling Katie.

"Instead of unloading this mess, let's drive the Corvette," Wyndom suggested to Ruth. He maneuvered the Bermuda into the garage and they transferred to the other car. Violin music drifted from the cassette player, the piece was one of Ruth's favorites and she tried to relax, concentrate on the music. Wyndom snatched furtive glances in her direction. Somehow their relationship had changed; maybe that was the issue at hand. Before they had just been getting acquainted now he knew that he wanted a relationship with her.

What did Ruth want? He hoped they were in agreement on that point.

Wyndom wanted the woman beside him, wondered how he would manage to respect her wishes and still fulfill his fantasies. Maybe he should try and fulfill her fantasies instead.

Being close to her played havoc with his libido. He had not desired another woman since the fiasco with Cindy. He'd thought about dating, encountered any number of willing companions but he had always been too numb to even try.

Ruth changed all of that. He wondered if he might be falling in love with her. One thing was sure, Wyndom did not want to inadvertently do anything that might ruin the relationship developing between the two of them. He planned to let her know the depth of his commitment. He wanted to spend time with her. Wanted her to understand his willingness to respect her right to set the pace for their future dates.

And somehow, some way he had to find the courage to explain his ex-wife's part in her parents' death. He wished he had explained it when they first met. Back then he'd been unsure of her reaction to Jason, once she knew the truth. "I'm a coward," he murmured before he shoved the worry from his mind, reluctant to say or do anything that might cause Ruth pain. Wyndom reached over and covered Ruth's hand with his own. She fought the urge to curl up in a ball and hide, instead she raised her eyes to look into his. His smile ignited heat clear to her toes. She wanted this date to be perfect, worried it might still turn out to be a kiss off or worse yet an attempt at seduction, an attempt to ride roughshod over her principles. She studied his hand. It covered hers so naturally. She used the index finger of her other hand to trace the back of Wyndom's fingers.

She loved the look and feel of his hands. She never realized how sexy a man's hands could be. Wyndom's fingers were long and slender, their backs dusted with dark, curly, hair. She ran her finger lightly up and down each of his. Pleasure shot up her arm. She saw him flinch, noticed a tremor flash along his fingers and knew he was not impervious to her touch.

"You realize that tickles. You're driving me wild," he said to her and squeezed the slender fingers resting beneath his. Their eyes met, held. Soon laughter filled the Vette, dispelling the tension between them.

Silence shifted, became comfortable, a warm cloak, one they donned willingly as they sped toward their destination. Wyndom had called ahead for reservations so, although the restaurant was crowded, their wait was minimal.

Seated at a quiet table, secluded from the others by greenery, Ruth and

Wyndom studied the menu. The waitress brought them each a soft drink and took their order. She slid the menus under her arm, hefted the drink filled tray, and rushed off to her next table.

"After you left last night, I thought I might never see you again," Ruth said quietly unable to keep her finger from worrying circles on the tablecloth.

Wyndom reached over and covered her hand, stilling her finger; "I needed a cold shower, Ruth. I desperately needed to cool off," he admitted.

Ruth lifted her chin to catch Wyndom staring at her with such intensity that it sizzled the hair on her arms, covered her flesh with goose bumps. Dark lashes rimmed his deep brown eyes and he held her gaze praying she could read into his heart.

"Bedding you has never been the paramount goal of our relationship," he said huskily and reached out to take hold of her other hand. "I am attracted to you, Miss Ruth Dennison and I willingly admit that I'm eager to explore that attraction."

Ruth smiled shyly, continued to hold Wyndom's gaze. "I know the feeling." Ruth whispered, biting at her bottom lip to keep it from trembling. Lowering her eyes she murmured, "I can't stop thinking about you."

Wyndom watched color bloom in her cheeks. His heart seemed to expand, grow tight in his chest. He was jolted by Ruth's innocent openness. Desire engulfed him.

"My first marriage left me feeling ineffectual and raw," Wyndom quietly admitted. "She wasn't ready for commitment, especially a commitment to me and my way of life. She wanted to spend her days and nights having fun."

"I...I was immersed in starting my own career, making something of myself. At the time I thought I was doing it all for her and Jason. Now I know a great part of that drive to succeed was personal." A smile tugged at the corners of his mouth softened his serious expression. "It's hard though to regret a marriage that brought Jason into my life."

"You love him a lot, I can see it when ever you're together," Ruth softly said. Wyndom released Ruth's hands to let the waitress place their food in front of them and ask if they needed their glasses refilled.

Once they were again alone, Wyndom continued. "What I'm trying to say Ruth is that I want to get to know you better and I am willing to let our relationship unfold at what ever pace you set."

Ruth's somber face bloomed. Joy flashed first in her eyes before racing like a drought feed fire to her lips. "Thank You, Wyndom. I want that too."

The food was hot and perfectly prepared. Ruth rediscovered her hunger now that she knew Wyndom was still a part of her life.

"You've really never been camping?" Wyndom asked, several bites later. He buttered his dinner roll and his fingers, his attention all on Ruth. "Haven't you ever been fishing?"

"No, I've never experienced either of those great outdoor activities," Ruth said between bites of baked fish. "I prefer being pampered and catered to."

"You could join us for Jason's birthday trip."

"You're volunteering to oversee another greenie," she said, looking up from her meal. "I hope you know what you're doing. Somebody should."

"Not really," he admitted, "but how hard can it be?" Ruth watched Wyndom arch his eyebrows. "Say you'll come, the four of us will have a great time."

"Four?" she said, momentarily forgetting her conversation with Jason last evening.

"Jerry Bartlett is coming along too." Wyndom reminded her. "Say 'yes,' Ruth. We'll have fun catching our meals, breathing the fresh country air and roughing it." Wyndom emphasized the roughing it part, issued the idea in a challenging tone.

"Sounds just wonderful. Fish three times a day," she teased.

"Do I need to get down on my knees and beg," he said, his tone soft but serious.

Ruth's face light up with laughter. Wyndom, catching, cleaning, and cooking fish, sounded much too simple to actually happen. She figured it might be worth a little inconvenience to discover how Wyndom handled the adversity of adventure. Her smile radiated sunshine at Wyndom's soulful pleading. She shook her head at his tactics and wondered at the wisdom of her acceptance. Her quiet "I'll come," was filled with mixed emotions as she wondered what she had just committed herself to.

CHAPTER TWELVE

Pink puffy clouds interspersed with tinges of gold, edged the early morning horizon. The eastern skyline emitted a rosy glow as the sun tossed its brilliance over the rim of the earth peeking light into a new day. Jerry had spent the previous night with Jason. This morning, Wyndom marveled at how easy it was to get them up and moving for their early departure. Since they'd packed the back of the Edsel last evening, all they had to do this morning was pick up Ruth.

Wyndom punched her number into the phone. She answered on the first ring. "We'll be there in ten minutes," he said.

"I'm ready." Wyndom, surprised and pleased at the eagerness in Ruth's voice, found he was looking forward to the day. At Wyndom's insistence, Jerry and Jason raced back up to wash off the remains of their hasty breakfast, both anxious to climb in the wagon and begin the trip.

***

Mammoth oak and maple trees surrounded each secluded campsite in the state park. Wyndom parked the Edsel in the shade at the edge of their assigned area. They all worked together to unload the back of the wagon. Wyndom sat on his heels reading the instructions for assembling the tent. They were penned in English but were couched in innuendo and impossibilities.

"Can we help?" Jason and Jerry said as one. They laughed, swatted playfully at each other as they waited for Wyndom to spread out the canvas.

"If each of you grab a corner, we'll drag the tent over there and get it set up," Wyndom said. After several mis-attempts, much consulting of pictures and disregarding of instructions, the three males stepped back to admire their

113

efforts.

"Good job," Ruth praised. She unzipped the door, removed her shoes and stepped inside.

And the tent collapsed. Ruth was still laughing when they pulled her from the pile of canvas. Wyndom excused himself once he too had stopped laughing and disappeared for half an hour. When he returned, he attacked the tent once again. Assembly accomplished, he stood back and watched Ruth enter the canvas domicile with caution. She circled the interior carefully, then they all helped carry the sleeping bags and their luggage inside.

Ruth backed out of the tent and secured the entrance against intrusion. She put her shoes back on and stooped to buckle the sandals. Wyndom's agonized groans caught her attention and she grinned at his exaggerated antics.

"What do you have in here, Ruth?" he said. "It weights like gold bricks," he teased, setting the large cooler she insisted on bringing beside the tent.

"Just a few things we might need," she said choosing not to indulge his curiosity.

He considered lifting the lid for a quick peek but the container was locked and he would not give Ruth the satisfaction of asking for the key.

"What now, Dad?" Jason said, hoping for a peek at the lake.

"If we want to eat, we catch fish," Wyndom said. He handed each of the boys a fishing pole. He offered a rod to Ruth but she declined. "I intend to watch you three play with worms while I read my new paperback."

He grinned at her, "Chicken. You just might get hungry."

"Sticking worms on a hook is...is..."

"Don't worry. I'll catch enough fish for both of us," Wyndom said with a confidence born common to all men. He led them single file along the trail to the lake. Birds sang joyous greetings to each other and small creatures scuttled through the grass all around them. It had turned into one of those perfect summer days that Iowa is famous for: the sun was brilliant, the sky, shimmering like blue silk, was cloudless, the breeze was whisper soft and filled with the scent of wildflowers.

Ruth sat in the shade of a tall tree, her head resting against the rough bark, and watched Wyndom bait the boy's hooks and show them how to handle their poles.

Jason and Jerry chatted quietly as they watched their bobbers drift in the serene water. Wyndom distanced himself from the boys and their giggles before tossing his line into the lake. Making himself comfortable in the grass, Wyndom spent the next few hours alternately watching his pole and Ruth, who lay stretched out on her stomach in the grass, quietly reading.

The boys had grown impatient and Jason was jiggling his pole, watching the reflection of the bobber in the water when the red ball disappeared altogether and he felt a tug on his line. "Dad, I got a fish," he said excitedly. The fish Jason yanked from the water was judged too-small-to-keep and the seven-year-old reluctantly tossed it back into the lake.

Ruth excused herself, "I'll be right back. Don't let those fish catch you while I'm gone."

Wyndom glanced at his watch. He hated to admit defeat but if they didn't catch something soon he would have to drive them over to the other side of the lake where there was a concession stand. He figured the boys would be demanding food any minute.

He reeled his line in to check on the worm. The hook was empty. After rebaiting his line, Wyndom helped the boys check and bait theirs. Jerry had just plopped his line back into the water when Ruth returned, loaded down with a paper platter of individually wrapped ham and cheese sandwiches, apples and individual packets of fruit juice.

Humor washed a quick smile on Wyndom's features. "The contents of the cooler?" he said, reeling in his line and laying the pole on the ground. "You had no faith in our fishing talent?" he chided. "Smart woman." He walked over to help her set out the feast as eager to eat as both boys.

"Food!" The boys dropped their poles and ran for Ruth.

"Get your lines out of the water first," Wyndom, gently ordered. He pulled the quilt from Ruth's arm, shook it out and settled it on the ground. He helped to set the load of food on the blanket then both of them dropped down beside the boys to eat.

They devoured their meal and the boys tossed their lines into the water and settled back to watch their poles. Within minutes both were asleep, their poles held loosely in their hands.

Wyndom stowed the wrappers, apple cores, and the drink packets in a plastic bag and carried it to the trash barrel he'd noticed up the trail. Returning, he knelt down beside Ruth and planted a quick kiss on her mouth. "I thought you'd never been camping," he said, "yet you are the only one who thought to bring food. You really didn't have much faith in our fishing ability."

Ruth's grin was contagious. "My father loved to fish he just wasn't adept at catching the elusive creatures."

"I'm determined," Wyndom said, lightly tugging at the wayward curl that lay against her cheek. "I want fish for supper."

Ruth returned to her reading. Wyndom picked up his pole and sat along the bank enjoying the peacefulness of the park. He lay back on the grass relaxed enough to drift into a nap. Wyndom set the rod on the ground and raised his arms to shield his eyes from the sun. He yawned repeatedly and fought to keep his eyes open.

Wyndom rolled over and sat up. "It's nice here," he said to Ruth. She closed her book. Looked all around. He was right about the park.

"Where did you disappear to this morning?" she quietly asked, not voicing her suspicions.

"I...no place special." He looked at Ruth, shook his head. "Okay, I went tent watching. It was easy once I studied an expert." He confessed. Her grin told him she suspected the truth all along.

Wyndom watched the rippling water; three aimlessly drifting bobbers shimmered their colors on the lake's surface and danced a rhythmic jig in the cooling breeze.

"Wyndom!" Ruth said and pointed toward the water.

The bright blue ball submerged and Wyndom's pole started to slide toward the lake. Moving quickly he lunged for the rod. His fingers closed around the slender pole moments before it disappeared under the water.

Ruth voiced her encouragement as Wyndom struggled with his catch. Soon two very excited boys added their voices to the drama.

The large mouth bass—Wyndom had brought along a book with pictures to aid in identification—put up a good fight.

"Boys, why don't you bait your lines and move over to that shaded area," Wyndom said. He pulled the bass free of his hook.

Within minutes Jerry was caught in his own battle. The fish he hauled out of the water was a smaller version of the seven-pound fish Wyndom caught. Still Jerry's fish weighed enough to be edible. Wyndom pulled in another fish to add to their cache. Jason continued to work his line for a while but all he got were unproductive nibbles.

"We have enough fish for supper," Wyndom said. Both boys eagerly agreed when he suggested that they put their catch on ice and don their swim clothes. They all were ready for a walk around to the beach.

***

Water dripped from Ruth's face. Wyndom and the boys had surrounded her and were using their hands to hydroplane water. She dove under and resurfaced behind Wyndom, cascading water over his back. The boys joined in her assault and soon all four were soaked.

After their session of play, Wyndom and Ruth took time to help the boys in their swimming and floating technique. Finally the boys were moaning for food and they all climbed from the water. While they wandered leisurely back to their camp, the warm June breeze dried their suits.

"Come on guys I'll teach you how to clean fish," Wyndom said, surprised at how easily his grandfather's lessons had resurfaced

Ruth managed to figure out the camp stove. She wrapped potatoes and carrots together in foil and slid them close to the heat. Soon she had everything ready to pan fry their catch. Sizzling-hot crispy fish fillets, baked vegetables and lemonade completed the meal and left all of them feeling satisfied.

"That was great," Jason said, licking his fingers clean then crumpling his plate and shoving it in the bag of garbage Wyndom had started.

"If you three will get us four slender branches, I'll fix you a great dessert," Ruth said busying herself with clean up.

By the time the boys and Wyndom returned she had everything ready for the standard camp treat. Marshmallows, Hershey bars, and graham crackers were devoured until they all four groaned with overeating. Once everything was cleaned, faces and hands washed, the four sat under a darkening sky and watched it fill with stars.

"Tell us a story, Dad," Jason said into the music of the night.

Each took advantage of the opportunity to relate their favorite story. Ruth was last. She held the boys and Wyndom spellbound with a story of the Hobyahs and their little dog Turpie. (Ruth's story can be found at the end of the book.) The fluctuations in Ruth's tone captivated her audience. Silvery glow from the moon broke through the foliage overhead and bathed her face. Heat, unrelated to the evening air, swept through Wyndom as he studied her features.

Fire flashed from her eyes, her hands mimed the actions of her story. She was as entranced with the telling of the tale as her audience was with the listening. *She is very beautiful*, Wyndom thought. He drew air into his lungs, enjoyed the heady sensations he was experiencing just looking at and listening to Ruth. Wyndom felt great. He could not remember ever being this content.

Ruth was a natural storyteller. Her voice was low, a touch husky, and it poured over her listeners like warm honey. She wore her hair up in a ponytail but, by evening, several tendrils had come loose, they curled around her face, softening her features. Their jaunt in the lake had removed all her make up. She barely looked twenty years old sitting bathed in the moon's gloss. The tragic twists of her tale enchanted Jerry and Jason and they sat mesmerized at her feet. A smile curled Wyndom's lips as piece by piece Ruth zipped Little Turpie back together.

Storytime over, Ruth was afforded the privacy of the tent to change for bed then Wyndom and the boys took their turn. Jerry and Jason crawled into their sleeping bags and were soon asleep.

Ruth and Wyndom sat in the opening of the tent, their fingers intertwined, and listened to the mingled voices of the night's creatures echoing all around them.

Distant croaking of frogs mingled with the "hoot" of an overhead owl and in turn their cries blended with the chirping of crickets and the raucous sound of cicadas.

"My back yard sounds like this when I step out on my deck to wish God a good night," Ruth whispered.

"I'd forgotten the joy of summer evenings," Wyndom quietly admitted. "I haven't experienced this wonder since my grandfather and I went camping so very long ago."

"The grandfather that owned the Edsel wagon?" she said.

"Ironic isn't it? " he reminisced. "The best times of my life revolve around that old car."

Wyndom lifted her hand and placed a kiss on her knuckles, their eyes locked. He wanted to pull her into his arms and make mad passionate love to her but sensed the magic between them was too precious to destroy. As the heat of his desire flowed from his eyes to hers, shooting through her body to ignite in the center of her femininity, she watched him struggle with his emotions, temper and slough them off. She savored her next breath, relieved that he also understood and sensed the timing was wrong. Still wrapped in the heat of their emotions, they separated and moved to the sleeping bags that bracketed the boys. It was a long time before their breathing slowed its rhythm, freed them to drift into a passion filled sleep.

She was wading in a lake, was surrounded by cold water. She turned full circle looking for the shoreline but all she saw was water. Water that grew wind rippled began to churn. The waves grew. She struggled to retain her footing, fought the waves pulling at her legs. Blackness around and above her split, rent by a flash of hot, jagged light. Water, no longer tugging at her knees, crowded upward instead, enveloping first her waist then slowly, insidiously, it circled her neck. Fear filled her, surrounding her like the black raging sea of water holding her captive. She tried to move but her body was loaded with lead. Just as the ugly brine closed over her head she unfroze enough to silently scream herself awake.

Ruth rubbed her eyes, struggled to fight off the dread of her nightmare. She clawed herself out of the mantle of sleep enveloping her body and opened her eyes to more darkness. Moisture splashed onto her nose. Rain. It was raining and their tent was leaking. Relief eased the tension caused by her dream. Rain's rhythmic cadence against the canvas dulled the sound of the drips seeping through, invading their sleeping area.

Thunder rumbled in the distance. Ruth sat up, ran her hands down the length of her sleeping bag checking for moisture, pleased to find the bag still fairly dry.

Wyndom jerked awake. Moisture leaked from his forehead into his eye and he too struggled to sit up.

"This canvas domicile is not waterproof," Ruth's whisper quietly chided Wyndom.

"The label said weather proof. I forgot to ask about a guarantee," he chuckled at the hilarity of their situation and used the sleeve of his pajama's to dry his face. "Probably explains why the tent was so reasonable." He could barely discern Ruth's outline in the shadowy darkness.

"Any suggestions?" he inquired of Ruth.

"Station wagon," slipped simultaneously from both their mouths. They crawled out of the bags and fumbled for their shoes. Each folded their own sleeping bag, tossed it over one shoulder and hurriedly bent to lift a seven-year-old into their arms.

Wyndom lead the way.

The boys woke briefly but curled back into sleep immediately when Jason was placed on the front seat and Jerry on the back.

Ruth and Wyndom scooted over the seats. He unzipped their bags and spread his over the floor. He pulled Ruth's back against his chest and they curled spoon fashion in the limited space in the back of the wagon.

Wyndom tugged her sleeping bag over them. "It's early, we'd best try and get some more sleep," he said. "We have two active boys to keep up with."

Heat from her body seeped through the thin material of her pajamas to warm and awaken Wyndom's body. The subtle movement of their bodies as they drew in each breath and released it was more seductive than either of them could have imagined.

Silently each fought against heightened desire.

Wyndom sighed against her ear, "This isn't going to work."

They sat up and pulled apart. "Tell me about yourself," Ruth said, wrapping her arms around her drawn-up legs and resting her chin on her knees, eager to gain control of her thoughts.

"What would you like to know?" he said in hushed tones, trying not to disturb the boys.

"I've only heard you mention your mother once, are your parents still living?"

"They're fighting hunger somewhere in Africa. I haven't seen them since I graduated from Iowa State and Dad turned the reins of the company over to me." Ruth noticed a hesitant catch in his voice, a bitter tinge he tried hard to cover.

"They've never seen Jason?"

"They didn't even come back to the states for my wedding," Wyndom said. "Mother has always been more interested in her causes than in me."

"Your father?" Ruth waited for his answer, sad at the loneliness she heard in Wyndom's response. He tried to sound matter-of-fact. He failed.

"He was a shadow in my life. The longest conversation we ever had happened the day he retired. I was twenty-four. They left town a week later."

"My parents were wonderful," Ruth said. "I always knew how much they loved me." She sighed. "I miss them terribly."

"That summer I spent with my grandfather, I understood finally what was missing in my life." Wyndom almost envied Ruth's whispered emotions, knew her sorrow was more intense because of the parental love she had grown up with, love he had not known.

Once again, he heard the catch in Ruth's voice when she mentioned her parents, sensed it was a part of her grief. Overwhelmed with guilt, he thought about the part his ex-wife had played in her parent's death. Wyndom knew he should tell Ruth about Cindy. Knew she had a right to know.

He visualized her pain at hearing the gruesome details and froze. How could he add to the pain already evident in the wobbly tone of her voice? Mentally, silently he railed at himself for his display of cowardice. Sometime soon he would have to explain the situation to Ruth. If their relationship was to continue, grow into more than friendship as he hoped, Wyndom knew he would have to be honest with her.

He shook his dreary musings from his mind and concentrated on the words slipping from Ruth's mouth, wondering what he had missed of her conversation.

He could hear a smile flowing through her unshed tears when she talked about the love her parents shared. "I want that 'forever' kind of relationship," Ruth said. "The kind I witnessed between my parents as I grew up."

They continued to quietly talk through out the early morning hours, moved away from grief toward their years in school and the effect it had on their lives.

Sunshine pierced the edge of the new day throwing its glow upward to lighten the sky. Rain diminished to mist then stopped altogether. "You're a good listener, Wyndom Winters," Ruth whispered, laying her hand lightly against his stubble-crusted cheek. "Thank you."

She looked over his shoulder to the water-sodden tent barely visible in the dawn light. "I wonder if we still have any dry clothes?" she softly said.

Wyndom turned his head to follow her gaze, said, "We best venture out to determine the damage." They ran barefooted through the wet grass to the tent.

Ruth grabbed her damp swim towel and used it to wipe moisture from the top of her case. When she finally lifted the lid, she was pleased to discover its contents were dry.

Thank heaven their luggage proved to be waterproof, something Wyndom knew he should have demanded in a tent.

Ruth and Wyndom sopped up the excess water inside the tent. Wyndom wrung the towels as dry as possible and tossed them over nearby bushes. "You first," he motioned to Ruth when he exited the still dripping structure.

She dressed hurriedly, donning slacks and a simple sleeveless blouse. Zipping her suitcase shut, Ruth walked out into the early dawn. She busied herself making coffee for the two of them as Wyndom took his turn in the privacy of the tent.

The coffee, though instant, was good. They stood relishing the sounds of early morning in the woods and savored the hot brew. "The concession stand advertised an early church service at the lake's edge," Ruth said quietly, a question in her eyes.

"I saw that. We have forty-five minutes," Wyndom said after a quick glance at his watch. "I'll wake the boys."

He dumped the last of the coffee from his cup and handed it to Ruth. "Do you have breakfast in your magic box?" He asked. Her quick smile delighted him; he rubbed his stomach vigorously and turned toward the wagon and two sleeping boys.

Forty minutes later, Wyndom backed the Edsel into place at the edge of the clearing. He stepped out of the wagon and lowered the tailgate. They each found a comfortable position in the back of the Bermuda. Their vantage point was excellent and the two adults studied the scene playing out before them with interest as they waited for the service to begin.

Other vehicles skirted the edge of the circle. People of every age had come together and were seated within, waiting in expectant silence. Lawn chairs and blankets covered the sand almost to the water's edge. People waved to each other but basically the crowd remained respectfully subdued.

Suddenly a young man appeared at the lake's edge and all eyes turned to watch him move through the crowd. He wore casual attire and his shoulder length, rust-colored hair rippled in a light morning breeze. When he neared the edge of the water he stopped to remove his sandals.

A young child took the shoes from his hands and cradled them in her lap. With nonchalance born of confidence and youth, he stepped out into the water, then turned to face his audience.

His dark eyes blazed fire. His voice, deep and resonant, invited them to join him in an old familiar hymn. Water lapped at his pant legs. Their material drew moisture upward toward his knees. He seemed unaware and unconcerned, intent only on leading the crowd in the words of Blessed Assurance.

"'He Lives,'" someone in the crowd suggested when the first hymn ended. Unaccompanied voices mingled joyfully. Their singing carried across the lake and throughout the park.

"One more," the preacher said and pointed to a young girl seated in the sand at the waters edge. She chose without hesitation.

"I come to the garden alone..." they sang, filling the morning with the beauty of their music.

The audience grew quiet, spellbound by the young man. He preached about the significance of water in Christ's life. His words were simple; still he captivated his listeners. He was not handsome yet his face glowed with beauty. He talked to the crowd about Jesus. His words, tone and manner conveyed the message that he was memorializing about a personnel friend.

At the close of the service he led them in prayer, giving Ruth a heady feeling of renewal. There was an aura about the man that set him apart and Ruth hoped that he would be able to retain that humble image he exuded once the power of his presence projected him into the limelight.

The experience had helped her to feel closer to God and she was reluctant to leave the serenity that he had created with his presence and his words. The quiet peacefulness of the speaker had ensnared and enveloped his audience.

Wyndom spied a young boy moving through the throng with an upturned hat and he dug in his wallet to contribute to the offering. He felt lighter somehow, closer to heaven, and he knew this morning's service was one he would gladly repeat.

The young preacher disappeared as suddenly as he had arrived. Ruth wished she had heard his name, wondered if she would ever chance to meet up with him again.

Slowly the crowd dispersed, Ruth figured they had all been as touched as she by the service and the man who had drawn them together. Quiet joy, a sense of peace remained with all four of them as they returned to their sodden campsite. Ruth realized how deeply the boys had been effected when Jerry asked if that man had been one of Jesus' disciples.

"He was definitely a friend of our Lord," Wyndom said, holding the car door open while they exited.

As they worked together to dismantle the camp, they encouraged the seven-year-olds to talk openly about their perceptions of God and Jesus.

Ruth set out the remaining contents of the cooler and they all helped create a picnic lunch. Together they walked to a secluded edge of the lake where they spread their blanket out on a grassy knoll. Each one seemed to savor the sense of communion with God and with nature as they knelt to eat. Conversation was sparse; no one wanted to interrupt the magic of the view splayed out before him or her.

Although the boys were reluctant to leave, they helped load the wagon without complaint. The drive back to town took very little time. Jerry politely thanked Wyndom and Jason for inviting him. He grinned and waved from his own front door as they drove away.

Ruth noticed that sadness had returned to Jason's face as he sat huddled alone in the back seat. Obviously he was not happy to be going home. She decided to question Wyndom about Jason's home life the next time they were alone together.

Wyndom carried Ruth's cooler through to the kitchen.

"I'll call you later tonight," he murmured against her cheek before returning to Jason and the wagon. He shook his head, sighed with the thought of all the unloading he and Jason had to accomplish when they reached the house. He wondered what Evelyn would think when he draped their soggy tent over her pristine patio furniture to dry.

The motion light on the garage was already ablaze when the Edsel entered the driveway. Wyndom noticed movement at the top of Katie's stairs, then his headlights impaled a disheveled Jeffrey, his fist raised to bang on his mother-in-law's door.

Katie opened the kitchen door stood framed in the light and waited for Wyndom to step from the wagon.

"Where is Karen?" Jeffrey yelled. He stumbled haphazardly down the stairs. He tried to press the wrinkles from his shirt with his hands but he gave up, shrugged his shoulders when it had no effect. He reached out, grabbed the stair rail to keep from falling. He brushed hair from his eyes, as if it were the cause of his clumsiness and stumbled toward Wyndom and Katie.

She stepped out onto the porch. "I told you when you phoned this afternoon that Karen wasn't here," she said quietly.

"I think you should leave," Wyndom said. He reached out to steady the man. "Katie, go in and call Jeffrey a cab."

"I'm not going home without my wife," Jeffrey said, his tone belligerent, his words slurred. "Besides, my car is out front."

"Karen doesn't want to see you, Jeff. If you want to get your wife back," Wyndom said, "sober up and get some help."

Jeffery huddled into himself and his anger seemed to drain away. Tears streamed down the young man's face and he mumbled, "I didn't mean to hurt her, really I didn't. I love her...her and the baby," he muttered.

"If you really mean that, Jeff, get some help. Make sure you never let it happen again," Wyndom said, shoving the drunken husband toward the cab pulling up out front.

Wyndom demanded and received Jeffrey's keys before shutting him in the cab. "You can pick these up at my office in town once you are sober," he told Jeffrey before shutting him in the cab.

Jason and Katie were already unloading equipment when Wyndom walked back up the drive. "Bruce has been trying to reach you," Katie told Wyndom, thankful that he'd arrived when he did. She helped him stow the dry camping paraphernalia in the catchall closet off the kitchen and drag the damp tent out of the back of the wagon so he could drive the vehicle into the garage.

"He's called several times since you left." Katie said and handed Wyndom Bruce's number.

Wyndom and Jason spread the damp tent over several chairs on the patio. Wyndom hugged Jason and sent him upstairs to bathe. He locked up outside then shut himself in the den and called Bruce.

***

Ruth sat in the middle of her bed, her hair still damp from showering and, now that it was free of snarls, attempted to pull it all back into a single braid. She flexed her muscles repeatedly and tried to rub away the ache in her neck.

She had enjoyed the weekend trip but after a sleeping bag on hard ground, her bed felt marvelous. She turned up the tiny braid end and secured it with a bright band. A Robin Cook paperback lay in her lap but when she stifled the second yawn in as many minutes Ruth decided she was ready to curl up under the sheet and sleep.

She set the book on her nightstand, reached for the lamp switch and the phone rang.

Wyndom's soft husky "Hello" sent delightful tremors skittering down her spine.

"Thank you for inviting me along this weekend, I really enjoyed the experience," Ruth said into the phone cradled against her ear.

Wyndom sighed. Ruth could picture the grin playing across his mouth when he whispered, "Having you alone for a whole two days would be even better."

"Jason wouldn't have liked being left behind," Ruth murmured, sliding down to sink into her pillow.

"What I have in mind is definitely X-rated," he said.

"You'll make me blush with that kind of talk, Sir."

"You're beautiful when you blush," he teased, "I wish I were there to kiss your blush away."

The husky tone of Wyndom's voice effectively relayed his desire and Ruth felt a longing that left her reeling and feeling unsettled and lonely.

"I have to fly to Chicago in the morning, Ruth. I hate to leave Jason. He seemed so happy on the trip. Would you call him, maybe take him out for ice cream?" Wyndom asked.

"How long will you be away?" Ruth said, missing him already.

"I don't know."

"I'll watch over Jason while you're gone." she pledged.

"We'll have dinner, go dancing, the day I get back, promise," Wyndom said his voice barely above a whisper. "I'll call you from Chicago."

"I'll miss you," Ruth said, cradling the phone between her ear and her shoulder.

"Sweet dreams lovely lady," Wyndom whispered before disconnecting.

Wyndom went in search of Evelyn to let her know of his plans. She listened, said not a word. *How strange*, he thought, and hurried upstairs to pack.

He had just put a dress shirt in his suit bag when he remembered Jason's birthday. Wyndom wondered if Evelyn had anything special planned, wondered if he should mention it to her. He hated being out of town for the occasion, prayed Jason would understand. Wyndom zipped the medium sized carry-all, draped it across the bench at the foot of his bed, and, knowing he could not put it off any longer, went in to tell Jason about his trip.

CHAPTER THIRTEEN

Ruth smoothed the hair back from her face before stepping from her convertible. Jason sat on the back porch waiting for her. She noted that his face warmed with a smile when he recognized her car and she realized that she greeted him with the same pleasure.

"Should we go tell your Grandmother that we're leaving?" Ruth said.

Jason took the hand she held out to him. He straightened his shoulders and led Ruth around the house to the pool area.

Evelyn Carlyle studied the young woman walking with Jason. So this was her grandson's teacher and the new woman in Wyndom's life. Her hair was pulled back in a childish ponytail. She wore no makeup and appeared totally lacking in sophistication. It was evident to Evelyn that Ruth Dennison would never be the proper mate for her son-in-law.

***

The furniture clustered in seating groups around the Olympic size pool was opulent, its colors a cool serene combination of yellow, blue and green. The woman seated at the round table, sipping daintily at a frosted glass of amber liquid, did not appear matronly. Her intricately detailed coiffure and designer bathing-ensemble seemed to fit perfectly with the scowl marring her artfully made up face.

"There is nothing grandmotherly about this woman," Ruth said silently, as she followed Jason toward Mrs. Carlyle.

Jason stumbled through introductions and Ruth said, "I'll have Jason home before ten." She watched the older woman shrug her shoulders as if the information was none of her concern. Ruth shivered inwardly as the woman's cold eyes swept her from head to toe.

"I'm hosting a birthday party for Jason tomorrow afternoon, please join us," Evelyn stated, her frosty tone more a command than an invitation.

Ruth resented the aura of coldness emanating from the woman and wondered why she bothered to tender an invitation that she did not mean. The woman was decidedly unfriendly. Ruth hesitated. Finally she nodded acceptance, realizing it would give her an opportunity to observe the interaction between Mrs. Carlyle and Jason.

"Three o'clock," Evelyn said in clipped tones. "Come suited, it's a pool party."

Ruth was as eager to leave the Carlyle estate as Jason. The drive calmed her and she began to wonder if her reaction had all been in her mind. Time would tell. She determined to ignore the feeling of unease at the invitation and concentrate on having a good time with her young companion. Food was the first item on the agenda.

Jason wiped pizza sauce from around his mouth and eyed the last piece. Ruth shoved the pan across the table, "Help your self, please, Jason, I couldn't eat another bite."

She watched as the seven-year-old devoured the cheesy slice and wondered where he found room.

"We have to decide what we want to do next," Ruth said. "We can visit the Historical Museum, see a movie, or play a round of miniature golf. Which sounds best to you?"

Ruth waited for Jason to choose.

Jason drained the root beer from his glass, carefully wiped his mouth again. When he finally lifted his eyes and looked at Ruth, she was puzzled by his expression, until he said, "I don't know how to play golf."

"You've never played miniature golf?" Ruth said in mock surprise.

Jason lowered his eyes, slowly shook his head.

"I refuse to leave you, a grown man of eight in this sorry state, I will teach you," Ruth exaggeratedly teased. She handed the bill for the meal and twenty dollars to Jason. He seemed to stretch up another two inches standing proudly at the cash register.

Jason offered the change to Ruth. "Leave it on the table for the waiter," she said and added another dollar to the tip.

Ruth unlocked the driver's door, pleased to find Jason already strapped in his seat belt by the time she slid in beside him. The afternoon heat dissipated in the gentle breeze that signaled evening. Ruth drove leisurely through the edge of town enjoying the reprieve. She'd lowered the top of her '69 Cougar before leaving the Pizza Hut and was enjoying the cool air.

Although Jason seemed unusually quiet once again, Ruth noted that he did not seem unhappy. It dawned on her how unique it was for a child of this age to remain so still. She hoped he would relax and have fun with learning the game.

Ruth helped Jason choose a putter. "Do you want to go first?" she said to him as they walked to the play area and waited their turn.

He shook his head.

Jason studied her every move. Watched as it took her three tries to hole the ball. Then it was his turn. He gnawed on his lower lip as he studied the situation and lined up the ball. It shot down the green, rolled over the hole, bounced several times from one side of the play area to the other back and forth then rolled slowly to the center and dropped gently into place.

"Good shot," Ruth said, smiling brightly and clapping her hands.

Jason, who knew he had done well, fought to hide his pleasure.

As the two worked their way through the various play areas, Jason relaxed. He showed he was having fun when he began to laugh at his own mistakes.

Jason's smile grew euphoric. He grinned from ear to ear and sank his ball in the last hole. "I won," he said, definitely pleased by that fact.

After checking her watch, Ruth paid for a second round. "One more game," she said, pleased to see Jason eyes light up.

This time Ruth won.

"I had fun tonight," Jason said once they were back in Ruth's car. He groaned, stifled a yawn, leaned back in the bucket seat and watched the street lights flash by.

Jason thought back to his memories of his mother. She had been very beautiful, he didn't really remember her that much but the pictures of her in Grandma's living room all attested to that fact and when Jason asked, his father agreed that she was beautiful. Jason played through the scenes stored in his mind: his mother seated before a mirror putting on make-up, the swirling skirt of her red party dress as she swept into his room, the way she blew him good-bye kisses. He could not remember sitting on her lap. Could not remember being hugged by her. In fact, he could not remember any time when she had even touched him. Jason looked at Ruth sitting behind the steering wheel and recalled all the times she reached over to ruffle his hair, squeeze his shoulder or bent down to draw him into a quick hug. Jason wondered if that was why he enjoyed spending time with her.

Ruth reached over and patted Jason's knee, "You'll be eight years old tomorrow, are you excited about your party?"

"Not really," he murmured, "the stuff in the pool makes my eyes burn and plugs my nose."

"You're probably allergic to the chlorine," Ruth calmly offered.

Jason was surprised at Ruth's acceptance of his situation. Grandmother always said he was being a baby when he complained and she would order him to his room.

"We'll have a good time tomorrow, I'm sure." Ruth said.

Jason quietly hoped that she was right.

***

Jason walked into his room as the phone was ringing. He spent the next fifteen minutes telling his father about playing miniature golf and winning.

Listening to Jason expound on his evening with Ruth gave Wyndom twinges of longing. Longing for time with his son, for time with Ruth.

"I'll challenge you both to a match when I get home," he promised "Happy Birthday, Jason, I...I love you," Wyndom whispered into the phone. "I'll be home soon."

Jason clutched Wyndom's words of love to his heart while he undressed and prepared for bed.

***

Ruth sat on her deck; the tall glass of iced Russian Tea forgotten in her hand, and replayed her meeting with Evelyn Carlyle, Jason's Grandmother. There was something menacing in the woman's attitude and Ruth promised herself to remain alert at the party tomorrow afternoon. Her observations could be important for Jason, a help to Wyndom. Jason's problem could be too close to home for the man to notice.

A drop of moisture slid down the side of her glass and plopped onto her bare leg. She took a sip of the iced drink and let its coolness wash through her. Warm air brushed against her cheek. Ruth lifted the hair from the back of her neck, let the light breeze dry the perspiration beaded there. She scanned the star frosted heavens splayed dramatically above her and wondered what Wyndom was doing at this exact moment.

The wind whisperings turned to loud mutterings that whipped through the trees skirting the edge of the deck. Ruth prayed the changed weather would bring them a much-needed rain. Her lush lawn was growing brown at its slender tips its root system thirsty for water. She searched the horizon for clouds but the sparkling midnight blue blanket over head was unmarred. Setting her empty glass on the floor at her feet, she stretched contentedly then placed her fingers over her mouth to stifle a yawn. She jumped, startled from her thoughts by the sound of her phone.

"Hello, Beautiful."

"Wyndom?"

"Does that questioning tone in your voice mean there are other men addressing you as, 'Beautiful'?"

Her responding chuckle was light and merry.

"It doesn't sound like I woke you."

"I was out on the deck enjoying the night." Ruth's voice held a wistful quality, a hint of aloneness that added to Wyndom's longing to be there with her.

"Wish I were there," he said and Ruth heard the longing in his voice.

"Me too. I hope you aren't working too hard," Ruth said into the receiver.

"I'm in a hurry to get home," he replied huskily. "I hope you've missed me."

"Maybe just a little," she said. "Although, I did spend a lovely afternoon and evening with a very attentive and attractive gentleman."

She heard Wyndom's low, sexy laugh. "It seems I have competition. My own son at that."

The smile curving Ruth's mouth transmitted itself through the phone line when she whispered, "This Lady has enough love for both Winters men."

She heard the catch in Wyndom's voice. He said, "I wish I were there to kiss you good night."

A blush rose across Ruth's face when he detailed how often his day was interrupted with dreams of holding her near.

Ruth told Wyndom about Evelyn's invitation and sensed his surprise at the woman's offer. Wyndom promised to return soon and sent Ruth a goodnight kiss through the phone line. Her preparations for bed were slow and methodical as she indulged in fantasies of the handsome, dark haired, brown-eyed man, who seemed to be stealing her heart.

***

No clouds marred the brilliance of the day. Ruth understood her gloom was all inside, a reaction that confused her. She stewed over the perfect attire for the birthday celebration. Something that did more than make her look good, today's outfit must make her feel great as well. Ruth sensed that her attire was more important today because of Mrs. Carlyle. She'd spent the morning choosing just the right gifts for Jason, now they sat wrapped and waiting for her beside the front door.

Ruth's one piece black swimsuit sported a wide slash of bright tropical flowers. She buttoned on the companion skirt and slipped into a plain hot-pink blouse, buttoned the two top buttons and tied the front tails at her waist. The blouse matched exactly the hot-pink shade of several of the flowers that graced the skirt and swimsuit.

Ruth could not shake her unease. She was sure her apprehension had nothing to do with Jason and she pushed it aside, vowing to do her best to insure that he enjoyed the day.

She brushed the wispy brown curls that escaped from her single braid away from her eyes and slid a colored lip-gloss across her mouth. After one last glance in the mirror, she gathered her courage, stuffed sunscreen in her bag and started for the party.

***

Evelyn pulled her sunglasses off and relaxed, wiggling once to achieve the proper pose at the round umbrellaed table. Her perfectly coifed hair was very blonde and obviously a wig. She sipped daintily from a frosted glass laced with vodka. The ensemble she wore, a designer original definitely made for viewing had obviously been created for a younger figure. Several other richly dressed women sat around the table with Evelyn, all sipped at iced drinks.

A young male lifeguard, hired especially for this party, sat at the end of the diving board watching the antics of the youngsters splashing in the pool.

Ruth stood quietly at the edge of the lawn; the gaily-wrapped gift she clutched was the only present in evidence. Her arrival went unnoticed by the ladies clustered at the pool's edge and the revelers in the water. Only Jason, sitting forlornly with his feet dangling in the water, noticed when Ruth entered the back yard. She wondered if he had been watching for her?

He jumped to his feet and rushed over to greet her. "You brought me a present," he said, the only change in his expression, the gleam in his eye. He accepted the gift, waited for Ruth's permission before he started to open the colorful package.

Ruth knelt in front of Jason. Watched him carefully remove the paper. His expression turned questioning when he uncovered two separate gaily wrapped gifts. He pulled paper from the smaller of the two, discovered a blank-paged leather bound journal.

"A place to write your stories and private thoughts," Ruth explained. "Open the other box." Jason's eyes registered pleased surprise and he studied the 3-D puzzle in the shape of a medieval castle.

"The next time it rains you have a perfect project," Ruth said, kneeling to pull the eight-year-old into a swift hug. "Happy Birthday, Jason."

"Do I have to wait for it to rain?" he asked eagerly. "We could work on it right now."

"Maybe later," Ruth said. She suggested he take the puzzle up to his room and promised to wait for him to return before she joined the party.

The children and their mothers were all strangers to her, Ruth realized, when she and Jason joined the group by the pool. Not one of the boys was from Jason's class at school.

Evelyn invited Ruth to join her at the patio table, scowling at Jason when he drew up a chair next to Ruth. "You aren't making friends with any of the young people I invited," Evelyn accused Jason.

"I...I don't know any of those kids," he stammered.

"They attend the best schools. They should be your friends," Evelyn said. "Wyndom has no idea how to raise a child," Evelyn pointedly said to Ruth. "Cindy would've put her foot down about private school if she were alive." The older woman dabbed dramatically at her eyes.

Ruth noticed a pained expression on Jason's face, assumed it was caused by the mention of his mother's name.

"Have you been practicing with your Hula-Hoop? Practice is important," she gently reminded, in an attempt to distract Jason. She gave his hand a squeeze, smiled when he excused himself and went in search of plastic circle.

"You must miss your daughter," Ruth murmured hoping to offer comfort to Mrs. Carlyle.

"Yes, I do. Cindy was so beautiful. She had such a fiery spirit, so wild and free," Evelyn sighed. "Wyndom loved her desperately. He was heartbroken at her death," the older woman stated.

Ruth was surprised by Mrs. Carlyle's observation. She had not gotten that impression from Wyndom. "I thought they were divorced," she quietly said to the older woman.

"It wasn't Wyndom's idea," Evelyn said. "Cindy was so young when they married, too young really. She had just decided to mend her marriage, recommit to Wyndom. Then she died." Mrs. Carlyle carefully wove her lie. Ruth listened to Mrs. Carlyle ramble on about her daughter, wondered how much of what she spoke was actual truth.

"The accident was so senseless," Evelyn murmured with just the right inflection of emotion in her voice. "But then you understand, I'm sure it was as tragic for you as well dear," she said and patted Ruth's hand.

Ruth looked at the woman opposite her, confusion written across her features. "I'm sorry, I don't understand."

Evelyn swallowed her glee and let the pause build, extending the drama of her actions.

"Surely, Wyndom has explained that it was Jason's mother driving the car when your parents were killed."

Ruth stared at Evelyn, silence eddied and built between them as Evelyn's words slowly penetrated.

Evelyn knew, by the pained look on Ruth's face that she had guessed right.

"The other driver's name was Addison," Ruth whispered trying to make sense of it all.

"We did what we could to protect Jason." Evelyn said, malice lacing her tone, the glow of pleasure in her eyes giving lie to the commiserating tone of her voice.

Tears slipped unchecked from Ruth's lashes blinding her as she pushed away from the table. Confusion stilled her movements for a few seconds while she swiped at the tears then she bolted for her car. Ruth rushed passed a wide-eyed Jason who was also caught up in the drama. She was so wrapped up in her own pain she failed to notice his presence or his reaction to his grandmother's words.

Why hadn't Wyndom explained all of this to her? She felt used, lied to, deceived. She fought to control her emotions as she drove mindlessly toward her home and refuge. She was on the verge of falling in love with the man, how could he do this? He had no right to keep such information from her, she thought, rubbing moisture from her eyes enabling her to stay on the road, find her way home.

***

Jason stared at his Grandmother, not believing a word she said. It was not true. Must not be true. "Why did you tell her that. It's a lie! You're a liar," Jason sobbed. He confronted his grandmother. He stared at her, his fists clenched and prepared for battle.

"Don't you yell at me young man," Evelyn stood in front of him and shook her finger under his nose. Her haughty expression had no effect on Jason's anger.

"You made her cry." His tone grew hushed, deliberately intent.

"Good, maybe she'll stay out of our lives," Evelyn said. She put her hands on her hips and continued to stare down at Jason. "She doesn't belong in our society."

"You drove her away. I hate you. I hate you," he said his voice trembling with rage.

Jason clenched and unclenched his fists. He was so angry he felt like he could explode. He sputtered. Wished he were not just a kid, a powerless kid. Jason looked at his grandmother, at her smug satisfied countenance, the smirk gracing her lips and his rage exploded. In one quick move, not even stopping to think, he reached out and shoved.

Evelyn's wail of surprise assaulted his ears and then he was watching her struggling in her fancy old pool. She sank from view. When she resurfaced, her blonde wig, its wilted curls dripping water, slid down the side of her face and floated slowly down out of sight. Laughter erupted, rippled once around the pool then abruptly ceased as hand after hand reached up to stifle the sound.

Evelyn sluiced water from her eyes and glared up at Jason. "Heathen bastard," she sputtered, "wait until I tell your father."

Jason saw the hate flash from her eyes and he turned and fled from her sight.

"Get back here you little brat," she yelled after him, a contemptuous scowl twisting her red lips.

"Help me out of this pool," she demanded of the young lifeguard.

Her outfit had not been designed to actually get wet. Now the material seemed to shrink painfully into her voluptuous curves. She splashed awkwardly along the pool's edge, working her way toward the steps. By the time the young man pulled her from the water her mind was already plotting proper punishment for Jason.

She pretended not to notice the barely controlled grins being suppressed by her society crowd. Her rage increased. *I'll get you, Jason, for humiliating me like this.* She stomped her way toward the house. Evelyn's anger would have increased two-fold if she had spied Katie, doubled over with laughter, just inside the patio door.

Evelyn, water squashing nosily in her shoes, stomped her way up the stairs to her room. She prayed she would require no assistance to get off the swim attire, another embarrassment she didn't need. Her anger at Jason abated momentarily as she relished the memory of Ruth's reaction to her news. She was convinced that that relationship was over for good. She looked at her reflection in the mirror and her rage at Jason returned. Evelyn stewed and stomped through her ministrations, knowing that she must return to her guests in order to salvage what she could of the afternoon and her reputation.

***

Jason sat in a corner of his room, worrying about what his grandmother would do to him once she escaped the pool. She had upset Ruth with that lie about his mother. Jason knew it was a lie otherwise his father would have told him.

Jason knew his mother had been killed in an accident. That was all that his father, or anyone else for that matter, had confided to him. At the time Jason was too upset by the news to ask questions. Later it did not seem to matter.

Ruth hadn't even noticed him when she ran from the yard. Jason wrinkled his forehead, frowning with the notion that his teacher might be angry with him. He listened to his grandmother squish hurriedly down the hall. Jason wondered how long it would be before she came looking for him.

Evelyn had changed, repaired the damage to her hair, now she hesitated at Jason's door, even struggled to gain control of her anger before shoving the door open. He lay curled into a corner of his window seat, his arms wrapped around his knees.

Jason's eyes, blazing with emotion, impaled Evelyn. She ignored his irritation and stepped into the room.

"I told Miss Dennison the truth young man. You get busy and pack your bags; they have military schools for disorderly, mannerless brats like you. I promise you that you will never again get the chance to embarrass me. By tomorrow you will be out of my house." She tilted her head, smugly, and swept from the room. She did not even bother to close the door.

Could she do that? Jason wondered after she marched out of his room. As much as he hated her, she was right, it was her house. Jason decided not to stay around and give her the opportunity to send him away. He moved quickly to the closet, stuffed his new puzzle, journal, and his jacket into his back pack. Jason started to leave the room then he turned back and grabbed Scruffy and his Hardees hat from the shelf. He stuffed the bear in the pack with his other things and slipped quietly down the back stairway.

With very little effort Jason slipped unnoticed from the front door. The eight-year-old walked away from the house not even sure of his destination. He wandered aimlessly, his mind continuously replaying the earlier scene and occupied with the repercussions of the afternoon's incident.

***

Ruth huddled in a corner of her sofa, sipping tea. She was wrapped in an old afghan of her mother's in an effort to stem the chill that had invaded her mind and body. She felt so alone. She suspected that it was already too late for her, suspected that she already loved Wyndom. She had even begun to dream they might have a life together. Now all she felt was rejection, rejection and deceit. *Why didn't he tell me, why?* Slowly she replayed the events of the afternoon, even recalling the malicious glint in Mrs. Carlyle's eye. *What was going on with that lady?* she wondered.

It was hard to accept that the drunk that had killed her parents, robbed her of their presence, was Jason's mother. Tears pooled at the corners of her eyes as memories surfaced. She worked through picture after picture of her mother and father. They had both been so happy so full of life. Ruth still missed them terribly. She missed the sound of their laughter filling the house. Mostly she missed the attention they lavished on her day after day since she returned home. Memories of her childhood, good memories occupied her thoughts for several hours. She wallowed in self-pity, silently railed at fate and now and then she muttered her contempt for Wyndom Winters, the cowardly rat.

A gunshot-reverberating clap of thunder jolted Ruth from her reverie. She set the cup of cold tea on the coffee table and moved to the patio door. Sunshine had dissolved into a bleakness that scurried the creatures out in her back yard into a riot of action. Birds flew hurriedly for cover as angry gray clouds bumped each other, birthing brittle bolts of lightning that bounced out loud peals of thunder.

The awesome power playing itself out in the sky held her mesmerized. Bold drops of rain began to pelt the earth. Ruth experienced the storm with awe, riveted by its frenzy. Its raging furor matched her mood; its fiery display afforded her a measure of comfort.

As the gray storm-blanket choked light from the sky, an eerie darkness seeped over the earth. Finally the combustible center of the storm passed overhead and the rain's fierceness diminished into a soft gentle rhythmic cadence. Ruth drifted toward the kitchen unsure if the ache gnawing at her stomach was despair or hunger. She figured what ever she put in her mouth would resemble unseasoned mush still she felt propelled to pull the last homemade double cheese pizza from the freezer. She popped it into the hot oven and set the timer.

Ruth wandered aimlessly from room to room waiting for her supper to cook. A knot, no a fist, a cold hard fist was gripping her heart squeezing all the emotion from her being. It was as if her tether on life had been severed. She sensed the void clutching at her being but did not have an inkling of how to escape the morass. Unconsciously she prayed for something to jolt her out of this dungeon of numbness. She prayed for peace.

***

Jason's raging thoughts so obsessed his mind he missed the fury of the storm brewing overhead. The first drops of rain mingled unnoticed with the moisture already gracing his cheeks. Finally he stopped under a broad-leafed oak tree and pulled his school jacket from his pack. He plopped the overlarge cap on his head and listlessly continued his journey.

He wandered, one foot in front of the other, in a mindless haze. The turmoil inside his head blinded Jason to the impending storm. He neither saw lightening nor heard thunder. His feet ached and he had grown a blister at his heel from the sloshing motion of his wet shoes. Jason, sodden and drippy, had no idea of the time or of his whereabouts.

Only when the light began leaching from the storm-gray sky did Jason experience his first inkling of trepidation. He stopped. Turned slowly in each direction, trying to determine his next move. A car passed him and drove slowly down the street and Jason was sure the man inside stared strangely at him. Jason shivered. Cowered into his wet clothing and studied his surroundings.

That tree and that house across the street seemed almost familiar to Jason. When the streetlight flared to life, he began to worry. Jason paced briskly to the next corner and once again searched for anything familiar. *It's impossible,* he thought, clenching his jaw to keep his teeth from clattering as a chill overwhelmed him. He halted, took a deep breath. He recognized his surroundings. Jason was both happy and frightened to discover he was not far from Ruth's house. What should he do?

In an instant Jason knew that he had to see Ruth. Had to apologize. Had to find out if she was angry with him.

Jason was thoroughly soaked by the time he stood at the bottom of Ruth's front steps. He ascended slowly, step by step, stood before her front door, hand raised, afraid to knock.

***

Horse began to whine. He scampered to the front door and assumed an attentive pose. Ruth halted her rambling and listened. Someone or something was on her porch. The bumps and clomps, though barely audible to Ruth, had garnered Horse's attention. The cat leaned his front paws against the door and swiveled his puss to stare at Ruth as if trying to implore her to come open the door.

Light flared around Jason stilling his motions. Ruth gasped in surprise at the sight of the soaked and disheveled child she spied through the peephole. She quickly unlocked the door. "Jason, how on earth did you get here?" Ruth said pulling him into the warmth of the house.

Water dripped in rivulets from his jacket and too-large hat. Jason held his head at an awkward angle to look up at her because the bill of his hat drooped clear to his nose. Ruth used two fingers to lift the offending bill out of his face so she could see his eyes. He stared up at her. His lips were blue and wobbled with tension or cold, maybe weariness she wasn't sure which. From his appearance probably all three. His eyes seemed to radiate questions. Ruth flashed him a smile.

"My but you look wetter then Horse did after he tangled with the water hose yesterday. Stand still," she said in a calm quiet voice.

Jason watched her hurry from the room, amazed that she didn't seem angry. He was not sure how he found his way here but right this minute he was glad that he came. He felt weird, kind of floaty. The room faded in and out around him but he was so relieved at being inside and safe that he ignored the sensation. Delicious smells wafted through the room tantalizing his nostrils and he remembered that he had not eaten since breakfast. Jason's stomach rumbled loudly just as Ruth returned with a load of towels.

Jason began to shake making his teeth clack with his shivers. Ruth dropped to her knees and wrapped a huge fluffy towel around him, used another to try and dry his face and hair then she pulled him into a body warming hug until he stopped trembling. When he was less drippy she led him into the bathroom and left him to change into one of her old flannel shirts.

"Drape your wet things over the bath tub," Ruth instructed from outside the door. "Then come to the kitchen. Our pizza is about done." She hoped that he had the energy to get out of his wet clothes without her help, knew she had to trust that he did in order to preserve his dignity.

Ruth picked up his sodden backpack as she walked back through the living room. Once in the kitchen she unzipped and emptied the bag. The cellophane wrapped puzzle and leather journal she had given Jason, along with a very damp fuzzy toy bear, slid to the counter. Ruth toweled all of them dry, set the journal and puzzle on the table, and then carried the bear and bag into the laundry room. She put both in the dryer and set them on air-fluff to dry.

She had already assembled plates, forks, and glasses on the counter by the stove when the buzzer on the stove sounded.

"It smells good," Jason quietly said when he padded barefoot into the kitchen. They were the first words he had spoken since she opened the door to him. He looked even smaller in her old shirt and she sensed he was embarrassed at the dress like outfit.

"Shall we eat in the other room?" Ruth said, pulling the hot bubbly circle of melted cheese from the oven.

Jason silently watched Ruth cut and distributed pieces to their plates.

"If you'll carry in the plates, I'll bring everything else," she said and handed him both plates, gently pushed him toward the family room.

Jason held a plate carefully in each hand and wove his way around an exuberant Horse. He settled to his knees in front of the coffee table, put the plates down in front of him, then opened his arms to the waiting cat, burying his face in Horse's soft fur.

Ruth looked across at her guest. His blonde hair was still dark with moisture in places although shoots at the very top were beginning to spike. Jason's cheeks were red and as Ruth watched he grabbed a napkin to stifle a sneeze. Apparently he had been too-long out in the rain. How had he even managed to reach her house unaided, she wondered?

"Does anyone know you're here?" Ruth asked once she slipped to her knees across from him.

"No." He refused to look up at her, sat listlessly staring at Horse. Ruth's instinct warned her something was amiss.

"Jason, did you run away?" Ruth observed the subtle nod of his head and wondered what she should do. Jason's stomach rumbled loudly, solving their immediate dilemma and Ruth suggested they eat.

She licked sauce from her fingers and looked up to discover Jason eyeing her with a fierce intensity, his frown etching lines on his boyish features.

"Do you hate me? Is it true what my Grandmother said?" His voice was scratchy, his words a mere whisper. Sorrow flared from his aqua eyes as he studied Ruth.

"I could never hate you," Ruth said, holding his gaze, praying he would accept her words as sincere.

"You ran away. I saw that there were tears on your face," Jason said his voice hoarse and croaky, a pained expression gracing his features.

"Your grandmother told the truth, and it came as a shock. But none of this was your fault. I did not mean to desert you on your birthday, Jason. Please, Forgive me?"

"I ran away," he said and lowered his gaze for a minute, waiting for her reprimand.

"You walked all the way here alone? Amazing," Ruth said under her breath.

Jason slowly lifted his eyes. Ruth didn't shake her head or her finger at him. She did not even act angry. Instead he saw a smile begin to build on Ruth's face and bloom into a special look that warmed him. Her smile remained, seemed directed just at him and he felt the knot of tension in the pit of his belly ease.

Jason devoured the last piece of pizza, and drained a second glass of milk, sneezing twice in the process. Ruth quietly determined to keep an eye on him.

***

Evelyn sipped the vodka laced juice trying desperately to control her quaking hands. She realized the events of today would feed the gossip mill for awhile before being forgotten. Her anger at Jason had started to diminish still she wondered what Wyndom would do if she sent the boy away before he returned. The man had said he would leave if she forced the idea of boarding school. Did she dare push the issue?

Evelyn rang the silver bell she used to summon Katie. She sent her servant to bring Jason down. A smile curled her upper lip as she plotted through several deserving punishments short of sending him off, something that would teach the child who was boss in this house.

"What is taking the woman so long?" Evelyn slurred and finished her drink.

"Jason's not in his room. I couldn't find him anywhere upstairs," Katie explained when she stepped into the sitting room.

"He's just hiding. Find him," Evelyn ordered, firmly shooing Katie out from the room.

Katie went through every room, checked the closets and under the beds. There was no trace of Jason. The rain pounding against the roof increased Katie's worry. She needed to tell Mrs. Carlyle, but wondered what good it would do. Repeatedly she wished out loud that Jason's father were here.

What had that woman said to Jason that caused him to run away? Katie wondered. She should have gone up sooner to check on the boy. Katie knew she would have to call Wyndom. He had asked her to watch over the boy and she had failed. Katie understood that Mrs. Carlyle was already too inebriated to worry about her own grandson, wasn't even sure the woman would worry if she were sober. Katie had seen the tension between her boss and Jason, but could not fathom justification for the rift.

Katie frowned. Guilt stabbed her and she realized that Jason had probably slipped away while she hid in the pantry trying to control the laughter this afternoon's scene had created.

She walked into the den to look up Wyndom's number and the phone rang. Wyndom greeted her warmly and asked to speak with his son, wanted to wish Jason happy birthday.

"Disappeared? What happened Katie?" Wyndom's anxiety flowed through the phone line, his tone harsh with worry.

"I'm not sure, Mr. Winters. Whatever happened, that teacher fled in a hurry and Jason must have been pretty upset because he shoved Mrs. Carlyle into the pool." Katie described the episode unable to enlighten Wyndom as to its cause.

"I'm catching the first flight home. Check the garage, Katie, he could be hiding out there. He might have sought comfort in the Edsel."

"Right away, Mr. Winters." She hung up the receiver, hoping and praying that the man was right.

Katie ran her fingers through her shortly cropped, salt and pepper tinged curls. The wayward locks fell back across her brow, furrowed now with tension grooves. She wondered if there was any place inside the house she had failed to check. She replayed her search over and over in her mind as she moved through the plushly furnished sterile rooms toward the kitchen.

Katie rummaged through the back closet for an umbrella, switched the lights on inside and outside the garage and stepped out into the storm. After a thorough search of the garage and the cars it held, the grooves etched in the housekeeper's brow deepened. Jason was not out here either.

The phone was ringing when Katie rushed in from the storm's fury. Puddles formed around her patterned canvas shoes with each step that she took inside. One set grew larger when she stopped and reached for the receiver. "Carlyle residence."

"Mrs. Carlyle?" The questioning voice was unfamiliar.

"Mrs. Carlyle is indisposed. May I help you?"

Ruth assumed Jason would know the person on the other end of the line and handed the phone to him.

"Katie."

Jason's voice flowed over the housekeeper's heart like warm honey. Relief suspended her tension, momentarily. "Where are you? Are you all right?" She listened to Jason's explanation, accepted his apology for frightening her.

Katie stooped to wipe the water from the floor, wondering how Jason had managed to find his way to his teacher's. The young lady insisted that Jason stay the night. Katie hoped she did the right thing by consenting. She pulled Wyndom's number from her pocket. Maybe she could catch him before he left the hotel.

***

Wyndom stashed his luggage in the trunk and climbed into the hotel limousine. He instructed the driver to hurry; he needed to make the scheduled flight.

Weather was atrocious, traffic sparse. Heavy rain impaired their visibility; still the driver rushed competently through Chicago's gaudily lit downtown district.

Wyndom's fists were clenched, jammed into the pockets of his raincoat.

Worry eroded all pretexts at polite conversation from his mind. He worked through a dozen different scenarios, each more deadly than the one before. Wyndom feared for Jason. Where could he be? What had motivated the boy's actions? Picturing Evelyn Carlyle sputtering angrily in the pool did little to relieve Wyndom's mind about Jason's disappearance. Thank God he had been able to get a direct flight.

***

Ruth studied Jason's flushed cheeks as he attempted to find the puzzle piece he needed. Ruth had agreed to help build the 3-D castle if Jason would let someone know of his whereabouts.

"You look feverish, Jason," she said. "How do you feel?" Ruth reached over and discovering the warmth of his forehead and cheeks, she went in search of some Tylenol to combat the boy's fever. Wind buffeted the ranch house, whispered at each window of some past adventure eagerly told and retold. The rain had ceased its onslaught, dwindling at last into a fine mist as the storm blew eastward.

Jason put down the piece of cardboard and grabbed for a tissue to catch his sneeze. His eyes felt gritty and his head ached. "My throat feels funny," he said when Ruth asked. Right now, more than anything, the eight-year-old wanted his father.

"It's after ten, Jason, I think you should pick up any loose pieces and get ready for bed. I laid a new tooth brush out on the bathroom counter for you."

Jason yawned. He closed the puzzle box and set it next to the unfinished structure. Ruth waited by the bed until he came out of the bathroom then she tucked him in, kissed him on the forehead and shut off the light.

"Goodnight, Jason," she said. "I'll come and check on you in a little while."

Jason's goodnight was slurred, already heavy with sleep.

Ruth vowed to check on him through out the night. His trek in the rain had caused a fever and she needed to make sure it did not escalate.

While Jason was awake she'd managed to shove her anger at Wyndom aside. Now she uncovered it, polished it until it glowed. She fumed. Wondered if the man cared for her at all. She thought back over their relationship. He had had several opportunities to tell her about Jason's mother. The man had ignored every one. Picturing Wyndom as a coward was difficult. For some unknown reason he chose to keep this awful secret from her. Maybe it was too painful for him to discuss because he still loved his ex-wife. That thought hurt. Maybe he didn't trust her or even worse maybe he just didn't care. Her emotions fluctuated between outrage, dejection and even despair.

Ruth struggled with her emotions. Finally, recognizing the magnitude of her torment for what it was, she admitted that she already loved Wyndom. She understood that otherwise his deception wouldn't hurt so much. Her feelings had crept up on her, left her vulnerable to this agony of betrayal that Wyndom had caused by his lie of omission. *Why, oh why did he lie?* She asked herself that question so often it became like a litany bouncing unchecked through her brain.

CHAPTER FOURTEEN

Ruth woke immediately. Someone called her from sleep, the voice, commanding and urgent. She lay blanketed in darkness and listened intently. The wind whistled and whined around the corners of her house in muted antipathy, its whisper not the sharp "Ruth, wake up" of her dream. The command seemed genuine. She discerned its urgency.

She shook her head to clear the webs from her mind. The clock on her nightstand blinked twelve, repeatedly, still her bedside lamp flared to life. Ruth pushed her arms into the cool silk of her robe, knotting the belt securely.

According to her watch it would soon be one a m. Ruth figured they had been without electricity for very little time. She rushed along the hall to check on Jason. It had not been his voice she heard but she knew she had been awakened for a reason and she was concerned.

Jason's raspy breathing met her ears the minute she stepped into his room. Ruth quickly knelt and placed her hand on Jason's brow. He was hot, much too hot. Ruth rushed through the house, turning on lights as she went. She sat at her desk, hurriedly leafing through the pages of her phone index hunting for Dr. Chase's number. He answered on the third ring.

Ruth poured alcohol into the pan of tepid water. She stopped in the living room and turned on the porch light, a beacon to the doctor, then grabbed a wash cloth from the bathroom and hurried in to be with Jason.

She bathed his face, arms, and chest, over and over. She worked feverishly to lower his temperature, all the while murmuring reassurance to her lethargic patient. Ruth offered up continuous silent prayers for him with each swipe of her wash cloth.

"Hurry, doctor! Hurry," she whispered against Jason's too warm cheek.

Ruth totally immersed herself in the task at hand, jerking in surprise when the pounding on her front door finally registered. *Thank God. The Doctor is here.* Ruth rushed to let him in.

***

Wind driven clouds parted momentarily, allowing the moon's silvery glow to illuminate the airport's parking area. Wyndom tossed his carryall into the trunk.

Katie called, said that Jason was with Ruth. He did not understand the black knot surrounding his heart, the sense of urgency that propelled him to hurry. He should feel relieved that Jason was safe with the woman he loved. He did not. Something had happened yesterday, something that caused Ruth to flee and Jason to attack his grandmother. Wyndom was baffled by the unexplainable worry driving him.

The car engine roared to life. Wyndom glanced once again at his watch. Ruth and Jason would be asleep. Still, he could not wait. Silly as it seemed he needed to see Jason and Ruth. Sensed that it was urgent he see them now.

Puddles intermittently edged the streets. Fierce winds battled and buffeted the Corvette mercilessly. Wyndom's hands, arms and shoulders ached with the effort it took to hold the car on the road. Tension knifed through him, increased with each mile, as he steadily decreased the distance between he and his son. The worry torching through him exploded into full-blown fear when he finally pulled into Ruth's driveway and noticed light blazing from every window.

***

Confusion suffused Ruth's face when she opened the door and found Wyndom with his hand poised to knock. He watched her confusion fade then flare into anger.

"Go away," she snapped. "I don't want to talk to you." She attempted to shut the door in his face. Anger radiated from every inch of her and she glared back at him, her fury so consuming it drove Jason's illness momentarily from her mind.

"What's going on here Ruth?" he quietly said, straining to keep the door open as he studied her face. He observed her anger; struggled to understand it when quite suddenly it drained from her face. Her attention was directed elsewhere, her relief was all he saw and he figured it had something to do with the car that just entered her drive.

Wyndom kept his foot in the doorway and turned around to scrutinize the new arrival. He was puzzled by the sight of an elderly gentleman exiting the black car, until he spied the black bag and it dawned on him that he was seeing a dying breed, a doctor that made house calls.

Wyndom grabbed Ruth by the shoulders, commanding her attention. "Who is sick?"

He studied her carefully. She looked fine, tired, disheveled but beautiful. "Jason?" Something was wrong with Jason; Wyndom read the truth of it in Ruth's attitude.

She ignored his question, shoved his hands away. Wyndom was perplexed by the look she flashed him, it was not conciliatory and definitely not loving. Ruth succeeded in barring Wyndom from her thoughts even managed to ignore his presence, concentrating instead on the doctor striding purposefully up her front steps.

Ruth motioned for the doctor to follow and hurried from the room. Wyndom slammed the door and followed in her wake. The doctor absentmindedly tossed his coat at the foot of the bed; his attention riveted on his patient. While the Dr. bent over the bed to examine Jason, Wyndom slipped unnoticed into the room.

Jason's eyes drifted open. He tried to smile when he spotted his father and noticed the worried expression. "Hi Dad," he quietly croaked, "I don't feel so good."

Wyndom whipped around to the other side of the bed and knelt beside his son. He clung to Jason's hand, surprised and worried by the heat burning through the boy's fingers, "It's okay, Jason, the doctor is here and I won't leave, I promise."

The adults in the room grew silent. The doctor busied himself with Jason while Ruth and Wyndom studied the man's every move in silence.

"Were you out in the rain this afternoon, young man?"

"Y...yes."

"Thought so." The doctor pulled a syringe from his bag and withdrew fluid from a small bottle. "Ruth this young man needs to spend time with a vaporizer." She nodded. Went to search through the bathroom closet.

"Jason, I have to give you a shot." The doctor explained and rubbed Jason's upper arm with an alcohol soaked cotton swab.

Jason grimaced at the needle piercing his skin, but he made no sound. He was obviously tired still he struggled to hold his eyes open.

"You're his father?" the doctor asked, turned to face Wyndom. "I'll write you a prescription, get it filled in the morning."

"May I take him home?"

"See how he feels in the morning, better not to move him tonight." Ruth heard the doctor's words when she returned with the apparatus. The vaporizer had yellowed with age and she wondered if it would even work. All three of the adults breathed a sigh of relief when the plugged in machine hummed appropriately and steam began to fill the air.

Ruth and Wyndom, silently working together, used a sheet to form a tent over the bed, encasing Jason.

The doctor nodded his approval, tipped Ruth's face up to study the dark circles around her eyes and shook his head. "You get some rest, now, young lady. I certainly don't need another patient in this house."

"Yes sir," she smiled, and leaned in to hug the man who had watched over her since birth. Ruth walked the doctor to the door, thanked him and locked up after he left.

She reasoned that Wyndom would refuse to leave Jason but right now she could not deal with him or the issue raised by his mother-in-law. Ruth dug out an extra blanket and pillow, tossed them into Wyndom, then fled to her bedroom. She closed the door, leaned against it as she endeavored to get away from his questioning glare.

***

Wyndom assumed the chill in the room was more a result of being iced out by Ruth's attitude then the weather. Although the wind still huffed at the night, turning it cooler then normal for a July evening, it was Ruth's reception that curled like an icy fist around his heart.

He moved to the bed and checked on Jason. His breathing was still raspy and rugged but he was sleeping.

Wyndom stewed over the matter for several minutes. He paced the confined space of the small bedroom working through his options. He realized he had to face Ruth now. The problem would only amplify if left untended, could become insurmountable if left to simmer until morning. Wyndom could not sleep worrying over this anyway. He stumbled into the hallway listening at closed doors for a sign of her movement. Light filtered meagerly from under the last closed door and Wyndom assumed he'd finally found Ruth's room. He swiped a hand down his face. He was weary, bone tired. He'd pushed himself for days in order to return home. Home to his son and Ruth. What a homecoming this was?

He stood there for several minutes pondering Ruth's attitude, contemplating what might have gone wrong. Consternation and concern fought for prevalence and he plotted his approach.

Relationships took so much energy, Wyndom wondered if he had any left. Maybe it wasn't worth the effort. He thought about Ruth pictured her in his mind. Wyndom gathered his resolve, shook his head to clear the worry from his mind and remembered the way Ruth looked when she smiled at him. His body immediately responded to the mind picture and he groaned his despair, knew he must make things right with her. He wanted and needed her in his life, permanently. He wanted her bad enough to wage war if necessary.

***

Ruth pulled the light blanket up to her knees, totally unaware of the mental pandemonium being waged outside her bedroom and reached out to extinguish the light. Wyndom's knock rattled both her and her door.

"Go away," she ordered. She watched the doorknob swivel, wished she'd thought to engage the lock and then he stood in the entryway, his eyes devouring her features.

"I didn't know I had to lock my door in my own house," the timbre in her voice attested to her anger while exposing her exhaustion.

"We need to talk. I doubt a locked door would have stopped me." Wyndom said, his voice, quiet but firm. "I need to know what happened today...yesterday to cause such...such repercussions?" He studied her expression. "Was It Evelyn? What did she say to upset you, you and Jason? Whatever it was, it upset Jason enough that he ran away." He perused her features, waited for her to respond.

She silently, determinedly stared back at him and said not a word.

"Jason attacked his grandmother then ran away from home. And look at you Ruth, you're angry. Why?" he repeated as calmly and quietly as he could manage with a wagonload of fear clutching at his heart like an iron fist. "You're angry with me, Ruth. Why?" He prodded more forcefully at her continued silence.

"Ask your mother-in-law." Ruth said, her tone brittle, her emotions barely in control.

151

"I'm asking you." His words came out in a whispered plea. His eyes never wavered from her face. "Please."

Shadows rimmed her brown eyes. Sadness oozed from her expression. Wyndom watched her brush stray wisps of hair from her forehead, noted that her hand trembled with the emotions coursing through her petite frame. He perceived she was on the brink of tears still he refused to relent. This matter was way too important.

"I don't want to talk...I...I...I don't even want you in my room." Exhaustion and anger deepened her tone, turned it harsh. She glared at him, menace in her manner.

"Fine. Join me in the living room...we can talk there..."

Her stillness denied his request and he finished his sentence. "Or I'll come over and join you on the bed. We are going to talk. I'm not leaving until we do," he firmly said.

He stood a moment longer waiting for her response. When she failed to move, Wyndom turned and enclosed himself in her bedroom.

Ruth skittered to the furthest corner of the bed as Wyndom walked toward her. Defiance that flashed from the depths of her brown eyes seemed to heat the whole room. She looked bone weary but Wyndom knew he was right, they had to have it out. Ruth gnawed at her bottom lip, brushed invisible devil webs from her eyes and watched Wyndom settle on a corner of her bed. *What do I say to him?* she thought, pondering how to begin. She refused to look at him, angered even more because she still ached to be in his arms.

"Why didn't you tell me about your wife?" Her voice was gruff and wispy when she finally spoke.

"Tell you what about my ex-wife?" he said, stressing the ex.

"The accident!" Her words became a hiss that she spat at him.

"Evelyn told you Cindy was responsible for the death of your parents?" Wyndom groaned, his tone attesting to his astonishment. His fists clenched, he held his body rigid, perplexed and angered by his mother-in-law's motivation. Silence hung in the air, stretched between them, turning the atmosphere in the room a crackle with electricity. Wyndom paused, weighed his thoughts, and sought for words. Wanted words that would absolve him of any wrong in the matter. He found none.

Sorrow seeped in a swirl around them. Wyndom knew the information had reopened the wounds death had thrust at her, wounds that had finally begun to heal. When he spoke, at last, Ruth strained to hear the words that slipped softly and hesitantly from his mouth.

"When we first met, it was because of Jason, because he was having problems. You knew his mother was dead. If I'd told you then it might have affected your response to him. I didn't know you then and couldn't take that chance. He was already under stress. I had no way of knowing if somehow you might be responsible for the change in him. It didn't seem likely but I couldn't take that chance.

"I'm not proud for thinking that of you. As our relationship developed, as you began to fill the void in my life and Jason's, I struggled with the desire to tell you the truth about Cindy. Started to, many times. Then I'd catch a glimpse of the pain still evident in your eyes. You seemed so sad. How could I add to that sorrow? I realize it was cowardly of me but I couldn't add to the sadness already there. "

Ruth watched his agony twist his face. When he raised his head to meet her eyes, he held her gaze, capturing her, holding her as immobile as if he held her with his hands. "You fill my life with joy, Ruth, with hope. You're so sweet and wonderful. I'll admit it, I was afraid.... I didn't want to loose you. Suddenly I couldn't imagine my life without you a part of it."

Contrite. Wyndom's every movement; every expression shouted his remorse. Contrite, that word blazed at her like a neon sign. She hunched against her headboard, dizzy from exhaustion, strained to hold her eyes open, to remain alert. Thinking grew difficult and she floated in a fuzzy haze. He seemed sincere but Ruth was too tired to care or to even think properly.

"Does Jason know?" he quietly asked.

Ruth sighed and rubbed at her gritty eyes, "I'm sure he heard Evelyn...overheard our conversation."

"Just what did she say to you?"

Ruth struggled to recall the words, wondered why it mattered. She could not trust him, would not trust him, she had promised herself that much.

"She explained how beautiful your wife was, how broken up you were at her death, then she said how sorry she was about the accident. My confusion elicited her quick admission that Cindy had been driving the car that killed my parents. I was shocked. I panicked and ran. I was angry with you, with her, with all of you so I left. I don't know how much Jason heard but he does know." Ruth crossed her arms and hugged herself as if there was a chill in the room and she needed warmth.

"I had no feeling left for my ex-wife by the time of her death, Ruth," Wyndom said. "She may have been beautiful but she was self-centered, spoiled and quite often, not a nice person."

"You don't have to tell me this. It's none of my business."

"Yes, Ruth, it is important. I want you to know the truth," he said, exasperation evident in his tone. "Cindy was pregnant when we got married. She thought a baby would be great fun, her own personal plaything. That didn't last long. Cindy quickly developed distaste for motherhood. I came home one afternoon to find Jason soaked, hungry and crying loudly for attention. Cindy was locked in her bedroom dressing for a party. She had turned her stereo up to cover the sound of our child's cry.

After that I hired a full time nurse. Tried to spend more time away from the office caring for Jason. Cindy asked for a divorce that night. We'd been married all of ten months." Wyndom brushed his hand across his face and absentmindedly combed his fingers through his hair.

"I held on, fought the divorce for Jason's sake. Nothing changed; she ignored both of us for an incessant round of parties. When Jason was three, I gave in. It was obvious she didn't want me, Jason, or our life."

Ruth tried to concentrate on the words coming from Wyndom. His voice was laced with anger and a touch of sadness. Ruth wondered if Evelyn was right and he unknowingly still loved Cindy. If only she could think clearly.

"You miss her?" Ruth's question was barely audible.

His laugh was harsh, more a dry croak from deep in his chest. "Just the opposite. I was relieved when she left, I felt guilty about it but by then I knew I was not in love with my wife. I was infatuated for a while with her looks, her wild spirit but the magic was over long before the marriage."

Wyndom reached out and his fingers traced a path along Ruth's cheek. His touch was gentle. Heat coiled along her nerve endings. She felt tingles every place he rested his fingers.

"Evelyn Carlyle is trying to drive a wedge between us. I don't know why exactly, but she is a lonely, selfish woman. Don't let her win, Ruth."

Wyndom curled his fingers around her neck and drew her against him. He held her for several minutes, delighted to have her in his arms even for a short time.

"I know you're wiped out," he whispered against her hair. "I'm going to check on Jason, you go to sleep. We'll talk more in the morning. I want you in my life Ruth. Please remember that."

Wyndom drew the light blanket up around her shoulders then tiptoed from the room extinguishing the light as he departed. Ruth eyes drifted shut and she was asleep before she could make sense of the situation, before she could decide what she should do, too weary to rekindle her anger.

Wyndom added water to the vaporizer, pleased to note an improvement in Jason's breathing. The wind careening around the house forcefully enough to rumble the windows carried a coolness that nipped at Wyndom and he was grateful for the cover Ruth had tossed at him. He stretched out his long legs, his whole body weary. He leaned back into the large overstuffed chair, nestled in a corner of the room, and determined to try and rest.

He doubted his ability to quiet his emotions long enough to fall asleep in such a cramped space but he'd promised to be here when Jason woke up. He planned to stay. He deemed it imperative that he and Jason talk. Wyndom understood the pool incident much better now but wondered if there was more to the story, something else that had prodded Jason into running away.

Wyndom closed his eyes, Ruth's image flared to life in his mind. Her eyes were already drifting shut with sleep when he last saw her. Even then her beauty had struck him. He wanted nothing more from life right now than to join Ruth in her bed. He wanted to hold her, comfort her until he could claim her, heart, body and soul. He imagined unbraiding and fluffing her hair. Pictured the way it would curl around her shoulders, tickling the rounded curve of her breasts.

A sigh of frustration slipped from his lips at the thought that because of his own cowardice he might loose her. He refused to contemplate the end of their relationship. He took a deep breath and sought to temper the tension of the last few hours, at last he slept.

***

Jason looked around. Nothing seemed familiar. He wandered hall after hall, found no one familiar. He realized he was at school but he could not find his classroom. He knew he was late but could not remember where he was supposed to be? He wandered aimlessly, until he finally found his locker. He struggled to work the lock but try as he might the combination alluded him.

Understanding came slowly; this was not his school. Everything was different Panic griped him, clogged his throat. Grandmother promised she would send him away. Fear overwhelmed him. He ran through one long hall after another, seeking escape, there were no doors. No way out. He tried to cry out for help. No sound would come from his mouth.

Wyndom woke with a start. Sun streamed through the window pushing waves of heat into the bedroom. Jason struggled on the bed, moaning and thrashing in his tangled bedding. Wyndom hurried to the bed and shoved a corner of the sheet tent aside. What if Jason's fever was worse?

Relief washed through Wyndom at the coolness of his son's forehead. Wyndom pulled away the makeshift tent and gently shook Jason awake.

"Dad?" Jason appeared startled, disoriented.

"A bad dream?"

"The worst." Jason's mouth felt dry and fuzzy. He was thirsty.

"How do you feel this morning?"

"I'm okay, just thirsty," Jason said, recalling the events of yesterday.

"I'm sure Ruth has juice in the kitchen, let's tackle juice and breakfast first," Wyndom said and went in to wash up before going to the kitchen. Jason was just leaving the bathroom when Wyndom returned with a glass of orange juice.

***

The smell of coffee, hot and fresh brewed teased her nostrils, drew her toward wakefulness. Ruth fought to stay in the oblivion of sleep with out awareness of why. The scent swirled near and she sniffed in its delightful aroma. Fresh brewed coffee brought back dreamy memories of her mother's blueberry muffins and shared breakfasts. That's impossible? Her parents were dead. Her nose twitched. She definitely smelled coffee. She rolled over and struggled to open her eyes. Then memories of the party and Mrs. Carlyle's harsh words pushed the fog from her mind. The horror of yesterday and Jason, Jason was here and he was sick. And Wyndom!

Oh Lord, Wyndom was here too. Ruth opened her eyes, pushed herself up in bed. There on the nightstand by her bed was a cup of steamy coffee. Her anger flared anew at the thought that he had been in her room. Ruth propped a pillow at her back and picked up the peace offering. She savored the hot brew, delightfully embellished with vanilla, and mentally practiced all the scathing sentences she intended to throw at Wyndom. She had been too wiped out last night to let him know how devastated she had been by his betrayal. Last night he had tried to apologize, she remembered that, but his words were a jumble, a jumble she refused to try and piece together.

Ruth drained the last of the coffee, stumbled out of bed and into her bathroom. She stripped and stepped into the shower. After adjusting the water nozzle onto blasting beads, she lathered her body with the special scented soap she preferred. She yawned once and stretched the sleep from her lithe body, letting the water pelt her into total awareness.

As Ruth tossed the band from her braid on a shelf and pulled the strands of hair free, she berated Wyndom for his cowardice. She held her head under the water and proceeded to shampoo and rinse all the while she spouted her venom at the man she had earlier dreamed off loving. Then she recalled that Jason was in her house and she knew she couldn't say these things to his father while he was around to hear and be hurt again.

Ruth piddled with dressing, took time to blow-dry her hair. Anything to avoid a confrontation with Wyndom. Worry about Jason niggled at her, however, so she finally tied her hair into a ponytail and slipped from her room intent in checking on her young patient.

The vaporizer was unplugged, the bed made. The extra covers were folded and stacked neatly at the foot of the bed.

The room was empty.

"Pancakes." The raspyness of her voice surprised her and she prayed she was not catching Jason's cold. She sniffed again, convinced that she smelled pancakes.

The scent niggled at her nose and nudged her forward, drew her through the living room toward the kitchen. Pain stabbed at her chest at the domestic scene she encountered at her glance into the kitchen. Emptiness was all she had found in that room since the death of her parents. Now Wyndom stood flipping over golden cakes, Jason ate with vigorous disdain of all but the cat. For the first time in months the kitchen appeared warm and friendly, a comfortable place to enter. Tears came to Ruth's eyes and she blinked them away. She had longed to have this become an always reality but Wyndom had ruined that.

He looked up at her and smiled when she finally padded barefoot into the room. Breakfast smelled delicious. Jason, eyes clear and alert, nose no longer edged in red, forked a piece of pancake into his mouth, dribbled syrup on his chin and Ruth watched him lick up the sweetness, never losing the grin from his mouth. Obviously Jason had overcome his illness.

Wyndom took the empty cup from her hand, refilled it and set the mug of coffee on the table before he pulled out a chair for her. Horse had parked his front paws on the seat of Jason's chair and was busy purring his pleasure at the tasty morsels the boy secretly shared with him when Wyndom's back was turned.

"Enjoy your coffee, Ruth. I'll have a stack of cakes ready for you in minutes." The hair falling over Wyndom's forehead was uncombed and still damp adding a hint of youth to his features. He wore a pair of well-worn jeans that hugged his hips and thighs like a second skin. His shirt hung unbuttoned and the brown curls frosting his chest drew Ruth's gaze. Her fingers itched to play in the field of curls. She lifted her eyes to his, read desire in his coffee colored orbs that left her mouth dry and her heart pounding in her ears.

Confusion consumed her. She wanted to hit and hug him. How would she make it through the day if he continued to unnerve her? *How can I sustain my angst when his presence in the same room gives me such provocative ideas?* She searched for her fury, grabbed for the elusive ends of her irritation and discovered only numbness. Why had he lied to her? She watched him looking comfortable and at ease in her kitchen, really her parents' kitchen. They would have approved of Wyndom. That thought splattered her acrimony right back in her face yet for a brief moment her parents seemed to surround her with their love as if to let her know they trusted in her judgement. She was not sure she could or was even ready to forgive Wyndom. He set a plate of fragrant fluffy cakes in front of her and consuming their cottony cloyness with out choking took all her attention.

Wyndom insisted on cleaning the kitchen. Ruth made her bed and put the vaporizer in its place. She cleaned and straightened both bathrooms before gaining the courage to rejoin Wyndom and Jason in the living room.

The two of them knelt beside the coffee table, studying the pieces of the half-built puzzle. Horse, the traitor, was wrapped around Wyndom's neck like a ladies mink stole. The cat's front paws searched Wyndom's shirt pocket. Ruth could hear his contented purrs from across the room.

Wyndom added a piece to the castle, "I hear you shoved your grandmother into the pool." He hoped that the matter-of-fact tone of voice he contrived to maintain would come across to Jason as non-threatening.

Ruth was surprised by the information and looked at Jason, watched a smile tug at the corners of his mouth.

"Jason?" The curiosity in her tone relaxed the boy. He shrugged his shoulders.

"She deserved it, Dad. She made Ruth cry."

Wyndom looked back and forth from Jason to Ruth. He covered his face with his hands, took a deep breath then looked at each of them again. "I'm sorry you had to hear about your mother that way. I...I should have told both of you myself," Wyndom said. He drew Ruth down to the table beside them. The three worked silently for several minutes and the walls of the 3-D puzzle began to resemble the pictured structure. All three of them maintained their silence, concentrated on the task at hand.

"Why did you run away?" Wyndom asked. He observed a myriad of emotions wash across Jason's face, watched his son struggle with information he was reluctant to reveal. "Jason?" Spoken softly, his eyes and voice exuding reassurance, Wyndom waited for Jason's answer.

Moisture threatened the corners of Jason's eyes and he swiped at them. What would happen if he told, Jason wondered. He stared at his father and knew he could not evade the issue or lie. Jason trembled, lowered his eyes until he saw nothing but his own trembling body.

Barely speaking above a whisper, Jason responded. "She...grandmother told me to pack. She was going to send me away."

"Has she threatened to send you away before?" Wyndom kept the menace from his tone.

"No." A tear slid down the boy's cheek, he scruffed it away with a clenched fist.

"What has she been telling you, son?" Wyndom's voice deepened, throbbed with concern.

Jason flung himself at his father, dislodging Horse. "She said you'd leave me if I'm bad, just like my mother did. I try to be good, Dad, I don't mean to make her mad."

Wyndom held Jason tight against his chest; his anger at Evelyn Carlyle pursed his lips and furrowed his brow.

Ruth sat hunched on her knees unable to relinquish the sight of a father comforting his son. Wyndom's patience, his strength, his gentleness all served to tighten the net of love ensnaring her heart. She struggled to sustain her anger, felt it crumble at the edges.

"Is there more Jason?" Wyndom asked quietly.

Both Wyndom and Ruth strove to hear the boy's whispered reply. "She said you would send me away to school if you married Ruth."

"Has she ever done anything more than threaten you, Jason?" Ruth asked. She brushed the tears from his cheek.

"She...she hit me when I wrecked her cake. Usually she just makes me go to my room without supper."

"Why didn't you tell me about this before, Jason?"

"I was afraid if you knew how bad I was you would leave too." Jason's voice wobbled turned into a trembling whisper.

"Your mother left me, son. It had nothing to do with you or your behavior, I promise."

Wyndom settled Jason on the carpet. This conversation had to be man to man, eye to eye. "You and I are a team. I may not always approve of your behavior, Jason, but I will always, always love you. Remember that."

Jason threw himself at his father. "I love you, Dad," he said, his face buried in Wyndom's neck.

"I think it's time for you and I to have our own place." Wyndom said, appalled that he had been so blind to Evelyn's abuse.

He assumed that despite her drinking she was a decent person, a bit selfish, yes, but he had not imagined mean. He had not suspected mean. Surely this was the cause of Jason's personality change at school.

He met Ruth's eyes across the table, "Thank you for being here for Jason yesterday."

Wyndom quietly voiced his reluctance to take Jason back to the Carlyle residence to Ruth and she agreed to let Jason stay for a while. Wyndom went to get the prescription filled before he went home to what Ruth suspected was a confrontation with Evelyn.

She let her eyes wander over Jason where he lay sleeping on the couch. Horse was nestled on the boy's legs, arrogantly cleaning first one paw then the other. How would it be to have an eight-year-old child as part of her life? She longed to hold him tight and protect him from the hurts of the world. The knowledge blossomed that both Winters men had stolen her heart. Ruth shoved the idea out of mind, not yet ready to accept its truths.

***

Evelyn was already drinking and it was not yet noon. She tried to ignore Wyndom's presence in the room, the man radiated anger and he stared at her as if she had suddenly grown an extra nose. She turned to face him at last, defiance written in the set of her mouth. "I presume you found Jason."

"Yes."

"The child is no longer welcome in this house, he is unmannerly and rude. I suggest you accept the arrangements I've made at Brenhurst."

"You made arrangements, Evelyn?" The chill in Wyndom's voice raised the hair on her forearms. He continued to glare at her and she lost what little poise she had maintained.

"You needn't concern yourself with either of us again, Madam. We are leaving."

"Leaving?" Her haughty demeanor toppled.

"I explained all this once before, Jason and I are a package deal. We will have our things removed from your house as quickly as possible." Wyndom swept from the room, eager to separate himself from his mother-in-law before his anger scorched the arrogant hussy hairless.

Evelyn shivered. She was alone again. But then she had been alone even when they were here. It was always that way, she could never remember not being alone.

Wyndom cornered Katie and explained the situation. She offered to help pack up their clothes and Jason's toys. Wyndom and Katie were working together in Jason's room when the phone in Wyndom's bedroom rang.

"Katie, that was Bruce. Jeff found Karen. Bruce needs us to meet them at the hospital," Wyndom said. He shoved his wallet and keys in his pocket and ushered Katie out to the garage.

"Did he hurt her again?"

"Katie, I don't know. Bruce didn't explain. He just said hurry." Wyndom said, gratified that he had thought to drop off the prescription earlier.

He hustled Katie to the Edsel. He could offer no reassurance to the salt and pepper haired lady seated beside him tensely wringing her hands.

July sun zapped earth and mingled with the storm's moisture, evaporating dampness along the curbs into a willowy mist. Traffic was minimal. They sped street after street toward the hospital. Wyndom's foot reached for the accelerator and he prayed that there were no police cars lurking in the area.

Katie's lips moved with every silent prayer she had ever learned and several new ones.

"Damn, damn, damn," Wyndom railed against the red light. How had Jeff managed to find Karen? They had all been so careful.

The parking lot was overrun with vehicles. "I'll leave you at the emergency entrance, Katie. I'll be in once I've parked."

No one was in attendance at the emergency room desk and Katie was still waiting, tense and pale, when Wyndom walked into the hospital.

"Come on, Katie, we'll find her."

They stopped at the doorways of several rooms before Wyndom spied Bruce, pacing circles in a small cubical. Curtains were drawn enclosing the sterile cot. Voices were evident from behind the cloth screen. None of the words were discernible. Wyndom motioned for Katie to join her daughter before he pulled Bruce into the hall.

"What happened?"

Bruce rubbed his face, his scratched and bloody knuckles attesting to battle. "The bastard followed her home from her doctor appointment yesterday. She didn't even see him. He drank up enough courage early this morning to confront her and he turned vicious."

"Is she hurt bad?"

"I just don't know." Bruce's voice was ragged with emotion, his movements abrupt and jerky as he tried to pace in the narrow hallway.

"You're taking this rather personal, Bruce."

"So, sue me, I think I'm in love with the lady. We've been working together. I've been attending Lamaze class as her coach. If I hadn't come to work early this morning that drunken bastard could have killed her. The man's abusive curses were what drew me toward the trailer. He'd knocked her down, was trying to kick her, when I pulled him outside."

"He attacked me and I knocked him flat. Karen was having pains by the time I reached her. I cleaned the blood from her face, packed a bag for her and carried her to the car."

"Jeffrey?"

"His car was gone by the time we got outside."

"Mr. Overton?"

Bruce rushed to the white-coated woman, "Is Karen okay?"

"She's in labor. She claims you're her coach."

"Will she be all right?" Bruce tried to push the issue but the doctor ignored him.

"We're taking her up to delivery. Follow me. We'll get you suited up. She needs you."

"It's too soon isn't it." Worry etched brackets around Bruce's mouth and he hastily trailed the doctor.

Dr. Lucas heard the fear in Bruce's voice and decided to offer what consolation she could, "The baby's just three weeks early, everything will be fine."

Wyndom watched his foreman follow in the doctor's wake. Karen was wheeled from the cubical and he and Katie were directed to the proper waiting room.

***

Wyndom had been gone for hours. Ruth watched Jason move aimlessly around the room. Nothing seemed to hold his attention. He had picked at his supper and ignored Horse's antics. Something powerful was disturbing him.

Ruth knelt in front of Jason, detaining him from his pacing. She laid her hand on his forehead and discovered no fever. "Something is troubling you, Jason, talk to me."

His eyes appeared haunted and he avoided her gaze. He stared out the patio door into the black night, his expression bleak. "What if he doesn't come back?"

"Your father?"

Jason nodded. A single tear slipped down his cheek, caught in the corner of his mouth, and he unconsciously licked it away as he gave voice to his fears.

Ruth hugged the eight-year-old and tried to console him. "Your Father loves you. I saw love written across his face when he held you this morning. He said you were a team, remember? He needs to find you a new place to live. I'm sure he's making preparations." Jason slipped his arms around Ruth's neck. She smelled nice and it felt good to be held. It was nice to be hugged.

Horse shoved himself between Ruth and Jason. He was tired of being ignored. He bit down on Jason's sneaker lace and tugged. The boy dropped and drew the cat into his arms. Jason was wrestling with the arrogant beast, his fears forgotten, when Ruth went to answer the phone.

"Your father is at the hospital with Katie and Karen. He said Karen is having a baby. Katie is your grandmother's housekeeper, right?"

"Karen is her daughter," Jason said. "She stayed with Katie after she got hit by her husband. Karen's nice. We played games together and she read to me." Jason concentrated on the cat, scratching the black bundle of energy lightly on his underside.

Jason's tone and the scowl on his face both became serious. "Why do people get angry and hit?" he asked Ruth.

It was quiet several minutes before she knelt down beside him, "I don't know the answer to that, Jason, I just don't know."

"Dad gave Karen a job and a place to live. They didn't think I knew but I heard them talking. Her husband hurt her." Jason sat down on the floor beside Ruth. He sat with his elbows on his knees, his chin resting in his hands and watched Horse extended his long sleek body into a full stretch. He remained motionless for several minutes. "Dad said her husband had a drinking problem. My grandma drinks," Jason said in a hushed voice. Ruth slipped her arm around Jason and pulled him close.

***

Evelyn rang the bell again. This was the fourth time she'd tried to summon Katie. The woman was getting lazy and Evelyn wondered if she should start looking for new help.

There was no ice at the bar, all the glasses were dirty, and Evelyn wanted her dinner. She looked at her watch. She had skipped lunch and dinner was hours past due. She pulled herself from the confines of the plush chair, searching from room to room, upstairs and down. She was alone in the house. Fleetingly she wondered what had happened. It was obvious that Wyndom was packing to leave but he was gone as well.

She found a neatly wrapped plate of fruit in the refrigerator. Carrying the food into the den, she made herself comfortable. The plate of melon and berries, ripe to perfection, disappeared quickly. Evelyn shoved the dish aside and sipped at her drink. The doorbell rang repeatedly but Evelyn ignored the noise. Wyndom and Katie both had keys. Evelyn didn't want to see anyone else.

CHAPTER FIFTEEN

Katie was tense, nervous. Wyndom watched her move restlessly from one side of the waiting room to the other. He brought sandwiches and coffee back from the cafeteria and firmly suggested Katie try to eat. It had been hours now and Wyndom understood her worry.

She stood, paced, looked out the window. She clenched and unclenched her fists murmuring prayers repeatedly. She finally spied Bruce's reflection in the glass. Katie turned, stared anxiously at Bruce as he pushed open the doors of the waiting room.

"You have a granddaughter. A sweet perfect little girl," he said, awe written in his weary features and wobbling his tone.

"Karen?"

"Karen is fine too, she's tired but both of them are wonderful."

Minutes later the doctor walked in and made arrangements for Katie to see both of them.

"I'm taking Bruce to the cafeteria, Katie. You go spend time with Karen, when you're ready I'll drive you home."

Karen was holding the baby, counting fingers and toes, when Katie entered the room. She spent the next half-hour admiring her granddaughter and discussing names with Karen. Half an hour later the nurse carried April Ann back to the nursery and Katie, watching her daughter struggle to stay awake, gave her a quick kiss on the cheek and left her to rest.

Once in the cafeteria she accepted a cup of coffee from Wyndom and while she sipped at the thick strong brew, she studied Bruce. "Thank you for watching out for my daughter," she said and fleetingly wondered about Bruce and Karen's relationship.

Apprehension flashed across Katie's features as she thought of her

165

employer for the first time since Bruce's phone call. "I have to get back to the house, I forgot to let Mrs. Carlyle know I was leaving," she explained to Wyndom. True to his word he rushed her home.

***

A police car pulled into the drive behind Wyndom's Edsel. "I wonder what has been happening here since we left," he muttered with a scowl and watched two police officers step from the black and white.

The events of the last twenty-four hours left Wyndom tense and over weary but one look at the ominous expressions on the officers faces and he knew there was more trouble to come. "Katie you go and get some rest I'll take care of this," he said, turned Katie toward her apartment. "It's probably some foolishness of Evelyn's."

Katie thanked Wyndom for his help and turned to leave.

"Wyndom Winters?"

The officer's manner skittered fear down Katie's spine like sorghum over warm biscuits. She swiveled slowly to face the man-woman team. Some inner sense held her firm, commanded she stay.

Wyndom acknowledged the officers with a nod of his head. "Yes."

The officers stopped a few feet from Wyndom. "Do you know someone named Jeffrey Warren?"

"He's my son-in-law," Katie said, stepping closer to Wyndom.

"What's he done now?" Wyndom asked.

"Could we go inside? There's been an accident and we need to ask both of you some questions."

Wyndom slipped his hand under Katie's elbow and led them into Mrs. Carlyle's kitchen.

Katie slid down into a chair. "Is he all right?" She was unable to hide her disgust.

"No Ma'am, he...he's dead."

"Dead!" Katie said, too weary to cover the sound of her shock.

"Maybe you should tell us what happened," Wyndom said. He stood behind Katie's chair and settled his hands on her shoulders in reassurance.

"Did he have some grudge against you, Mr. Winters? He damaged a trailer at the construction site in Ames." Wyndom hesitated, unsure of how to respond.

"Was he an employee, Mr. Winters?" the female officer asked again her hand poised over a small notepad.

"No."

Silence stretched the tension in the room into a taunt unspoken "why." Shaking the webs of weariness from his mind, Wyndom explained that Karen was living in the trailer.

"We need to speak with Karen Warren. Where can we find her?"

"Karen is in the hospital. She just gave birth," Wyndom said.

"What hospital?"

"It would be better if you let her mother break the news about Mr. Warren."

Katie's hands rested on the table, her knuckles white from the pressure with which they were clasped. "What happened?"

"Mr. Warren used his car to demolish a trailer. There was an explosion and a fire. He was trapped in his car. Heat and fumes finished him before we could pull him from his vehicle."

"He'd been drinking," Wyndom said to the young male officer.

"Our problem, Mrs. Bowen, Mr. Winters, is the scars. Mr. Warren's body showed evidence of an altercation. Scaring that was not consistent with the accident."

The female officer looked at Katie, her questions blazing from her eyes and stretching the silence once more. Wyndom squeezed the older woman's shoulders.

"Karen and Jeffrey were separated. He followed her home from a doctor's visit yesterday. Early this morning he'd drunk enough courage to confront Karen. When my foreman, Bruce Overton, got to the job site he had to pull Jeff off his wife. Jeff was attacking Karen with his feet and fists. Bruce shoved him out of the trailer then rushed Karen to the hospital," Wyndom calmly relayed.

"Did they get into a fight?"

"I don't know. Bruce was with Karen at the hospital. He was concerned for her and the baby. We really didn't talk about Jeff."

"We all spent the day at the hospital," Katie said, breaking into the conversation wearily. "Because of Bruce, my daughter and granddaughter are alive."

"We'll have to question both of them but it can wait until morning." The female officer turned the page of her notebook, "We need an address, phone number for Bruce..."

"Bruce Overton, " Wyndom supplied before pulling Bruce's card from his wallet and handing it to the officer.

"We'll try to contact any other relatives, if you'd like," the young woman said.

"Jeff's parents died several years ago. He's an only child, I don't think there are any relatives," Katie said quietly.

"Someone has to make an official identification, make arrangements for the body."

Wyndom assured the police officers that they would come down, take care of everything. The female handed him a card with instructions and they excused themselves.

Wyndom sent Katie off to get some rest and went in search of Evelyn.

Evelyn Carlyle lay sprawled in a recliner, empty liqueur bottle at her side. He pulled a throw off the love seat and covered her gently. In the morning he would sit down and have a blunt talk with the lady. He had to make her understand what she had done.

Wyndom hated the idea of spending another night under this roof but Evelyn needed to have him here and he doubted that he would be welcome at Ruth's. Wyndom hoped he could convince one lady to get help and the other to forgive. Regardless of the fact that Evelyn had tried to break up his relationship with Ruth and had treated her own grandson abominably, Wyndom felt a responsibility toward her.

***

Ruth calmed Jason's fears and managed to read him to sleep, now she was restless, unable to put aside her tension. Thoughts of Wyndom kept crowding in on her. She was so confused. One minute she wanted his face wiped from her brain the next she wanted him to walk in her front door and wipe away all her doubts. She prepared for bed her mind a scrambled clutter of 'what ifs.'

He'd apologized. Ruth did remember that. But she had been so fogged with exhaustion his words were just a jumble in her head. If only he had been the one to tell her about Cindy. She reached over and pulled her Bible from the drawer by her bed. Ruth opened the book at random and began to read.

Love is patient and kind, never jealous or envious, never boastful or proud, never haughty or selfish or rude. Love does not demand its own way. It is not irritable or touchy. It does not hold grudges and will hardly even notice when others do it wrong. It is never glad about injustice but rejoices whenever truth wins out. If you love someone you will be loyal to him no matter what the cost. You will always believe in him, always expect the best of him, and always stand your ground in defending him.

Moisture glazed Ruth's eyes at the significance of the words floating before her. *Love doesn't hold a grudge, love understands, love forgives.* Her Bible had fallen open to the Thirteenth Chapter of First Corinthians. God's words sounded so easy. Ruth knew it wasn't.

Ruth reread the chapter several times, struggling to fight the power of the words. Words that seemed to shred layer after layer of anger from her mind. Now she had to convince her heart to follow. God's truth about love seemed to be written for her alone, for just this moment and she wanted to believe that she was open to the Lord's guidance.

Ruth accepted another truth. Acknowledged that she had been living with anger and resentment since her parents' death. Those feelings had become impregnated in her thoughts and responses for so long that she had become numb to their presence. Ruth knew that resentment and anger made poor companions. But knowing that truth and accepting it, letting it change your life was not as easy.

"I do not want to live my life filled always with bitterness, Lord. Teach me forgiveness," she prayed. "Open me up to a greater understanding and acceptance of your kind of love." Ruth sat motionless. Calmness and a sense of peace drifted from the top of her head down to her toes. Tranquility settled in overpowered the despair she had claimed as her own. Now, at last, she could rest.

Ruth tissued her eyes dry and slid the Bible back into its resting-place. Extinguishing the light, she curled under her sheet, confidant that God would let her know how to react when she next saw Wyndom.

***

He stood at the window watching the quiet peace of the night enfold the earth. He wanted serenity in his own life. His bedroom was dark except for the illumination of the cloudless heaven; its symphony of soundless stars a combination of silent joy. The beauty of earth's star glazed night-bonnet filled him with longing.

Wyndom wanted love back in his life. He wanted a wife, a home, wanted to be part of a family. There were so many dark, empty, lonely corners in his life, he wanted them exposed and filled with laughter and love. Wyndom knew that even if he lost Ruth, he and Jason were going to have a home of their own. Wyndom vowed to become the kind of father to Jason that he himself had never had. As he stared out at the deep blue velvet sky, a star flashed a trail of light across his vision. A shooting star, it had been a bucket of tears since he had seen such a glorious sight.

Wyndom turned from the window, reassured. Praying silently for God's assistance with tomorrow's tasks, he succumbed to exhaustion.

She felt wonderful in his arms. Her smile was warm and he knew it was there just for him. Her dress was frothy, effervescent as moon glow, and appeared to be stitched of moon rays. The garment swished around their knees as they swirled together over heaven's royal blue carpet. White rose petals embellished her umber mane; now and then one fluttered, lifting up to drift away on the warm celestial breeze. Soon bits of flower cascaded around them like snowflakes.

Ruth and Wyndom flowed in perfect harmony across the star studded milky way. They danced through the royal velvet night with such grace, Wyndom figured he was dreaming. Love shone from her eyes as they circled through the sky and Wyndom prayed Ruth might experience the dream with him.

Sounds kept trying to intrude; Wyndom fought at the noise. He tried to force the blaring clamor from his ears. Its intrusion persisted. Wyndom reached to silence the alarm only to remember he had not set the clock.

Groaning, he grabbed for his Levi's. *Someone was leaning on the doorbell.* Wyndom rushed through the house. It was early, too early for anyone he knew.

Bruce, disheveled and obviously upset, pushed his way past the opened door. "The bastard trashed her trailer, everything she'd accumulated for the baby is ruined. I should have killed the creep when I had my hands on him yesterday," Bruce said, slamming his fist on the table.

Wyndom wiped the sleep from his eyes before he reached to scoop coffee grounds from the can and draw water from the tap. "Coffee will be ready soon. Sit. Calm down," he ordered Bruce.

"You haven't been to the job site, you haven't seen what he did." Bruce's anger escalated the pitch of his voice.

"Was there any other damage?" Wyndom asked calmly in an effort to pacify and tone down the man's irritation. He ushered Bruce to a chair, pushed him into it and patted him gently on the back.

"No, we were lucky that way. The trailer was far enough away from the new construction, but the trailer is demolished. He left his burnt out old hulk of a car in the yard. Wait till I get my hands on the creep. He doesn't deserve his wife or his sweet new baby."

"He's dead." Wyndom stated quietly. He stood across from Bruce, watched his anger dissolve into first puzzlement than shock.

"What?" Bruce said, staring open mouthed at Wyndom.

"The police were here when we got home from the hospital last night, Jeff died in that fire he created. Seems he was trapped in the car."

"You're not kidding. Sweet Lord, what a mess," Bruce said. He finger raked blonde hair from his eyes, rested his head on his table-propped arms and struggled to assimilate the information. "Does Karen know?" Bruce quietly asked, deeply concerned about her reaction to the news.

Both men looked up as Katie slipped in the back door in time to answer Bruce. "Not yet. I have to go and talk to her now before the police make it worse with their questions."

"The police want to talk to you as well, Bruce. They have questions about your incident with Jeff yesterday morning," Wyndom said. He set a cup of steaming coffee in front of Bruce.

"Sit Katie," he ordered, "you have time for coffee."

After sipping at his coffee for several minutes, Bruce looked at Katie. "I want to go with you. Please. We can take my truck. I think I should be there when you tell her about Jeff."

Wyndom carried his second cup of the strong brown brew with him while he walked them to Bruce's truck. "Once I've seen Karen," Bruce said, "I'll stop by the police station. No sense putting it off."

"Why don't I meet you both there at 9:30. I can help you with any arrangements you have to make, Katie," Wyndom said, assisting her into the truck and shutting the door. The lines etching the housekeeper's face eased and she nodded her thanks to Wyndom.

Hot water pelted Wyndom's naked body, driving fatigue from his muscles and his mind, and beading the shower door with rivers of water drops. Memories of his dream swirled through the hot mist to heat his loins. He imagined Ruth in the mist with him. His hands leaving soap over her curves. He wanted her: in his bed, his bath, and his life. Permanently!

Wyndom hurried with his shower. He wished for time to telephone Ruth before he left the house. He had put off his confrontation with Evelyn as long as possible, silently rehearsing the appropriate words. Words that would be hopeful, helpful and most of all, effective.

***

Ruth poured blueberry nut bran into her cereal bowl. It was early. Dreams of dancing through the stars in Wyndom's arms had unnerved her and she woke feeling lost and lonely. She sipped her hot tea, tried to picture what Wyndom might be doing this very moment. She heard unplayed music, the reality of the dream still vivid in her mind. Her eyes closed and the dream images resurfaced. Once again they floated, bodies pressed, arms entwined, eyes locked, their feet carrying them effortlessly over a starry carpet.

The phone bell jolted her back to earth, she leaned over the table to grab the receiver.

Jason, still wearing one of her oversized T-shirts and rubbing sleep from his eyes, ambled into the kitchen in time to see her replace the receiver.

"Was that my Dad?"

Ruth set a bowl, spoon and glass on the table as she explained that Wyndom would be over after lunch to take Jason home. "Karen had a baby girl last night. Your father plans to take you shopping, wants you to help him pick out a gift for April Ann."

"April Ann?"

"Your father said that was the baby's name."

Jason followed Ruth through the house helping make up beds and dust the Living room. Though quiet, he eagerly accomplished any task she gave him.

Their talk, when it happened, consisted of appropriate gifts for a newborn. Once chores were done, the two busied themselves by putting the final pieces of the castle in place, a task that they had barely completed when they heard Wyndom's car in the drive.

***

Wyndom slid from the wagon, his movements slowed by tension. *Is Ruth still angry?* He thought back over their morning conversation, while her voice had been comforting to him, he had not detected the usual warmth in her voice or a smile in her tone.

He knew they needed to be alone, needed to talk. Wyndom prayed she would accept his invitation for a late dinner this evening. A dinner to breach the rift between them before it grew into an unbreachable chasm.

He stared at the closed front door knowing he would achieve nothing if he were too afraid to try. He took a deep breath and bound up the steps, poking the doorbell without hesitation.

Ruth immediately noticed the dark circles rimming Wyndom's eyes. He looked tired. "Rough morning?" she asked as she stepped aside to let him enter. His eyes hungrily drank in her image.

His frank gaze heated her cheeks and curled her toes. Their eyes met, locked, and Wyndom breathlessly watched her smile flow from her eyes down to tease her lips where it blazed a path directly to his heart.

"I'm better now," he murmured, touching his lips to a very sensitive spot just below her right ear.

Wyndom turned and scooped Jason into his arms for a big hug. "No more fever?" he said after he rumpled Jason's hair, an excuse to lay his hand against his son's face.

"Did you see April born?" Jason asked, his eyes wide with curiosity.

"No, I was in the waiting room with Katie. Karen introduced us later."

"Will I get to see the baby?"

"When we go home." Wyndom watched Jason's face turn from sunshine to total stillness. Seconds later it dawned on Wyndom that the word "home" did not have a very nice connotation for Jason. "Your grandmother won't be there Son."

Wyndom set Jason on his feet and knelt down in front of him, "Your grandmother isn't well. I just took her to the airport. She's going to a special place where she can get help. I promised Evelyn that we would stay at the house and caretaker the place until she could come home."

Wyndom studied Jason's face while he talked. Sadness lurked in the depths of his son's eyes. "I invited Karen and the baby to stay at the house with us. I thought you might help Katie take care of April. Karen needs to recuperate."

"Okay," Jason quietly said. Wyndom realized it would take time and an enormous amount of love to heal the wounds inflicted by Evelyn.

"There was a fire in the trailer where Karen lived, all the clothes and furniture that she had acquired for the baby were destroyed. I told Katie we would go shopping for a few necessities. She gave me a short list."

"I don't know what a baby needs," the eight-year-old said.

"What say we at least make a valiant attempt," Wyndom said. "A baby crib is the first item on Katie's list, we can start there."

"Ruth knows what to buy, she told me a whole bunch of things you need for babies," Jason said. He smiled up at Ruth and Wyndom could see that Jason trusted Ruth's judgement.

An hour later the three of them were walking together through a large department store. Ruth silently marveled at how easily she had let herself be coerced into the Edsel and into shopping. Infant furniture surrounded them. Wyndom and Jason stood back, trusting her judgement, waiting for her to pick the appropriate items for this tiny new baby girl. A white lace skirted bassinet became their first purchase.

With Ruth's help they selected a crib and dresser, sheets and blankets, undershirts, diapers, sleepers, sweaters with matching bonnets and the tiniest little booties Jason had ever seen.

Wyndom studied Ruth as she chose each item with supreme care. Eyes sparkling, her whole face aglow, she tackled the task with enthusiasm. "You're enjoying this aren't you?" he teased when she held up a frilly, emerald-green top.

"Didn't you know all women love to shop for babies," Ruth said, reading the top's label to determine the garment's size.

"Cindy didn't," Wyndom said, too softly for anyone but Ruth to hear.

Their list of purchases grew. They assembled bottles, diaper bag, infant carrier and last of all, a monitor to save Karen steps.

The store's manager agreed to deliver the bulk of the items by 5 o'clock.

"You should take these things now," Ruth said, gathering the few items she thought might be needed immediately.

They left the store with their arms full, easily stashing everything in the back of the wagon. Car door locks were disengaged and everyone scooted inside. Jason stretched out on the back seat and Ruth joined Wyndom in the front on the passenger side.

Wyndom drove with traffic and tried to forestall mental pictures of Ruth with a baby in her arms. Not just any baby, his baby. The idea stole his composure and he ached with awe at the thought. By the time the Bermuda wagon pulled up in Ruth's driveway, Wyndom was wondering if Ruth even wanted a baby, a family. It was something they had never discussed.

Ruth helped Jason gather his clothes, coat, backpack and his prescription. "The doctor said to take all of these," she reminded Wyndom when he stuffed the bottle in his shirt pocket.

"Better load your things in the wagon now, Jason. Katie was fixing a room up for Karen and the baby when I left. She may need our help."

Jason, grabbing an armload of clothes, still had to make two trips to the Edsel.

Wyndom reached for Ruth's hand. "We need to talk, I...Have supper with me tonight Ruth. I'll tell you about the lovely dream I had last night," he said, caressing her cheek with the back of his hand.

Fire spread through her body at his gentle touch. His eyes deepened in color and glowed with passion. His gaze held her captive and willed her to accept.

Ruth struggled with her emotions. Ultimately total forgiveness must be her decision. Was she ready? A whisper in her ear, that tiny voice we all hear and generally ignore suggested life is just to short to harbor resentment. Ruth listened. She lifted her hand, let her fingertips graze his lips. Passion sizzled between them and Ruth swallowed the moan that threatened to escape her mouth. She consciously pushed her hurt and anger aside.

"Say, yes," his plea echoed.

"Yes," slipped from her lips and she moved into his arms. His hands, splayed across her back, were warm and gentle. They shared an embrace.

"Dad, what about the puzzle?"

"Tonight. Seven o'clock," Wyndom whispered, his mouth brushing against her ear.

Wyndom pulled Ruth around to nestle at his side, "If Ruth doesn't mind, we will leave it here until I can find a foundation for the castle, then we can move it with out taking it apart. That's quite a building you have there, Son."

Ruth stood framed in the doorway and lifted her hand to return Jason's wave. She missed the eight-year-old already.

Horse rubbed against her leg and she bent down to comfort him, aware that the cat would miss Jason too. Laughter bubbled up inside Ruth when Horse stretched his front paws to her shoulder and placed his furry head against her cheek, as if to offer her some cat-comfort. Ruth cradled Horse in her arms while she closed the door then she carried him in to the kitchen for food.

Ruth and Horse ambled through the backyard, moving from one flower patch to another snipping dead blooms from various stems and bushes. Horse was fascinated with the puffy balls of dandelion fluff interspersed throughout the back yard, especially the ones that drifted apart when he breathed on them or just bumped them with his nose. Ruth watched the cat's game, totally relaxed and at peace. Now and then she would stoop to pull out a thistle. Luckily she'd thought to grab a pair of gloves when she walked out the door.

Brilliant summer blooms bobbed their welcome to the pair as they strolled along the perimeter of the immediate yard. Grass Eaters, the service she'd hired to tend the lawn, were due to come and mow tomorrow then all the empty dandelion heads would disappear. Today the breeze carried the fluff off, carried the scent of summer, of green plants overlaid with layer after layer of the fragrance of roses, mums, lilies and spicy marigolds. Their delicate aromas tantalized Ruth's nostrils and she breathed deeply, taking pleasure from the special perfume of each. She settled on the bench placed beneath the rose arbor and watched Horse paw at each puff still intact in the yard.

Everything around her was brilliantly alive and lush after the other night's storm. Ruth reveled in the peacefulness, wishing only for someone with whom to share the beauty. Rumbling echoes in her belly drew her from a lovely daydream, alerted her to the passage of time. She called for Horse to follow and went inside to dress for her evening with Wyndom.

She donned a vibrant hued sienna dress with copper threads stitched through out, to add sheen and twinkle. Matching fabric buttons decorated the front opening from breastbone to hem. The dress had a deep v-shaped neckline, no sleeves, a bodice and waist that hugged her curves like second skin, and a short flippy skirt, that swished around her knees.

Ruth anchored her hair atop her head with a multitude of colorful clips, letting wispy curls slip down to brush her cheeks. Humidity had left the night air muggy so Ruth decided to go barelegged. She sat on the edge of her bed and pulled a pair of two-inch strappy sandals on her feet. She placed a few essentials into her evening bag, snapped it shut and went to answer the door. Wyndom, his hair still damp from a shower, was leaning against the porch rail waiting for her.

His glance lingered appreciatively as he perused Ruth from top to toe. She tingled with the heat of his gaze. He held out his hand, palm up. She slipped her fingers into his and watched, entranced, as he lifted her hand to his mouth. He pressed his lips against the back of her hand then he nibbled his way across her knuckles. Lightening streaked up her arm and she broke out in goose flesh before she managed to pull her hand away.

Witnessing the effect of his attention put a smile on Wyndom's face and he drew her into his embrace and covered her mouth in a kiss steamy enough to ignite forest fires. Both of them were breathing heavily by the time Wyndom released her, giving her time to lock her front door. Silence surrounded them as they walked side by side toward the car. However both noticed that the ease with which they had previously communicated was damaged.

Every window in the Edsel was open to gather the slightest stray breeze slithering through the steamy night. Soon Ruth had almost as much hair down around her cheeks as remained atop her head. Verbally they circled each other in a tangled dance of hurt feelings and an attempt to restore trust. Wyndom wondered how long it would take to get back their comfortable yet exhilarating familiarity.

***

Wyndom wore form fitting gray denims and a bright coral, short-sleeved pullover that he'd left unbuttoned at the throat. The bright color accentuated his dark umber hair and eyes, and his marvelous tan. He reached up to adjust the rear view mirror and his arm muscles rippled with power, straining the material of his shirtsleeves, causing Ruth's breath to stall in mid-chest and swallowtails to invade her stomach. She wondered how it was possible to derive such joy from watching Wyndom and the ease with which he controlled the old car.

She remembered the way his arms felt wrapped around her and a tiny sigh escaped her pursed lips, she tried to summon a bit of the anger she been steeped in the day of Jason's party but it eluded her. Wyndom had apologized that night, but she had been so wiped out that she barely recalled his presence in her bedroom. She could call up his image swimming across from her, see the sorrow emanating from his eyes but the words that slipped from his mouth escaped her and she resented the lapse, convinced that his words had been impressive. Ruth lifted her gaze. Where are we, she wondered, studying the scenery around them. Automobiles and bicycles filled the parking area while several couples strolled leisurely along the grassy terrain skirting the drive. Wyndom found an empty parking spot and maneuvered the Edsel into position. Mammoth oak and maple trees surrounded the blacktop creating an overhead canopy that shaded the ground leaving an intricate pattern of sun and shadow for all to walk through.

"There's a free concert here at Greenwood Park tonight," Wyndom said, opening Ruth's door and helping her from the car. "I had Katie pack us a picnic."

Pulling a colorful old quilt from the back of the wagon, Wyndom turned and handed it to Ruth before grabbing the basket of food and closing the back of the Edsel. Hand in hand they strolled through the swirling sun and shadow patterns created by the canopy of trees.

Wyndom guided her to a spot of grass secluded from the bleachers fronting the amphitheater. Ruth watched people file into the seats as couples or in clusters of four or more. Many were family groups with children in-tow.

Wyndom shook out the quilt. Positioned it for shade and maxim acoustics but distant enough to make conversation possible. He settled himself and the basket then reached up to tug Ruth down beside him. She squirmed to get comfortable. She had not been in this park for many years and had forgotten how pleasant it was this time of year. The Science Center skirted the southwest edge of the park converging with the Art Center and its lovely gardens that bordered the western perimeter. Ruth's stomach rumbled loudly and in her embarrassment she could not control the blush that rose up her neck to heat and color her cheeks.

"The lady needs food," Wyndom teased. He opened the wicker container, pulled out two plates, silver, glasses and several bowls filled to the brim with an array of mouth-watering food.

Crispy-crusted bread sandwiches, stuffed to overflowing with sliced turkey, lettuce, onions, peppers, both green and hot, and thinly sliced radishes, were unwrapped and set on their plates. Ruth licked her lips in anticipation as she watched Wyndom slather Miracle Whip and mustard on one of the sandwiches before handing it over to her.

She savored her first bite and watched Wyndom embellish the second sandwich for himself. Between bites of sandwich, Ruth sampled potato salad, celery, and hunks of cheese. Wyndom uncorked a chilled bottle of sparkling apple cider and filled each of their glasses.

"This is a wonderful feast, Katie really out did herself," Ruth said, licking potato salad from her fingers. "How did she ever find the time with a new baby in the house?"

"April and her mom weren't home yet. Bruce is probably driving them both home as we speak."

Wyndom uncapped another container and offered a cookie to Ruth. "These are Katie's special salted peanut cookies and they're fabulous," he said.

"I'm stuffed," she groaned. "There's not an inch of space left, not even for a cookie."

"We'll save them for later, then," Wyndom said and kept busy putting everything away but the cookies. He refilled their glasses and they settled back to enjoy the music. Listened in anticipation as the orchestra began to tune and ready their instruments. Violinists filed into the string section, horn carriers moved toward the back seats and the woodwinds filled in the seats between the two. Several young men from the audience were drafted into helping get the piano on stage. Meanwhile, leaves rippled pleasantly overhead as a cooling breeze began to steal the mugginess from the evening air creating their own serenade.

Music that started softly, rose rapidly, roared to life and Ruth tingled with the effect of the crescendo.

Wyndom set his cider on the lid of the basket and shifted so he could draw Ruth back against his chest. "Comfortable?" he asked as his arms curved around hers. His hands sought and covered hers where they lay along her belly, his thighs and legs bracketed her thighs and legs and she was held gently within the curves of his body.

They sat listening, letting the music weave patterns of sound, first lilting, now haunting, through the soft shadows of early evening.

"I want to dance with you," Wyndom whispered against her ear.

Ruth opened her eyes, noted several couples drifting harmoniously in the grass surrounding the bleachers, and nodded her agreement

"The program is billed as 'Music for Lovers,'" Wyndom explained. He stood, drew Ruth up with him. She turned and stepped into his embrace. Grass restricted the ease of their movement still they swayed with the waves of music undulating around them like golden stalks of straw in an oat field.

Softly haunting strains of the flute echoed through the dancers, the listeners and the trees. Violins, with their human-like voice, joined in the melody blending to give it life. One by one the other instruments joined the mix until the music soared, reverberated through the park until even the trees seemed to throb with their own heartbeat. Rhythm rumbled in an ebb and flow of notes that set the audience into motion. Heads, shoulders, feet, all tapped out the lively tune until it slowed, softly muted, then escalated once again to intermingle with the night's nocturne as it whispered its own story of love to the listeners.

Ruth laid her head against Wyndom's shoulder; she seemed to fit in his arms with a perfection that left Wyndom longing to keep her there forever. "I meant every word I said the other night Ruth."

She pulled away so she could see his face, a look of confusion slipped over her features. "I know you apologized," she murmured, making him strain to hear, "but I was so wiped out I don't remember most of what you said." She couldn't understand why that made her feel guilty but she knew it did. Wyndom moved nearer.

The breath of his laughter tickled her ear, "You sure know how to wound a fellow," he said as he whirled her through the soft carpet of grass. Each step carried them further from the other dancers, from the music. He slowed his steps, stepped back from her, "Are you still angry with me?"

"No. Not any longer," she admitted, hesitating briefly. "I think I understand about that."

"Thank you, Lord," he humbly said.

Music continued to sift over them. The orchestra moved from one melody to the next with no break. Now and then a smattering of applause indicated a particularly favorite piece, but most listeners remained immersed in the sweet cadence of the music, either dancing or sitting, arms entwined.

Couples moved apart when a break in the program was announced. Ruth and Wyndom ambled, hand in hand around the miniature lake, mesmerized by the love talk of the breeze as it flirted joyously with the park's trees, its playful creatures and the advancing night. Perfume from summer flowers beckoned them and they chanced into the nearby Art Center's rose garden.

Wyndom selected a bench and they settled for a moment to enjoy the scents mingling with the gentle wind. The sky became a deep royal velvet that opened clear above them. First stars popped into view and the moon, a luminous circle, painted Ruth and Wyndom with its luster.

He reached over and captured her hand between both of his. His fingers caressed hers, his thumb stroked seductively against the soft flesh of her palm.

In the distance the sounds of the Orchestra wafted into the air. Wyndom's hand cupped Ruth's chin forcing her to meet his gaze. Heat blazed to life between them and Ruth trembled with its power, she read corresponding emotion in the depths of Wyndom's eyes.

"You moved into my life," he haltingly said, "and filled all the dark empty spaces in my heart with joy. Loneliness has been such a constant in my life, I wasn't even aware of its existence until you began to crowd it out. You've restored my joy at life, given me friendship. And you've given me back my son."

Wyndom's eyes caressed her face learning each crevice, each contour, loving her with his gaze."Don't let my mistakes drive a wedge between us," he said, his voice a whispered plea.

Ruth placed her fingers over his lips, "I'm still here, Wyndom, I want us to have a chance to mend, to get back to the trust we once shared."

She leaned closer their lips meet. His kiss was gentle, undemanding and very provocative. Wyndom's lips blazed a trail of fire as they nipped their way up her cheek to rest at her temple. Ruth understood what it meant to be cherished and she savored the hope that that feeling would return. Wyndom held her close to his heart and prayed for guidance in restoring their relationship.

Another couple drifted into the garden interrupting their tranquillity. Ruth and Wyndom rose, floated, half dancing half walking, back to their quilt. Their eyes sparkled with unspoken contentment as they munched Katie's homemade cookies and sipped at the tepid, no longer frothy with bubbles, cider.

Spontaneous applause resounded from every corner of the park at the close of the final number. As instruments were cased, Ruth and Wyndom cleaned up their small section of the grass and joined the throng of couples drifting toward the parking lot.

Wyndom found soft music on the radio and they sat, holding hands and waiting for the jumble of cars to diminish. The night settled silently around the Edsel. When the traffic subsided, the natural nocturnal night noises filtered through their open windows and Ruth and Wyndom stayed, reluctant to break the magic of nature's symphony.

"Are you still planning to drive the Pacer 2-door hardtop to the Nationals?" Wyndom asked, breaking into the magic that seemed to hold them.

"It seems like a good idea. Several people have called about my ad in the Edsel letter. They're all planning to attend the Buffalo Rally and they want a chance to see the car," she replied.

Wyndom started the Bermuda wagon, punched the drive button, and contemplated the hesitancy in Ruth's voice. "Worried about the long drive with an unfamiliar car?" he asked.

"I don't even know how long it's been since the car was driven any distance," she admitted.

Wyndom skirted the downtown area, maneuvered the wagon through one side street after the other. "If you'd like, Jason and I can stop by next Sunday after Church and check the car over," Wyndom said.

"Thank you. I really would appreciate your help," she said, watching the street lights illuminate his features. "I'll grill lunch," Ruth offered.

The trip home seemed short. Ruth and Wyndom discussed the upcoming International Edsel Club national meet. Ruth tried to describe the event but it was difficult to impart to another just how much she had always enjoyed the experience.

"Have you visited the northern part of New York?" he asked.

"No. Have you?"

"Flew through once on business," he said, remembering the hurried trip he had made the week before Cindy's death.

"Did you visit the Falls?" He heard the wistfullness in Ruth's question and figured that she was looking forward to visiting the national attraction.

"No," he said softly, "I wish I could see the Falls. I'd like to make that trip with you."

"Work on it," she whispered and squeezed his fingers.

He nosed the Edsel into her drive and turned off the engine, then thought of all the work piled on his desk.

Wyndom unlocked Ruth's front door and reached inside to turn on a light. Laughter bubbled through them both when Horse bound across the room to greet them. The cat rubbed against Wyndom's leg, purring out his welcome. Horse stretched up on his hind legs to lick at Wyndom's hand, blatantly seeking attention. "I think he missed me," Wyndom said before drawing Ruth near for a flaming goodnight kiss.

"Sweet dreams," he whispered. He stepped out, closed the door and waited to hear Ruth engage the latch.

Cold showers are becoming a habit, Wyndom thought. He visualized piles of snow lining the street, torrents of water cascading on him from an icy mountain stream, but nothing tempered the bulge in his crotch. He drove toward the Carlyle house however with a sense of relief that Ruth had moved beyond the rift between them. He knew he would endure much worse then cold showers to permanently stay in her life.

Light flaring from most of the mansion's downstairs windows hinted at disaster and Wyndom hurriedly garaged the Edsel. Bruce's car sat in the drive. "What now?" Wyndom muttered, double timing it toward the back door.

April's wails bombarded his ears the minute he stepped into the kitchen.

"Where's Karen? Katie?" he asked from the living room doorway. Jason sat on the edge of the sofa watching Bruce, frustrated and pacing, trying to soothe a seriously upset baby girl.

April was cradled in Bruce's arms, he was both walking and rocking the angry child. "I volunteered to take over so they could go to the funeral parlor. I haven't a clue what to do now."

"Is she dry?" Wyndom asked.

"She was the last time I checked."

"Hungry?"

"She just finished a bottle fifteen minutes ago. She doesn't seem to want more."

Wyndom took the sobbing baby from Bruce and cupped the tiny form against his shoulder, alternately patting and rubbing her back. Relief washed through the room when a man-size burp split the air and April's cries ceased. Wyndom cuddled the powder-scented baby another minute then settled her in the bassinet.

The three males were clustered around the bed, admiring the newborn, when Karen and Katie returned.

"I helped give April her bottle," Jason bragged to his father as they went up the stairs to their beds.

***

Ruth intermittently worked or brooded her way through the next few days. She renewed her license indicating her desire to be an organ donor, celebrated a solitary birthday (her 30th – old maid age) with tears and some mental self-flagellation. Wyndom's nightly phone call and his reminder that the Winters men were expecting a feast when they visited the next day, laid siege to her singular chastisement and she fell asleep smiling.

The daffodil-yellow sundress served to highlight Ruth's tan; she hustled to set out her preparations for their lunch. She checked the grill, turning and basting the butterfly pork chops, smiling to herself when she heard the Edsel pull into the driveway.

Ruth watched with an unexpected new kind of hunger eating at her insides, as Wyndom, in a soft blue shirt and faded, body-hugging Levi's, walked toward the entrance to the breeze way. Every inch of him vibrated male, predator male, at that. Just looking at him made her mouth go dry, her spine prickle.

Ruth licked her bottom lip wondered when had it suddenly gotten so warm.

"Ruth! Ruth, this is for you," Jason said, tugging on her arm. Ruth's eyes dropped to the eight-year-old, bouncing happily at her elbow, and the beautifully wrapped and ribboned package he offered. Ruth had been staring at Wyndom so intently she had not even noticed Jason. Now she looked from one male to the other, her eyes wide with questions.

"How did you know it was my birthday."

"Open it," Wyndom said, wishing he had known and hoping his news would help.

"Open it," Jason echoed.

Ruth set the box on the table and carefully removed the ribbon and paper.

"A CB radio?"

"We've got one just like it," Jason said before he grabbed a dill pickle and turned to pursue Horse.

"I rearranged my schedule," Wyndom said. "Jason and I have reservations. We'll be traveling to Buffalo. Hoped we could travel together," he said, a grin curving the corners of his mouth.

"Now that, I consider a present."

"It really is your birthday?"

"All day yesterday."

"That sounds ominous," Wyndom said. He slipped an arm around her waist studied her face trying to read the tone of her response.

"I turned thirty," she said. It was enough.

"I should have bought you a rocking chair," Wyndom said with a merry twinkle augmenting his raised eyebrows. Soon they were both trying to cover up their laughter.

Ruth picked up the radio. "I guess it's not a birthday gift."

"It's for the trip. We can keep in touch with the CB. I'll install it today when I check out the car," he said, wondering what she thought, what she would say?

"I hate CB's," she hesitatingly said, before looking over to see hurt in Jason's eyes.

"It really is a good idea," she said, pasting a smile on her troubled features.

Ruth observed Wyndom's eyebrows rise in question at her tone and she lifted her chin. "I'm a two handed driver," she said with a touch of defiance. "I never could figure out how to drive and talk in one of those at the same time."

Wyndom pulled her into his arms. "If you have problems, pull off the road and use the CB to alert us," he suggested. He rested his cheek against the top of her head, not wanting her to notice how much he enjoyed her pouting demeanor. Her pique was short lived and her menu satisfied everyone's hunger. All three were in a good mood by the time they adjourned to the backyard to work on the Edsel.

Three unordinary people stared back at them. Squat wide bodies, relatively legless and very flat headed, mirrored them. Laughter bubbled from Ruth, Wyndom, and Jason as they postured and preened, poking fun at their reflections in the highly polished surface of the car. They strutted around the Edsel, surprised by the changes in their appearance, and laughter filled the back yard. Ruth chuckled broadly, clutching her stomach and huffing to catch her breath, clinging to Wyndom for support, even Jason's giggles were effortless.

"Jenny looks beautiful," Ruth finally managed to gasp. She used the hem of her dress to wipe moisture from her eyes and wondered how long it had been since she had laughed so hard and so freely.

"Jenny?" Wyndom and Jason together chimed.

"Dad had names for all of his cars. Meet Jenny," Ruth said.

"What did he call our wagon?" Jason asked.

"Betsy."

'We drive a Betsy,' Jason sang repeatedly while he chased Horse around the old car.

Wyndom put the sponges, cleaner, polish and polishing rags in a bucket. "Were they all named after women?" he asked, putting the container in Jenny's trunk before turning to look at Ruth.

"Dad said cars and women had a lot in common, both were temperamental and needed special care."

"Smart man," Wyndom mouthed with a grin, dodging when Ruth threw a handful of dandelions at him.

Wyndom held the car door open for Ruth. She slid in, started the car easily. The engine purred. Thanks to Wyndom's efforts and the knowledge that she was not traveling alone Ruth suddenly felt more confident about the trip to Buffalo.

"See you in a couple days, Jenny," Jason said when Wyndom closed the garage on the newly polished Edsel.

Ruth reached over and brushed hair off Jason's forehead, "You're a good worker, young man. I'd like to hire you to polish up Jenny for judging when we get to Buffalo."

Jason expression brightened. "What are you paying me?"

Ruth studied him for a minute, winked and replied. "Banana splits with everything you want on them."

Jason stuck out his hand, his expression very business like. "You got a deal," he said and they shook hands.

"Are you trying to steal my assistant, Ruth?" Wyndom said as he slipped up behind her.

"Don't worry, Dad," Jason said, lifting his arm to display his muscle. "I'll help both of you."

CHAPTER SIXTEEN

Car dust and road grime covered Jason's grinning gamin face and Ruth pulled the eight-year-old into her arms for a quick hug.

She smells good, Jason thought as Ruth held him. He slipped his arms around her to return the hug then withdrew abruptly when he noticed the hand print he'd left on her yellow dress. Fear flashing in Jason's eyes puzzled Ruth until she followed his gaze to the smudge. "It'll wash out," she quickly reassured Jason.

How do I get him smiling again? Ruth wondered, bothered by the troubled expression on Jason's face. She reached down and slipped off her thongs.

"Race you both to the house," She challenged and sprinted toward the house. Soon the three of them were charging across the yard, chuckling and teasing each other as they ran through the grass. Wyndom sprinted passed Ruth, cut in front of Jason and immediately tripped over an eager-to-get-in-the-game cat. He rolled to his back hoping to soften Ruth's and Jason's landing as they piled together into a laughing heap.

"Anyone ready for a banana split?" Ruth said, finally managing to stem her laughter long enough to push up from Wyndom's chest. "Once we've all cleaned up."

Later, Horse and Ruth stood on the front porch waving good-bye while the Bermuda wagon inched out of the drive. The sense of loneliness that enveloped her when the car disappeared from view was brushed aside by a mental review of the day. Spontaneous laughter had been absent from her life far too long. Today had changed that.

She hit the rewind button on the VCR. While *Pocahontas* rewound, Ruth carried the empty popcorn bowls, ice cream dishes and juice glasses to the dishwasher. The Winters men had become a very important part of her life.

They had felt like a family today as they worked on the Edsel. It was a feeling that Ruth relished, a feeling too long absent from her life.

Wyndom had devoured her with his eyes before leaving but his kiss was gentle, quick, and passionless. Ruth put the videotape away, shut off the VCR and the living room lights. She brushed her hair and braided the heavy mass into a single braid, thinking once again about her perfect day. Wyndom, his easy smile, the relaxed, comfortable way they interacted gave Ruth hope for a more permanent relationship some time in the future.

***

Jason straightened in the seat so he could see out the front window. Although it was almost dark, other cars on the road were honking a "hello" to the old Edsel. Jason liked the warm feeling that washed over him when strangers responded with friendly honks or waves. "I'm glad you bought the Edsel, Dad."

Wyndom understood. He reached over and patted his son on the knee, what could more he say since he was in agreement.

Wyndom stopped at the red light. "Snazzy wagon. What is it?"

Wyndom smiled at the young man in the next car, making a thumbs-up sign. "A 1958 Edsel," he answered.

The light changed and once again they were moving. Wyndom concentrated on his driving, tried to keep thoughts of Ruth at bay until he was alone and had time to pursue them properly.

"Do you like Ruth?" Jason asked, interrupting his father's thoughts.

The question startled Wyndom. He knew immediately that Jason was asking more than his words implied. Wyndom turned into the drive and eased the car into its stall in the garage.

"How about we discuss Ruth after you've had a bath?" Wyndom said, hoping to give himself the time to compile his own thoughts into words appropriate for Jason's understanding.

Wyndom slipped into the bathroom and inspected Jason's face. He picked up the washcloth and swiped at a spot Jason had missed. He reached for the shampoo, smiling when Jason clenched his eyes shut against imagined suds. Wyndom adjusted the water temperature in the hand unit, shampooed and rinsed Jason's hair. He threw the boy a towel then leaned against the sink and watched as Jason rubbed himself dry.

"I'm very serious about having a relationship with Ruth," he said to his son. "How do you feel about that?"

"She smells nice," Jason said hesitantly not sure how to answer his father.

"I've been thinking about proposing to her," Wyndom said. He watched Jason freeze, remain motionless.

Jason did not look at his father. He stared at the floor, not moving, not talking.

Wyndom handed Jason his clean PJ's; "I can see you have a problem with this. Out with it son, talk to me."

Jason stammered, lifted his chin and looked up at his father. "What if she doesn't want a little boy?" he asked. His mind kept replaying the words, *"She won't want you any more than your own mother did."*

Wyndom knelt to button Jason's top, wondering what to say.

"Grandma said you'd send me away if you got married."

Wyndom put his hands on Jason's shoulders. They were eye to eye. "Jason remember, I said we were partners. I would like Ruth to be part of our family, but I promise that she'll know that you and I are a team. We come as a package, Son. If you don't want her as part of our life, Jason, tell me."

Jason was quiet; it was easy for Wyndom to see he was carefully considering the situation.

"Has Ruth ever done anything to make you think she doesn't like you?"

"No."

"Do you like her?" Wyndom asked. His voice was quiet and his tone serious.

"I like it when she hugs me or musses my hair," Jason said.

He looked at his father. "She never yells at me or seems angry. I had fun with her when you were out of town."

By the time Jason was tucked into bed, Wyndom knew that he and Jason were in agreement where Ruth was concerned.

***

Wyndom's "Ruth," caressed her ear and seeped through her senses like the thick, warm, sorghum that her father had favored for his homemade biscuits. She wondered how his use of her name could give her such pleasure.

"I wish I were there to tuck you between the sheets."

"After you heard my prayers would I get a goodnight kiss?" she said wistfully.

"Several."

"I doubt I'd get much sleep."

She heard him chuckle, "And I would need another stint under cold water."
Silence swirled between them, heated but comfortable.

His husky "Goodnight" and her whispered response ended the phone
conversation.

Ruth settled the receiver in its cradle and scooted beneath the covers. She
was making mental lists of the next days chores when she drifted into a
relaxed gentle sleep.

***

One week later, a week Wyndom spent quietly rebuilding the trust between
he and Ruth, four a.m. came quickly. Ruth shut off the alarm's clatter and
hurried into the shower. Her suitcase lay atop her bed, packed and ready for
travel. Her best dress was zipped into her hanging bag. She had laid out her
clothes the night before and after dressing she braided her hair quickly and
added the last of the items to her make-up bag. She had just finished loading
Jenny, the 2-door Pacer, when Wyndom and Jason arrived in Betsy, their
bright and glistening Bermuda wagon.

They were driving through to Pennsylvania today. Early tomorrow they
should reach Buffalo. Jason helped Ruth carry Horse and his cage to the
neighbors, and within minutes the two Edsels were traveling one behind the
other on the interstate.

Ruth rolled down her window. The cool morning air carried the scent of
freshly mown clover and row after row of cornstalks that stretched
heavenward, their tassels bowing gently too and fro in the early morning
breeze. The eastern skyline seemed to glow a palate of pink hues muting into
gold tinged reflections as the sun seeped its way into the day.

Ruth donned her sunglasses and trained her eyes once again on the red
boomerang shaped taillights of the Bermuda wagon. She settled against the
seat, relaxed and began to enjoy the trip, comfortable in the knowledge that
Wyndom was in the lead.

"Ruth. Ruth, there's a truck stop up ahead, we're stopping for breakfast,"
Jason's voice came through the air, a bit trembly but also filled with pride at
his first attempt on the radio.

Ruth starred at the CB-radio momentarily. She understood how it worked
still it was a few minutes before she depressed the button and said 'Okay'
into the microphone.

They had been on the road for several hours and had just crossed the Mississippi river. A break sounded good. After locking the Edsel, Ruth stretched the kinks from her body and watched as Jason bounced to her side, "Did you know it was me on the CB?" he asked.

Ruth enjoyed the boy's cheerful easy chatter while they waited for their breakfast to arrive. It was obvious that Jason was having a good time.

Wyndom pushed his plate aside and unfolded a map of Illinois. Their route was simple. The only problem Wyndom foresaw: 'Chicago traffic.'

"I don't want to lose touch with you Ruth," he said. "Traffic will be heavy and fast as we skirt the edge of Chicago, would you like to borrow my navigator to man the CB-radio for you?"

Her smiling countenance and quick "Yes," warmed Jason's heart. This was his first long trip and he relished the idea of riding in each of the Edsels. Ruth smiled inwardly her pleasure increased by Jason's spirited exuberance.

Cars kept crowding in front of her Edsel. Ruth could no longer see the Bermuda's taillights up ahead. Traffic slowed down to twenty miles, ten miles, then five or less an hour. Impatient drivers continually zipped from lane to lane, in their hurry to nowhere.

Ruth's knuckles gleamed white from gripping the steering wheel. She knew Wyndom was up ahead, the truckers were talking about the two old cars. Then she spied the distinguishing boomerangs ahead of her in the next lane. Her line of cars inched forward. Soon she was almost along side the wagon.

The eighteen-wheeler directly behind Wyndom slowed and made room for Ruth to pull in behind the wagon. She breathed a sigh of relief and Jason said, "Thanks, mister," into the mike.

The travelers stopped for gas, food, or both, often enough to relieve the aches from long periods in the same position and to escape the heat of the afternoon.

Jason switched cars repeatedly.

Temperatures climbed into the nineties and the only air conditioning in either car was an open window. Still, Ruth realized, she was enjoying the jaunt through the various states.

Dusk was settling in around the Edsel when Ruth turned on her lights. An hour later her interior lights dimmed. Ruth watched her generator light blink red repeatedly then her dash lights flickered and went out.

She reached for the microphone, surprised when Wyndom's voice came through the air. "Your head lights are getting dim, Ruth. Do you have a problem?"

"Yes," she said into the mike.

"We're almost there. The next exit is ours," Wyndom said. "Stay close."

"I'm fine. You just lead the way."

By the time they pulled into the motel where they were staying for the night, Ruth's Edsel had no lights at all.

A '58 Edsel sedan from Nebraska pulled into the parking lot while Ruth and Wyndom carried necessities into their adjoining rooms. Ruth waved at the driver stepping out of his car. "Hi Bill," she called to the older man.

Bill walked over and gave Ruth a swift hug. "Hi, Ruthie. I sure was sorry to hear about your mom and dad," he said shaking his head as if to fend off the grief. "It's good to see you here, I was afraid you might decide to forgo the rally maybe even leave the club."

When Wyndom returned to the parking lot, Ruth introduced the men. "I need to see if they have a room for me," Bill said. "I'll see you two later."

"Competition?" Wyndom teased, watching the stately white haired man walk away.

"Of course," she chuckled. "One of many. You'll meet them all in Buffalo." Suddenly her smile was gone and Wyndom saw the hint of sadness in her eyes.

"Mom and Dad had a lot of very good friends in the club."

Wyndom put his arm around her shoulders and she leaned against him. He kissed her temple. "You have good memories Ruth, cherish them."

"Dad?" Jason stood in the doorway watching them.

"Jason is starved. I promised him a trip to the snack shop," Wyndom said against her hair as he hugged her.

Ruth invited Bill Lawton, the man from Nebraska, to join them in their booth. Ruth and Jason concentrated on their French fries while Wyndom sipped coffee and described Ruth's problems with the Pacer to the older man.

The next morning after the travelers had breakfasted and reloaded their Edsels; Ruth's would not start. The Edsel had a dead battery. Wyndom switched batteries with her, waited for her to turn the key and the starter to ignite before pushing the hood down.

Bill offered to jump start the Bermuda wagon and the three Edsels headed for Buffalo. The Pacer, sporting Wyndom's new battery and Jason in the front seat with Ruth, was sandwiched protectively between the wagon and the sedan for the entire two-hour drive.

***

Ruth dangled her feet in the cool water. She watched Jason swim back and forth across the pool. It had cost her all of thirty-six cents to buy the part to fix her generator. Bill showed Wyndom what to do and once the car was fixed, Wyndom had signaled a thumbs-up to her and hurried into the hotel to clean up. Now Ruth was waiting for him to join them poolside

Jason stopped at the edge of the pool next to Ruth. He grinned from ear to ear and splashed water with his constantly moving feet. Ruth was pleased to discover that the remedy she suggested freed the eight-year-old to enjoy the chlorinated water.

"You want to race me?" a gamin-grinned Jason asked.

Ruth shook her head. She was still shaking it when she was shoved into the pool.

Wyndom hit the water right behind her, showering both Ruth and Jason.

Ruth swiveled, glared at Wyndom, and used her hand to shoot water at him. "You deserve this," she said.

Jason joined the attack and they soon had Wyndom pleading for mercy. They played together in the pool until the sun's rays heated and increased to a shimmering iridescence that could easily sunburn. Vacationers crowded into the pool to cool off and the three of them adjourned to the many well-shaded chairs bracketing one side of the swim area.

"I registered us for the bus tour to Niagara Falls," Wyndom said. He lay stretched out on one of the lounge chairs bracketing the pool, too mellow to turn his head and see Ruth's nod of approval.

"Dad, you want some of my Pepsi?" Jason said, offering his father the can of cold drink.

Ruth sat up and shifted her legs to the ground. "May I have a sip?"

Jason joined her on the edge of the chair and handed the can to Ruth. She took a drink and murmured 'thank you' as she lay the can against her forehead then cheeks to help her cool. She handed the can back to Jason, turned back toward Wyndom to ask, "What time tomorrow does the bus leave?"

Sun, brazen enough to suck the moisture from their swimsuits and their bodies, added laziness to the afternoon. They sat by the pool reviewing the scheduled events for the four-day function and watching the colorful array of Edsels drifting, alone or in small groups of two or three, into the hotel's parking lot.

"Look, Dad." Jason said. They followed the direction of his finger with their eyes and watched a yellow Bermuda wagon, with a Colorado license plate, pull in and park behind their Red wagon.

Wyndom had found a "for sale" sign to put in the window of Ruth's Pacer and they watched people stopping to look the car over.

Jason's growling stomach soon had the Winters men donning their shirts and Ruth tying on her wrap skirt for the short walk down the street to the sandwich shop. They sat outside, under a colorful umbrella, to eat their meal. Replete they walked back to the hotel.

It was Wednesday night and the first day of the rally was about to end. Music, undulating and wispy, wafted with the evening breeze around and among the twenty-seven Edsels parked sporadically through out the lot.

Wyndom twined his fingers with hers and Ruth wondered if his touch would always make her knees shimmy and her body tingle and vibrate. She took a deep breath and pushed her desire out of her mind. She watched Jason dance ahead of them, relaxed and smiling. Ruth turned toward Wyndom to comment on the Jason's happiness. Total contentment and joy were in the smile Wyndom flashed at her, he squeezed her hand and mouthed, "Having fun?"

I am, she thought, *I really am enjoying myself.*

The three stopped often to visit with other small groups as they strolled along the Edsels. It became obvious Jason was partial to wagons, he delighted in each one they encountered; Wyndom seemed to linger overlong in his perusal of the convertibles.

"I heard a woman say she thought Edsels were ugly, she didn't like their horsecollar grille," Wyndom said as they strolled among the cars.

"Each time I see a row of Edsels, I'm reminded of a choir, their mouths open in song." Ruth replied. They walked and visited until Jason and Ruth were both struggling to keep awake.

Wyndom opened the door to Ruth's room, ushered them inside and turned to secure the bolt. The door between their rooms was ajar and Wyndom sent Jason off to bed. "Will you need a wake up call in the morning?" he asked. He slipped his arms around Ruth pulling her into his embrace. She was pleased that Wyndom seemed content to just hold her.

"My internal alarm works fine," she said and slipped her arms around his waist. Her hair smelled of spring flowers, she fit against him like the other half of a heavenly puzzle. His lips brushed the rim of her ear, shivers wracked her slender frame and Wyndom knew she shared his emotional turmoil. His light nipping kisses turned eager and Ruth clung to him.

He stole her breath, her resistance. Fire licked at the outer edge of her senses. She felt boneless. She cherished Wyndom's gentleness, was overwhelmed by the emotional roller coaster created by his kisses.

He tried to ignore the voice in his brain. He knew he could make love to Ruth tonight but the voice persisted and Wyndom realized he wanted more from their first intimate encounter. Ruth was the woman he loved. He had vowed to show her just how much by restraining himself. Wyndom's kisses became less ardent. With stupendous control he drew Ruth back to the present. He held her quietly for several minutes before stepping back, "I doubt I'll sleep much tonight knowing there's just a door separating us."

His voice was rich with passion. He bent and lightly kissed the tip of her nose. "Sleep well my love," Wyndom murmured before he turned and walked into his own room.

***

The door clicked, leaving Ruth alone. She trembled from the loss of his arms, wondered what it would be like to spend the night wrapped in them. She moved around the room arranging her wardrobe for the morning and changing for bed. He had led her so gently back into the present with his kisses.

Pink flushed her cheeks when the knowledge hit. He understood her emotions, maybe even shared them. Momentarily she worried that maybe he was not as interested then she recalled his hushed "My Love," and grasped his gift.

It was five minutes later than the last time she checked the clock. Ruth tried to remember her dream but all that came to mind was a wave of roiling heat and sizzling passion. She remembered a sense of reaching for something just beyond her reach. She freed her legs from the twist of sheets and sat up on the edge of the bed. It was early, too early, but showering seemed more attractive than trying to remain still for another twenty minutes.

Ruth adjusted the spray. The water beat against her body, massaging muscles taut from her restless night. The fragrance of shampoo tickled her nostrils and filled the small room with its rich scent. Suds slid down and around her body when she rinsed the lather from her hair. All evidence of her sleepless night vanished while she lazed under the warm spray.

Ruth had just clipped a bow to the end of her single French braid when Wyndom knocked on the shared door. He wore a pair of brightly patterned shorts and the Edsel T-shirt he had purchased when they first arrived.

"We're wearing matching shirts," Jason said, prancing around to show off his shirt. Ruth chuckled at the coincidence and strapped her purse to her waist. Hand in hand the three chatted easily as they rode the elevator to the first floor in search of breakfast.

An hour later they walked out of the restaurant and headed for the lobby. Cameras were draped around the neck or pushing up from shirt pockets of most of the gathered crowd.

Ruth, Wyndom, and Jason were quickly drawn into the midst of the Iowa group standing in wait for the tour buses. The trip to the Canadian side of the falls was shortened by the friendly camaraderie that developed between the driver and his passengers. Sunshine glazed the scenery they drove through with a dusting of gold, enhancing the vibrant colors splashed in the fields along the roadway.

"You have four hours to explore on your own," the driver said to the sea of faces visible in his rear view mirror. He opened the door and stepped down.

"The bus will leave the parking lot at One. If you're late you'll be left behind," the driver repeated his warning before letting them off the bus.

The roar of water drew Ruth, Wyndom and Jason across the parking lot toward the falls. The river's water, green and turbulent, rushed nosily past them, drawing their eyes and steps forward along the concrete barricade toward the immense drop.

"Jason, stay close," Wyndom cautioned. He reached for Jason's hand and they moved along with the flow of the crowd. Nine fifteen and already the heat of the day beaded their bodies with sweat. Today would be a scorcher. Ruth dragged the Winters men into the shade of a nearby tree, shared her sunscreen with them. The three donned sunglasses and wide-brimmed hats, in the hopes of neutralizing the sun's rays.

Wyndom chided Ruth for "mother-henning" them at the same time he squeezed her hand in appreciation.

"Come on, Dad, Ruth, I want to see the falls," Jason said, yo-yoing up and down with eagerness.

A fine mist drifted over, on, and around them. They leaned against the concrete rail to better observe the water that was cascading over the brink and plummeting downward with enough force to create a white watery froth of fog at its base. The view and the power it displayed was hypnotic. Awesome didn't quite cover their impression of the scene. The view was definitely one of those they would store away in their memory bank for future recalling. The scent of the water, its change at the rim from semi-translucent green to churning brilliant white, its roar as it swept over the edge and rushed downward, all combined to create the wonderment and grandeur of the Canadian side of Niagara Falls.

"Dad, look," Jason said, eagerly tugging at his father's arm and pointing toward the boat bouncing below them.

"Look at that face, Ruth," Wyndom said. He cupped Jason's chin, turned it so Ruth could see his exaggerated plea, "Are you game for a boat ride?" Soon they joined the line of rain-coated revelers waiting for a ride on the Maid of the Mist.

"This must be how an ant feels," Ruth yelled into Wyndom's ear.

The roar at the base of the falls was deafening. Their yellow plastic rain gear dripped with spray. Ruth and Wyndom clung to the boat rail, Jason wedged safely between them, and stared at the expanse of white froth bursting over the crest and plunging swifter than their ears could detect into the depths of the river. Sound enveloped and reverberated around them in one crescendo after another, as it became a repeated echo. Iridescent rainbows rose, shimmied and vanished on the mist. Before them lay a panorama predetermined to humble, intimidate, and yet dazzle all viewers.

Ruth recognized the look on Wyndom's face and believed he shared her feeling of God's nearness. Encountering together the beauty and power of Niagara Falls seemed spiritual, left Ruth, Wyndom and even Jason moved beyond speech.

Once they were back on dry land, they continued to explore.

Jason's hair, damp from their excursion, began to dry in unruly spikes that showcased perfectly his constant grin. An elevator carried them up, up into the observation needle toward more spectacular viewing.

"Jason, hang onto my hand," Wyndom quietly commanded. They worked their way through the throng of tourists, moving slowly along the windows of the circular room.

"Jerry will never believe me when I tell him about this," Jason said in wide-eyed wonder as the three of them stood and looked down on the miniaturized scene.

Ruth put her arm around Jason. "I think we can solve that problem," she said, showing him a display of booklets filled with pictures.

Wyndom helped the eight-year-old choose a T-shirt for his friend, Jerry, and cautioned him to keep hold of his purchases.

"We just have time for an ice cream cone before the bus departs," Wyndom said. They stepped from the elevator and went in search of a confectionery. Jason had just licked the last bit of ice cream from his fingers when the driver appeared and they were allowed to board the bus.

***

Steamy heat rolled up from the concrete parking plundering Ruth's breath the minute she stepped from the air-conditioned bus. Blistering heat with temperatures that reached up over one hundred degrees caused those out of doors to swelter. Wyndom was disappointed at the heat (he wanted to check out the recent Edsel arrivals) still he ushered Ruth and Jason into the coolness of the lobby, stayed with them as Ruth led them from acquaintance to acquaintance.

The huge mirrored and carpeted enclosure housed a multitude of people separated into small clusters, Ruth, Wyndom, and Jason moved with ease from group to group meeting new acquaintances and visiting with old and new friends.

"Miss Dennison?" Ruth turned to study the young man moving through the lobby toward her. He was slender with close-cropped blonde hair. Although he wore an Edsel rally T-shirt, Ruth did not recognize him.

"I'm Ruth Dennison," she said and reached out to shake his hand.

"My name is Michael," he said, his hand enveloped hers. "Bill Lawton pointed you out, I'd really like to buy your Pacer."

CHAPTER SEVENTEEN

Ruth sat on the edge of her bed, the stack of hundred dollar bills clutched in her fist. "I never expected cash," she said, astonishment lacing the tone of her voice.

"Some people would have refused a check," Wyndom said. "That young man came prepared to buy an Edsel."

Ruth pulled out the top desk drawer, found an envelope and sealed the cash inside. She shoved the money in her purse; "I'll put this in the hotel safe on our way to supper."

"We have time to do it now," Wyndom said when he noticed the unsettled manner in which she handled the cash.

"Thanks." Ruth visibly relaxed. Minutes later she accepted a receipt from the hotel manager and watched him store the cash in the hotel safe. Then Ruth, Wyndom and Jason walked out to the parking lot, empty shopping bags in tow. Together they removed all her possessions from the Pacer before she turned the keys and a signed title over to the new owner, who promised to mail the license plates back to Ruth once he arrived home.

***

Thursday's heat wave dissipated in the fury of an early morning storm. Rain pummeled the Hotel's windows with the force of shotgun pellets. Thunder thudded and throbbed overhead intermingling with flashes of lightening that sizzled swiftly and snapped several occupants from their cozy dreams.

Ruth's bedside clock read four AM.

She snuggled into the light blanket and listened to the storm move from one side of the sky to the other, leaving a soft gentle rat-a-tat of rain to soothe her back into sleep.

Several hours later Ruth opened the massive drapes to her view of the outer world. Wyndom would be knocking soon for their breakfast date and Ruth needed to select her attire for the day. Big and little trees skirting the parking lot swayed and bowed in the brisk breeze that seemed also to bombard the sun with enormous gray clouds. People walking through the parking area wore long sleeves. Ruth chose a sweatshirt from the drawer. She was pulling it over her head when she heard Wyndom's knock.

Jason, his hair wind spiked, his cheeks red, bound into the room, "We've already been out to look at the cars. Dad and I counted 86 this morning."

Wyndom looked marvelous in black Levi's and a Hawkeye sweatshirt. Wind had mussed his hair and heightened the color in his face. His eyes, glistening with gaiety, served as quotation marks that offset his rakish grin and grabbed Ruth's attention. Her heartbeat escalated into double time as she drank in his image.

"Have you checked the schedule for today?" he asked. He put his hand at her waist and ushered her out into the hall, pulled her door shut, made sure the lock engaged.

"There's shopping at a mall across town and several seminars on Edsel repair this morning. Valve cover races began after lunch and tonight following the 6:30 business meeting there is a hospitality party. The last event listed today is a surprise in the parking lot," Ruth said, repeating the information she had just finished reading.

"What would you like to do?" Wyndom asked both Ruth and Jason while he held a chair for Ruth.

"I want to swim," Jason said, looking around the restaurant for Bobby Jacobs.

"Ruth may want to go shopping," Wyndom suggested.

"No."

"No?" Wyndom echoed.

"I hate shopping and I hate crowds," she admitted.

Ruth opened her menu, "I'd like to find a good book and a comfortable chair. How would you like to spend the morning?"

"I want to take in every seminar listed," Wyndom admitted.

The waitress took their breakfast orders and left with their menu's tucked under one arm.

Jason, the corners of his mouth turned down, slid back into his seat minutes before the waitress placed a plate of pancakes in front of him. "Bobby has to go shopping with his mom." He said, trying not to show his disappointment.

"Maybe Brenda will let him spend the morning with us at the pool," Ruth said. "I'll ask her when we've finished breakfast."

Jason's face lit up. He licked syrup from his fork and attacked his pancakes with renewed interest.

"Thanks," Wyndom whispered against Ruth's cheek before hurrying off to the meeting room for the first seminar.

Ruth guided Jason toward the gift shop where she purchased a paperback by her favorite mystery writer. Then the two of them went to collect Bobby and adjourn to poolside.

Ruth looked up often to check on the boys. They were in the indoor pool tossing a beach ball with the daughters of the club president. She marveled at Jason's relaxed and carefree manner, it was good to see him happy. His laughter intermingled with that of his new friends and it was music to Ruth's ears.

She sighed and closed her paperback, unable to concentrate. She wiggled into a more comfortable position, leaned back and closed her eyes. Vivid fantasies fogged her vision with pictures of the three of them; Wyndom, Jason and herself walking arm in arm into the future. *Is this the future I want? Yes, yes, yes, her heart cried.* She pushed the fantasy aside, afraid that if she wished too hard for the miracle it would vanish like moon dust in sunshine.

Water dripped on her hand, plopped on a bare knee, pulling Ruth from her daydream. "Is it time for the races yet," the boys, grinning impishly and bouncing to ward off the chill of leaving the pool, chorused eagerly.

"We only have twenty minutes," she said and hurried the boys to their room to change. Ruth reapplied her sunscreen and lip-gloss while she waited for them.

The sun had spent the day playing tag with fast-scudding bilious white clouds until Ruth and the two eight-year-olds stepped out into the parking lot and the cloud shadows disappeared.

Wyndom and Eric Jacobs stood together studying a black and red Citation convertible that had just pulled into an empty space. The boys ran to join their fathers, pulling Ruth with them.

Several men from the host club were busy assembling the ramp for the scheduled races. Valve covers, each decorated differently, caught the boys attention and they tugged Ruth with them as they went to view the contestants.

"I bet the red one that looks like a fire engine will win," Jason said. He and Bobby asked permission before leaving Ruth to pick a spot on the grass where they could sit and watch the hand built racers that came off the track.

"I think that yellow taxi's gonna win," Bobby said, after a prolonged study of all the entries. Soon the boys were jumping up and down cheering for their favorite racer.

Ruth's laughter, warm and spontaneous, teased Wyndom's ears as he sidled up behind her and slipped an arm around her waist. "Did you enjoy the seminars?" she asked, turning her head to look up at him.

The subtle scent of his after shave and the warmth of his body pressed against her back, started pleasure pulses along Ruth's spine. She shivered with delight.

"Immensely," he said, his lips brushing the shell of her ear.

The parking lot and it's occupants receded into the background when Wyndom slipped his other arm around her torso, and hugged her lovingly, tantalizing the nape of her neck with his breath. Ruth glanced down to see the hair on his arm spring to life. It pleased her to know they had a similar effect on each other.

"The fire engine won, the fire engine won," Jason shouted. He varoomed his way over to Ruth and Wyndom, his gamin grin showing his delight.

The eight-year-old turned and waved good-bye to Bobby. "Did you guys see that the racer I picked won," he repeated, skipping beside Ruth and Wyndom as the three of them walked to the eatery down the street.

Jason sucked the last of his milkshake up the straw. He turned to watch Ruth and his dad finish their drinks then he offered to carry the empties to the trash.

Sweatshirt after sweatshirt was removed as midday heated up under the afterglow of a spirited sun. Ruth, Wyndom and Jason drifted through the parking lot, stopping often to visit with other Edselers.

"I need to find some shade," Ruth quietly said to Wyndom. He squeezed her hand and shoved her toward the tent set up on the lawn. Ruth smiled at Amy Johnson, an Edsel owning friend from Illinois, and sat down by her and their new baby. "Hi Amy, busy year?" Ruth said, opening her bag and replenishing her sunscreen.

"Busy and baby seem to go together." Amy smiled and groaned.

"You love every minute of it," Ruth said, smiling when baby Sara wrapped her fist around Ruth's finger.

"Yah, I do," Amy said with a grin.

"Tell me about that gorgeous hunk I keep seeing you with," the new mother said after she settled the sleepy child in her carrier.

The afternoon passed quickly. Ruth visited with Amy and other friends gathered in the shade. Now and then she spotted Wyndom and Jason in the parking lot visiting or looking at the parts various members had for sale. It was good to see the two of them happy and spending time together. Slowly the parking lot divested itself of people, all drifting in to prepare for the business meeting.

Ruth sponged off the day's heat and slipped into her peasant blouse and fully flared poodle skirt. According to rumor there would be a fifties dance in the parking lot after the business meeting and the hospitality party, she was dressing for the occasion.

She had brushed her hair up into a ponytail and filled her small handbag before she heard movement in the next room. Ruth touched perfume to her pulse points and ear lobs, slipped a pair of sparkling dangles in her ears and turned to inspect her reflection in the mirror. She hoped the fluffy dice hanging from the laces of her saddle shoes would serve to complete the picture of a '50's rock and roller.

Ruth and Wyndom walked with Jason to the room set-aside for a *kid's* party then they joined the throng of adults gathering for the annual business meeting.

"I hope you'll be my date for the dance," Wyndom said, putting his hand on Ruth's back and guiding her toward an empty chair. Ruth mouthed her 'of course', the din in the room making it difficult to communicate.

Edselers from all over the United States filled the room. "I met a couple from Sweden out in the parking lot this afternoon," Wyndom said against her ear when they settled into their chairs. "He told me that the Aruba Edselers shipped their Edsels to Florida last year then drove them up to Ohio for last years duel meet."

"All true. We Edselers love to drive our cars and show them off," Ruth said. She nodded at several familiar faces as surrounding chairs filled in, all waiting for the meeting to start.

She looked over at Wyndom. He was evidently relaxed and content, often nodding recognition at members that he knew.

"I think you've caught the fever," Ruth said, laying her hand on his brow.

"Fever?"

"Edsel fever," she said and they laughed together.

"If my forehead is hot it's from 'Ruth fever,'" Wyndom whispered in her ear, delighting in the color that crept into her cheeks.

South Carolina was proposed as the site of the next national meet, current officers agreed to remain in office, and after several brief proposals were discussed and voted on, the meeting was adjourned.

Jason met them in the lobby eager to show Ruth and Wyndom the Edsel coloring book he won at the children's party. Ruth waited by the door to the Hospitality Party while Wyndom and Jason took the precious prize back to their room.

Ruth, Wyndom and Jason stood in the doorway listening to the jollity of the members and searching for three empty Chairs. Laughter floated around the room, mingled with the soft and loud conversations of the revelers. The three of them found a table and sat down to enjoy the mound of food on their plates.

"Do either of you want another beef sandwich... Hot wings... Fresh fruit or veggies?" Wyndom asked, standing up for a return to the dwindling buffet line.

Ruth's "No, I'm full," was followed by Jason's request for more strawberries. Already the music drifting in from the parking lot had set Ruth's toes tapping. She was enjoying herself more than she thought possible when she first decided to come. Grief was still with her it was just less intrusive. She waited for Wyndom and Jason to finish eating, chatting comfortably with the other people at their table.

***

The music was live, the group, a popular attraction in the area, was famous for their loud, vibrant and well-played selections. Jason sat clapping in time to the beat, watching his dad whirl Ruth around the makeshift dance floor. Although some couples danced out among the Edsels, most clustered in front of the musicians. Chairs circled the perimeter of the dance area and those not strutting out front could sit and cheer both musicians and dancers.

Gently the translucent dusk ebbed into darkness and the revelers thinned. The youngest and the eldest of the Edselers drifted off to seek pleasant dreams.

For the umpteenth time Ruth interrupted secretive smiles flash between Wyndom and his son. The Cheshire-cat grin on Jason's face puzzled Ruth. "What are you two plotting?" she asked Jason when she managed to coerce him toward the dance floor.

"I'm just having fun," Jason said. He began to twist and wiggle his body in time to the music of the Beach Boys, grinning up at Ruth for approval.

"You're pretty good at this Jason," Ruth complemented her young partner.

"I've been watching you and Dad," he admitted. The music ended abruptly and Jason stifled one yawn after another while he and Ruth walked back to join Wyndom.

"I think its bedtime for you, son," Wyndom said. "Do you want me to walk with you?"

"Aww Dad."

"We have a six A.M. wake up call, remember. You and I have to get the wagon ready for the judges. Let's go," Wyndom said.

"I'm not a baby any more, Dad. I can put myself to bed." Jason said, trying not to yawn again.

"I'll walk with you," Ruth said, "I want to grab a jacket." Wyndom watched until they were out of sight, then he joined a group of Iowa members and they finalized their plans for tomorrow evening's surprise.

Ruth and Wyndom stood side by side clapping approval of the lively rendition of Wipe Out just completed by the group's drummer. "I've noticed that 'Wipe Out' is one of your favorites," Wyndom said. He took her hand and led her out for a popular slow dance.

"Music is one of God's greatest gifts." She said, nestling deeper into Wyndom's embrace. The excellence of the music and the wonder of being held by Wyndom added to the glory of the night.

"Are you tired?" he said his mouth close to her ear.

"As long as there's music and I'm in your arms, I'll willingly forego sleep." She said smiling up at him.

Wyndom pressed his lips against her temple. He nipped his way to her ear, "with you in my arms, the whole world is enchanted."

Ruth, Wyndom and a few other hardy couples danced the musicians out of their music.

Later in her room, Ruth turned off the lamp and opened the curtains to let the moonlight illuminate and frame her in its glow. Wyndom returned from checking on Jason.

"Asleep?" she quietly said.

"Angelic imp face and all," he replied and handed her a glass of sparkling water. They stood there, silhouetted against the night's silver-sheen, sipping their drinks and watching a few die-hards still wandering the parking lot.

"They're guarding the cars, right?" Ruth said quietly.

"I took my turn at guard duty last night from two to four," Wyndom said. He set his empty glass on the table and reached for Ruth.

Backing away from the window, she whirled to step into Wyndom's arms. His mouth touched her lips, soft as rose petals he nibbled at her mouth crumbling her inhibitions and igniting her fantasies into reality. Her arm crept up his shoulder, her fingers tangled into the soft hair at the back of his neck and they clung to each other with their strength while sharing their body heat. Time suspended around them. He paid homage to her with his gentle adoration, stole her breath and her ability to speak. She looked up at him through the fringe of her lush lashes. He studied her up-turned face in the moon's glow, held her gaze with his own, relishing the blush that rose easily to her cheeks.

"I love you, Ruth Dennison," he whispered.

"And I love you," she said, her reply husky with emotion.

"Enough to marry me?" Wyndom asked. Her astonishment showed in her expression then melted into pleasure; still she stared at him, speechless.

Wyndom's hand cupped her chin, the callused pad of his thumb caressed her cheek and he whispered once more, "Marry me?"

Joy, wonder, a rainbow of emotions flashed from Ruth's face as she sought the right words. "Anytime anywhere," she vowed. "Always and forever," She continued letting her promise of commitment ring bell clear in the tone of her voice. She raised up on tiptoes, placed her hands on Wyndom's cheeks and initiated a shy kiss.

"I intend to hold you to that for the rest of our lives," he said. He pulled her hand away from his face and stepped back. He withdrew his closed fist from his pocket and opened his hand to reveal the gold circle. He slipped the emerald and diamond ring on her finger. Delighted at her surprised expression.

It was exquisite, fit as if made just for her. Marriage. Her own family. Ruth, overwhelmed by her joy, wiped happy tears from her cheeks.

Wyndom watched the joy change, watched the cloud of worry sweep over Ruth's features. "What if Jason doesn't approve?" she softly questioned.

"But he does, Ruth, he even helped to pick out the ring." Wyndom saw hope fill her eyes.

Wyndom chuckled. "Jason has been trying to bolster my courage all afternoon."

Ruth smiled. Tears slid down her cheeks and collided with her up turned lips. "I will marry you, Wyndom. Anytime, anywhere, I love you, Wyndom.

I love you both. Wyndom whirled her around the room and Ruth realized he was happy.

"I was afraid you would turn me down," he admitted. "I'd spend the night holding you and planning our future but Jason and I have a date to polish the Edsel in just a few hours. He kissed her lightly and slipped back into his own room.

CHAPTER EIGHTEEN

Buzzing from the alarm drew Ruth from a heavenly dream. She and Wyndom waltzed from one fluffy white cloud to another, moon music and star rhythm wafting around them. Amazed that she had even been able to sleep, her first action was to touch the emerald to her lips. The stone felt warm, soothing, quickly assuring Ruth that her memories were real. Time was wasting and she rushed through her shower, eager to be out with the men in her life.

Ruth stopped in the open doorway leading to the parking lot to don the dark glasses she'd stuffed in the neck of her tattered sweatshirt. Sunrays glared hot and shimmery off shining paint and gleamingly clean chrome.

Edselers filled the parking lot, all working to transform their pride and joy into a winning beauty. Judging started at nine.

Ruth carried a bucket of cleaning supplies that bumped repeatedly against her thigh; she swiveled, searching for the Bermuda wagon. "Ruth, over here," she heard Jason's voice and turned to discover the Winters men at the outside faucet.

Wyndom looked up at Jason's shout and forgot how to breathe. Ruth, in faded jeans and ragged shirt, stood bathed in golden sunshine. *She is beautiful,* he thought, unable to take his eyes from her as she walked toward them.

The honk of the next car waiting in line broke Wyndom's concentration and he shut off the faucet while Jason walked over to meet Ruth. "Dad has to bring the car back to our space, then we can dry and polish it." Jason reached for her hand. "Did you come to help?"

"I even brought my own polishing cloth," Ruth said, walking proudly through the parking hand in hand with Jason. They chatted comfortably as they worked together to ready the wagon for judging, each busy with a specific task.

"Wyndom sure has you trained," the national president chuckled, indicating the toothbrush Ruth was using to clean dirt from crevasses in the grill. "Hey, Wyndom, this one is a keeper," he shouted before he walked off.

Friendly banter filled the parking lot as the Edselers worked side by side, removing fingerprints and smudges from their Edsels, transforming them into row after row of gleaming, singing choir boys.

Eric Jacobs drew Wyndom out of earshot, they stood with their heads together quietly talking, Wyndom used his hands to emphasize his words and Ruth wondered what plot they were hatching. Club members had been stopping by all morning, drawing Wyndom aside. Their quiet conversation shouted at secrets that had Ruth feeling left out.

The Bermuda wagon glistened. All the Edsels did.

Ruth washed quickly and changed into matching T-shirt and walking shorts. She was meeting Wyndom and Jason in the restaurant for brunch. She walked through the mezzanine, surprised by the number of women lined up in the lobby, waiting to board a bus to a nearby mall. Ruth waved to the group, wondered briefly why shopping held no magic for her.

She heard her name and turned. Amy, seated in an enormous lobby chair, was bottle feeding the baby. "I've been watching for you," she said. "You've been keeping secrets." Amy set the bottle aside and positioned the baby for burping, her eyes never leaving Ruth's face. "Come on, girl. Out with it." At Ruth's puzzled look, Amy laughed. "Show me your hands, please. I can't wait to see your ring."

"How did you know?" Ruth questioned.

"I heard rumors," Amy said. "I wanted to know if they were true."

Ruth introduced Wyndom and Jason to her friend Amy before the three of them made their excuses and left for the dinning room.

Ruth lost track of the number of people offering congratulations and wanting to see her ring. Wyndom and Jason disappeared right after brunch, leaving Ruth to the mercy of a myriad of well-wishers, as the news of their engagement spread like a grass fire during drought.

"I want to attend the parts auction," Ruth explained and excused herself from the women surrounding her. Neither Wyndom nor Jason was in the tent when Ruth entered and took a seat. The afternoon heat and the rhythm of the auctioneer's verbal cadence lulled Ruth into a short nap.

"Wake up," reverberated through Ruth's head. She looked around but no one was paying any attention. She rubbed the sleep from her eyes, feeling wonderfully refreshed.

The auctioneer held up a model car. "What am I bid for this red Bermuda wagon," he inquired, slipping into his auctioneer's staccato singsong.

Ruth responded with an opening bid and minutes later a final bid.

She presented the auctioneer's helper with a wad of money and slipped the boxed model car and the new old stock '58 hood ornament into a brown paper sack.

If I'm lucky I'll get this stashed before I run into Wyndom or Jason, Ruth thought. She hurried along the corridor to her room carefully alert for the presence of either one or both of the Winters men.

Once she stashed the gifts in a drawer she walked through the hotel, stopping now and then to visit. She detoured at the gift shop to buy a new pair of hose, wondering once again where Wyndom and Jason were hiding. She had not seen either of them since brunch and she definitely felt deserted. She had visited with several friends this afternoon but none of them had been from the Iowa group. She was beginning to feel abandoned.

Even the hotel corridors were empty when Ruth walked back to her room. It was time to get dressed for the banquet. Tomorrow they would all say "Goodbye" and "See you next year" and head for home. Ruth looked at her ring. She hugged herself...A new life; she was going home to a new life.

Later, Ruth studied her reflection in the full-length mirror. She had chided herself earlier, when she loaded the Edsel for the trip, for including such a fancy frock, convinced she would have no opportunity to wear it. Tonight, the voice in her head had prodded her to take a chance and she had to admit the effort was not half bad.

The shimmering green silk of her dress replicated the emerald in her ring. Soft silk material gathered across the top of the bodice to form tiny sleeves that skimmed her upper arms leaving the better part of her shoulders and neck bare.

Her dress fit perfectly. The image smiling back at her from the mirror lifted her flagging spirits. The dress, with its neckline that edged the tops of her breasts, dipped discreetly to display a hint of cleavage. A deep 'v' formed the back of the dress, it dropped dramatically to just inches above her neatly sculpted waist. The smooth silky bodice clung to her curves with elegant simplicity while the skirt flared out from her tiny waist in row upon row of bouncy four-inch ruffles that cascaded to just above the knee.

Ruth piled her curls atop her head leaving a few tendrils loose to frame her face. She dabbed perfume behind her ears, at her throat and between her breasts, and wondered if all her efforts were wasted. The adjoining room remained silent. Where were Wyndom and Jason? Ruth pulled a tissue from the box to blot her lipstick and forced herself to stop her worry. Surly there was an explanation.

A knock at the door stalled her tension. Jason looked spiffy in his dark suit, white shirt and western bow tie.

"Dad is slow tonight so I get to escort you to the banquet. Dad said we should get in line and he would catch up," Jason said in a rush. He grinned and stared up at Ruth.

She grabbed her evening bag and stepped into the hall. Jason held his arm out to her just the way he had seen his father do, "You're sure pretty tonight," he said stumbling over the words in his embarrassment.

"Thank you, Jason, you look mighty spiffy yourself," Ruth said and put her hand on his arm.

"What have you been doing all day?" she questioned.

"Nothing much," Jason said with a shrug as he lead Ruth toward the banquet room.

A haphazard line had gathered in the hallway, Edselers assembling in front of the closed double doors. Ruth and Jason took their place at the end of the line and were soon laughing and visiting with friends as each joined in the gathering.

The hairs at the back of Ruth's neck lifted alerting her to Wyndom's presence seconds before his hand slid around her waist. He nuzzled her neck and whispered how beautiful she looked before she could turn and met his gaze.

His charcoal gray suit graced his frame with tailored perfection. The pale pink of his shirt accentuated his tan and Ruth knew immediately that he was the handsomest man present.

When he dipped his head and touched her lips in a quick kiss the crowd broke into applause. The good-natured teasing of their friends kept them occupied until the doors opened and they all filed in to find a seat.

Friendly chatter became a low hum that filled the room until silence prevailed for a short blessing then the buzz returned as they all settled in to enjoy their meal. Ruth watched Jason pick at his salad until he realized every one, including his father, was eating with relish. She smiled, as he tasted each item on the plate carefully as if he were sure to discover some repugnant bit of food. Still he managed to empty the plate.

"You did that very well," Ruth said to Jason so only he could hear. "You look very grown up tonight." His smile widened with relief when the waitress removed his salad dish and replaced it with a plate holding a huge hamburger and a mountain of French fries.

"Mmm good," Jason said, savoring the first bite.

"You brought that red Bermuda, right?" the man across from Wyndom said. He slid his chair back from the table. "I own the yellow one."

"Have you owned it long?" Wyndom politely asked.

"Bought it new. Took a lot of ribbing for a few years there but I've always loved the old girl," he said, refilling his coffee cup and adding cream and sugar.

"Wyndom Winters from Des Moines," Wyndom said and offered the man his hand.

"Forest Wright, from Canada," the man said as he shook hands with Wyndom. "We just drove down for the day."

"Robert Jones from Colorado brought his yellow Bermuda too," Wyndom said. "How many Bermuda wagons were built?"

"Fourteen hundred and fifty six," Forest said. He and Wyndom talked quietly. Ruth and Jason shared her dessert and enjoyed listening to the varied conversations at their table.

While empty dishes were cleared from the tables, the group was enticed into a rendition of "Oh Lord It's Hard To Be Humble," with rewritten words. Next trophies were presented. Door prizes were given out then instead of adjourning, everyone was asked to remain for an announcement from the president.

Wyndom stood and excused he and Jason from the table. Ruth decided that they probably needed to visit the restroom. When they did not return, she became concerned. She found it hard to concentrate on her surroundings. The national president walked up to the podium. He asked the club members to stand when he called out their state and announced their attendance. Table after table stood to cheer their state. But for some unexplained reason the president neglected to mention Iowa.

Ruth heard titters of laughter break out around her before she turned and noticed the tall scruffy looking bearded man wandering from table to table scrutinizing the face of each woman.

"You there, what do you want?" the president said into the mike, making sure everyone in the room could hear.

Every eye in the room was trained on the bearded man shuffling slowly to the front of the room.

"He's barefoot," someone snickered.

"There's a hole in his overalls," commented another.

"His beard ain't real," a child said to his mother, his voice loud enough for all to hear.

Ruth studied the man. He wore striped overalls and a ragged white T-shirt. The child was right, the beard was false. After several minutes scrutiny Ruth recognized Eric Jacobs.

"Are you looking for someone?" The president asked, barely able to suppress his own laughter. Still he made an exaggerated effort at being serious.

"I'm lookin fur a wuman," the bearded man said in feigned hillbilly fashion.

"We have a room full of women," the president said, using his hands to indicate the crowded room.

The man seemed to rattle as he vigorously shook his head and held up one finger. "You want just one woman?" The club president's voice wobbled with feigned shock.

The hillbilly's straw hat flopped down over his eyes with his vigorous affirmative nod.

"You can't come in here and expect to pick up a woman," the president said. He shook his finger at the hillbilly, "Shame on you."

"Awe don't git yourself in a hissy fit. It ain't fur me. I'm lookin fur the wicked city wuman what ruined my boy." Everyone in the room heard his loud response.

He pivoted slowly waiting for his words to register then he pointed toward the door with the stem of the corncob pipe that had been clenched between his teeth. "See!"

A group of hillbillies milled in front of the open double doors. Most were barefoot, their attire reminiscent of the Lil Abner cartoon strip. Corncob pipes hung from several mouths and most of the group sported scruffy straw hats. Wyndom stood in their midst, his hair combed down over his brow. His too-short stripped overalls, showing plenty of naked ankle and bare feet, stretched tightly over a protruding belly.

Ruth placed her fingers over her mouth to stifle the laughter that threatened to explode. It appeared that Wyndom was supposed to be in the last stages of pregnancy.

"Point her out boy." Eric Jacobs called out to Wyndom.

Ruth saw the big burly man behind Wyndom prod him in the ribs with what appeared to be a shotgun.

"I see her uncle Bubba," Jason said and stepped out from behind his father.

Jason was shirtless; his overalls hung on his lean frame by one buckled strap.

His gamin grin showed off blackened front teeth and Ruth could see him struggling not to laugh as he led the motley group forward.

"That's her," Jason said, stopping in front of Ruth and pointing.

She scrutinized the faces looking down at her, tension increased when she realized Wyndom was absent from the group. Bubba motioned with what Ruth prayed was a toy gun and she stood. She did not know whether to laugh or cry when she saw that two Daisy Mae clad women were leading Wyndom from table to table so the Edselers could pat his belly.

"Move," Bubba, said prodding her toward the podium, his voice giving away his identity as another of the Iowa group.

"What are you planning to do with Ruth Dennison?" the president said and Ruth realized by the twinkle in his eyes that he was part of this whole plot.

"Her has gotta pay," one of the Daisy Mae-clad women said.

"She stole his in-no-sense, our wimmin won't have nuttin to do wit him ever agin," a short stodgy guy at the edge of the circle said around the piece of straw he chewed.

"You ruined him," tall, bearded, Eric Jacobs said to Ruth. "Now you gotta keep him."

"What? How?" Ruth stammered, confused by the proceedings.

"Yur gittin hitched and none to soon by the look of my boy," Eric said.

"A wedding, a wedding." The words ricocheted through the room, chanted by one Edseler after another.

The crowd seemed to part and a gentleman wearing black and sporting a clerical collar sidled up to the podium. Wyndom and Ruth were shoved into position and someone stuck a bouquet of flowers in Ruth's hands. She did not realize how tense she was until she noticed the flowers vibrating.

"Give us a minute, please," Wyndom said then turned to Ruth.

"You said anytime, anywhere, Ruth," he quietly reminded her. "Thanks to help from the New Yorkers and the Iowa group, this part is real. All you have to do is sign this license and we can be married." He held her immobile with his pleading gaze.

"I want you for my wife... now... tonight." His quirky smile vanished. His manner, his voice grew serious. "Will you marry me tonight, Ruth?"

She stared first at Wyndom then at the sea of faces all holding their breath, waiting for her answer. She trembled, sputtered, her thoughts in chaos, she was ... she was speechless.

"Ruth. Ruth." Jason tugged on her arm to attract her attention.

She looked down at him. "I want you for my mother too," he said grinning to display his blackened teeth. Mischief glowed from Jason's face, mischief and more happiness than Ruth had witnessed there in many, many months.

Jason pulled the license and a pen from his back pocket and held them out to her.

"Wyndom Winters, you are one devious man," Ruth murmured, she cupped Jason's chin and looked from one Winters up to the other, her eyes bright with joy.

"Whatever it takes Ruth," Wyndom said devouring her with his eyes.

"I believe I'll have to spend the rest of my life keeping an eye on the two of you," she said to Wyndom then knelt by Jason and added her signature to the Xed line.

"I prayed you couldn't resist both Winters men," Wyndom teased lightly. He drew her close to his side and, with Jason standing just in front, they turned as one to face the preacher.

"Do you Wyndom and you Jason take Ruth to be your loving wife," the preacher indicated Wyndom, "and your loving mother," he nodded to Jason, "for now and for all time?"

"I do," they said in practiced unison.

"Do you, Ruth, take Wyndom to be your loving husband and Jason to be your loving son, for now and for all time?"

"I do," Ruth firmly said.

Thus their vows were exchanged.

Edselers staged an impromptu party and stuffed money in Jason's overalls for the privilege of dancing with the bride or the groom.

A huge wedding cake materialized and the crowd laughed when Wyndom, his pregnancy still obvious, had problems kissing the frosting from Ruth's lips.

"You're so agile," she said and patted his tummy.

Groaning his distress, Wyndom proceeded to pull a pillow and other padding from his overalls. "That's better," he said and captured Ruth in his arms for a kiss.

"Jason's spending the night with Bobby," Brenda Jacobs said when she hugged first Ruth and then Wyndom. "Congratulations you two."

Ruth and Wyndom watched Brenda and Eric herd the boys out of the room. "One last dance," Wyndom said and whirled her around in perfect time to the old waltz tune.

Once they were secluded behind their own door, the magic of the evening continued and Wyndom led Ruth in a new dance. The words love and cherish took on new meaning for both of them as they blissfully became one in heart, mind and body.

***

Ruth felt beautiful and tall enough to reach heaven as she worked with Wyndom and Jason to load the wagon for the trip back to Iowa. She walked through the adjoining rooms carefully to make sure nothing was left behind. She tucked Jason's Edsel hat under her arm and closed the door.

"Dad wants you to come see something," a beaming Jason said when he meet Ruth in the hall. He grabbed her hand, tugged her out to the parking lot. Wyndom stood at the back of the Bermuda wagon. He smiled and gave her a wolf whistle, motioned for them to hurry.

"Just married," was written on the side rear window in blue finger paint and Ruth shook her head and wondered what next. She and Jason hurried toward the back of the Edsel.

Wyndom drew her into his arms for a swift kiss then turned her so she could see the sign hanging on the back of the wagon.

The two Winters men and the new Mrs. Winters stood together, smiling. Ruth read aloud the words painted in bold red. "The love wagon."

It's true. Ruth thought. The Edsel wagon had brought her much love. She put her arms around both of her men, her face radiant with joy.

The end

Ruth's Campfire Story
A Tale from an AnonymousAuthor

Once upon a time there lived a little old man and a little old woman, in a little old house made of hempstalks. They had a little dog Turpie, who barked whenever anyone came near the house.

Now off in the deep, dark woods there lived some Hobyahs. One night when the little old man and the little old woman were fast asleep, creep, creep, creeping came the Hobyahs through the woods.

"Tear down the hempstalks, eat up the little old man, and carry off the little old woman," cried the Hobyahs.

Little dog Turpie, barked loudly and frightened the Hobyahs away. This woke the little old man and he said,"Little old woman, little dog Turpie, barks so that I can neither slumber nor sleep. In the morning I shall cut off his tail." So he cut off little dog Turpies' tail and hung it upon the wall.

The second night the Hobyahs came creep, creep, creeping along through the woods crying, "Tear down the hempstalks; eat up the little old man; carry off the little old woman."

Again little dog Turpie barked and barked and barked so that he frightened the Hobyahs and they ran away home. This woke the little old man, who said, "Little old woman, little dog Turpie, barks so that I can neither slumber nor sleep. In the morning I shall cut off his ears." So he cut off little dog Turpies' ears and hung them upon the wall.

The third night the Hobyahs came creep, creep, creeping along through the woods, crying, "Tear down the hempstalks; eat up the little old man; carry off the little old woman."

Again little dog Turpie barked and barked and barked so that he frightened the Hobyahs and they ran away home. The little old man heard little dog Turpie, and said, "Little old woman, little dog Turpie, barked so loudly I can neither slumber nor sleep. In the morning I shall cut off his legs." So he cut off little dog Turpies' legs and hung them upon the wall.

The fourth night, little dog Turpie, heard the Hobyahs come creep, creep, creeping through the woods. "Tear down the hempstalks; eat up the little old man; carry off the little old woman," they cried.

Little dog Turpie, barked louder then ever. The little old man sat right up in bed, saying, "Little old woman, little dog Turpie, barks louder than ever. In the morning I shall cut off his head." So he cut off little dog Turpie's head and hung it upon the wall. Then little dog Turpie, could bark no more.

The next night the Hobyahs again came creep, creep, creeping through the woods, crying, "Tear down the hempstalks; eat up the little old man; carry off the little old woman."

Little dog Turpie, didn't bark that night because he couldn't; so there was no one to frighten the Hobyahs away. But the little old man heard them and he was very much frightened. He climbed up into the chimney place. Soon the Hobyahs came and tore down the hempstalks. They looked all about for the little old man but they couldn't find him. They put the little old woman into a big bag and carried her off to their home in the deep, dark woods. There they hung the bag, from the rafters and they poked it with their fingers crying, "Hear Ye! Hear Ye!" When it came daylight, they went to sleep for Hobyahs always sleep all day.

As soon as the Hobyahs were gone the little old man came down from the chimney place. He knew now what a good dog little dog Turpie had been to guard the house at night. So he took down from the wall little dog Turpies' head and ZIP, it went right on. He took down little dog Turpies' ears and ZIP, ZIP, they were on. He took down little dog Turpies' legs and, ZIP, ZIP, ZIP, ZIP they were on. He took down little Turpies' tail and Z, - Z, - ZIP, it went right into its place.

Then little dog Turpie, ran out of the house and went sniff, sniff, sniffing into the deep dark woods. He found the Hobyahs' house and went right in. The Hobyahs were all fast asleep. He heard the little old woman crying in the bag, so he cut it with his sharp teeth. The little old woman jumped out and ran home as fast as she could go. Little dog Turpie got into the bag to hide.

The night came, the Hobyahs awoke. They went to the bag and poked it with their fingers, crying, "Hear Ye! Little old woman, we're going to eat you up." But just then little dog Turpie jumped out of the bag and ate up every one of the Hobyahs. That is why there are no longer any Hobyahs.

Printed in the United States
17357LVS00002B/279